FOUND

IRENE COOPER

FOUND

A NOVEL

atmosphere press

© 2022 Irene Cooper

Published by Atmosphere Press

Library of Congress Control Number: 2022913404

Cover design by Brigitte Lewis

atmospherepress.com

For the chickens

CHAPTER

1

The image permeates the membrane and flashes, in breaths, when she's awake as well as when she sleeps: it is only the two of them on the bus. The galloping vista from the window varies in geography but never in color: it is a psychedelic rendering of the coastal town of her childhood; it is a painted sandscape of a desert in the southwest; the colors: a saturated red, ochre, the blue of a pulsing vein; all undulating at speed, at shattering breakneck speed, toward an edge, an end, toward the drop. Awake or asleep, when they reach the sucking lip, she is drenched.

The martial blare of the telephone breaks the dark surface of the room, and the dream divides, disperses, retreats into the deep of Eleanor Clay's bones, absorbs into skin, settles in the limbic recesses tucked behind reason.

"Hello?"

"Eleanor, it's Gordon. Listen, I think it's time we brought you in on the Lizzie Barrett case. We're at the train station."

"What've you got?"

"Nothing, not a thing, that's just it. I hate to give up on a missing three-year-old, but we're about out of time. Best case scenario, you come up with nothing, too."

Even as Detective Gordon Stanislaus said the words, he knew Eleanor would do her job successfully. He didn't make the call until that outcome was all but inevitable. She would find the child, and the child would be dead, case closed.

She found small things, easily lost. An earring backing in silvery late summer grass, a key at the beach. Her ability to recover the small and precious missing thing—a domestic superpower. If the object were to be found, she would. Or it would find her. Eleanor didn't search so much as make herself available, put her body and its senses in the way of the lost article until a glint or break in the pattern of the landscape drew her attention. Every recovery felt like a conclusion. Restored to the one who suffered the loss, the object fell without a trace from her consciousness, as if it had never held it.

Eleanor found the first child, small and precious and missed, months after Freya drowned but before Emmett and Levi moved to Denver, away from Bristlecone Springs. The lost thing was not hers, but as with the jewelry and the keys, the finding was a certainty, a fact to breathe into being.

The child was dead, of course. They would be, these small people she'd been discovering on behalf of the Bristlecone Springs Police Department for the last decade or so, eighteen children to date. Eleanor had been called in to find number nineteen, which meant that the detectives were not expecting to find the missing little one alive. Eleanor didn't show up until all other options had been exercised.

A flash of red, a thread of yellow. In the bus station, Eleanor pulled from between and behind two rows of lockers at the rear of the terminal a chunky knit red sweater, about the size of a composition notebook, a yellow canary embroidered on the front.

"She's not here, but she's not gone," said Eleanor. A terrible force flapped her ribcage.

Stanislaus gave orders to the uniformed police. "Talk to the drivers and the ticket agent again." This was their third visit to the station since the child's father had reported her gone.

"She's not gone. Give me someone to go look by the river." Eleanor didn't elaborate.

She's not gone. "Well," said Stanislaus, "she's not here." And they were nowhere, he thought. The Amber Alert drew nothing credible. The sweater was new evidence. There might be more, he could retrace and review, put the dog to better use. But it was Eleanor who'd found it, not his regular team, and experience said that meant only one thing. *We got nothing*, he thought.

"Yeah, okay, Eleanor. Drubbs!" Stanislaus signaled to his detective and a uniform. "Go with Eleanor. She thinks the river." In all these years, he still felt a freight elevator drop into his bowels whenever Eleanor said she had something. He'd never known her not to come up with a body, and if Eleanor's antennae were tingling, a body was all he anticipated now. He'd never feel at ease around that woman, but he couldn't, and wouldn't, deny her record. Macabre talent, she had, and not much else, having lost one kid to the Roaring Fork, and another, plus the husband, to fallout.

"Bring the dog."

CHAPTER

2

Two weeks later, Eleanor sat at a high table in Nina Steuben's laboratory at CorpsPursuit, a private volunteer cooperative of forensics experts, renowned for recovering long-lost bodies in long-cold murder cases. Nina poured water from an electric kettle into two cups and sat one in front of Eleanor. Months before, Nina had reached out to regional police departments seeking volunteers. The letter had been printed out and posted on the Bristlecone Springs bulletin board and had since been nearly papered over with notices of community service days and for sale flyers. Eleanor stood staring at the board the day after recovering a second child. It hadn't occurred to her that someone else did what she did. She felt compelled, suddenly, to talk to another woman, any other person at all, who knew what it was to make these grim discoveries. She didn't hope to find out what had changed—she wasn't looking for answers, exactly. CorpsPursuit recovered corpses, not living bodies, but for the first time in a very long time Eleanor felt the need to ground herself with another human being, someone who understood something—anything—of her dark work.

"That's when it started," said Eleanor. "That's the night everything changed."

"Changed again, you mean, yes?"

"Yes, okay. If I'm marking my adulthood by catastrophic events, then it changed again when we found Lizzie. When I found Lizzie."

Stooped, Eleanor picked her way along the rocky bank of the river. A light rain gently needled the back of her exposed neck, created rivulets across her scapula and joined the stream of sweat from her armpits. The police searched the vegetation, poked their flashlights into the bushes and tufts. Not one of them believed they'd find anything where the rushing water would have claimed that thing for its own.

"Here!"

Detective Drubbs swung his flashlight in the direction he'd seen Eleanor last. He saw nothing.

"Over here!"

He lowered his beam into the voice.

Eleanor was on her belly, her head bent below the bank. Upside down, she peered into a culvert that ran beneath the train tracks and dumped its runoff into the Colorado. A woven basket appeared to hang from the corrugated wall of the sewer pipe, a dead muskrat wedged between the resin barrier and the metal. A length of twine or some hairy rope secured a bundle within the basket, thin synthetic folds of pastel fleece pinched between the bindings.

She pushed herself up onto her knees and sat back on her ankles as the police moved in to see what she'd discovered, then took a breath that choked like a sob and stood back from the now-focused crew. She monitored her body from a dry and distant place, as though she were observing a familiar experiment through glass, dispassionately felt her adrenaline levels peak and then recede into her own murky soup. She waited for Drubbs to confirm her success: the discovery and fact of another dead child.

She watched a few yards off, flashlight off, as the police crew extracted the basket and lifted it free, cut the wrapping from the body of a child who could fit inside a basket. "She's breathing! Get an ambulance down here!"

Lizzie, the owner of the red sweater, wore what had been a white ribbed cotton tank top with a tiny blue satin ribbon at the neck and panties printed with individual pink tulips, both stiff with mud and blood. Remnants of a Disney princess blanket stuck to skin that was otherwise exposed and showing signs of bacterial infection, including open, pungent sores on her thighs and feet. She was three years old and had been missing four days, with the roar of the California Zephyr and countless freight cars rumbling inches above her head.

Eleanor stood frozen in the early summer night as the air filled with the noise and swirling light of emergency vehicles and responders. Some indistinct unit of time later, Drubbs slapped the back of the ambulance twice and walked to her.

"My god, the kid's alive! Can you believe it?" he said like a man who could not quite believe it. "It's a damn miracle, is what it is. You really did good this time, Eleanor." He attempted an awkward pat on her arm, felt her shaking under her jacket, and drew back his hand. "Okay, then," he said quietly, as to a treed cat, "I'll just get one of the men to take you home."

"It must have been very gratifying to find the child alive. Lizzie, I mean, and then the other, after." Nine days after finding Lizzie, Eleanor discovered Maybelline Dodge, unconscious but breathing, wrapped and stuck like spider food in a damp and lonely crevice of a closed-off cave, minutes from the hot springs pool, the town's most popular attraction.

Eleanor bent over her cup to take a sip of tea. Constant Comment displaced the cold metallic air under her nose with hot orange vapor.

"Well, sure, after ten years of recovering the dead, finding a living child is a kind of miracle, or would be if I could believe any god had something to do with it. I imagine it's more like winning the lottery. You get used to the fact that losing is a certainty, and you play anyway. Winning isn't a reality you're prepared for. But that's not even it. How do I explain it, when I don't understand myself? Yes, the last two children were alive when I found them, but somehow I felt like my proximity put them closer to death, like I brought it with me. I was certain—not with Lizzie, she was the first—but with the next child, that I would discover her only in time to see her die."

"Hm. Well, the living body is in so many ways fragile, and those children had already suffered considerably by the time you got to them. Dead bodies are far more resilient work subjects, in my experience, or parts of them anyway. At least, I am not overly concerned about a critical change in their condition." Nina nodded at the table before them, across which lay most of a reconstructed adult human skeleton.

Eleanor was unsure whether or not to laugh, until Nina winked.

"Despite this being a profession I gladly chose, in my forty-plus years as a forensic anthropologist at CorpsPursuit, I'll admit I hoped for living tissue every time we recovered a missing body, no matter how many years it had been lost to its family, no matter how long I knew it to be hidden. Death was a certainty, always. And still. I've come to think, in the hearts and minds of the families, the body was alive, maybe, as you say, until just before we uncovered it, when it could rest at last."

"Rest in peace, you mean. Now there's a concept."

"You're talking about sleep now, yes? I don't sleep so much myself, although I like a catnap in the office on the cot. My colleagues say it makes me a poor communicator, being always at work. But what should I do? This is what I do. I would like to continue our talk, but maybe not in the company of the bones. If you haven't made arrangements elsewhere, allow me the pleasure of inviting you to my home. I have one, you see, and you can bear witness to the fact when I introduce you to our little team."

"Thank you, I'd like that, if you're sure I'm not imposing."

"Ach, imposing." Nina removed her lab coat and hung it on a hook by the door. She wore a collared, short-sleeved, knit shirt and belted trousers, neat and trim, Eleanor thought, like everything else about her. As Nina slipped into her jacket, Eleanor noted the tattoo on the inside of the older woman's left forearm.

It was barely a glimpse, but Nina caught it and held it as though it was a train she'd been expecting and was satisfied had arrived on time. "Buchenwald. I and a brother were luckier than most."

"I'm sorry."

"Ja. But we go on living, if we live, yes?"

CHAPTER
3

Elan DePeña swung a leg off his Trek Powerfly and came to a standing sidesaddle stop at the bike rack in front of the police station. He loved his job, as long as he was on the bike. The fresh mountain air, the perennial festival feel to the Colorado tourist town, his minor celebrity—the gig was near perfect. If only he never had to get off the bike, as he had to now, to present himself to his sergeant. It was in moments like these, steeling himself for certain conflict, that he regretted the one course of study he'd so far completed—the police academy training that qualified him for bicycle patrol at Bristlecone Springs PD. He wondered if he'd seen it to the end of basic welding or baking arts at Colorado Mountain, if he'd be hanging on the scaffolding of that new hotel going up, or aiming a blowtorch at a creme brûlée downtown at La Boule. He'd look hot in work pants and a construction hat. Maybe not so much the apron. He looked pretty hot right now, he felt, in his shorts and jersey, though it took some of the shine off his performance polyester to be bracing for another sarcastic reprimand from his superior.

"Sarge? You called me in?"

"DePeña, yeah! How are you, son?"

"Good, sir."

"That's good, that's good. Because I've been a little worried about the chafing, all day in the saddle."

"Sir?"

"If we were earning points for pageantry, DePeña, you'd have the department way ahead. People love seeing you wheel around, especially the tourists. You'd think the Chamber of Commerce signed your paycheck. What I'm saying, son, is you got to get off the bleeping bike now and again. There is actual criminal activity going on that needs your flat-footed attention."

"Did I miss something on patrol, Sarge? On the radio?"

"Cars answered two calls this morning on your patrol, one for possession with intent, one public nuisance."

"But, Sarge, sir! I rolled on the scene for both those calls."

"Well after the fact, DePeña, and Schmidt and Rivera report you never disembarked, checked on their status with the bike between your legs. Don't go trying to dance with me, DePeña. I need you to do your job. Be a cop. It's time to stop thinking about what you're going to do when you grow up. You carry a gun, for crying out loud."

"Yes, sir. Is that all, sir?"

"No, DePeña, I have more good news for you. You're reassigned to special tasks for the next few shifts, effective immediately."

"Special tasks, Sarge?"

"Yeah. Detective Stanislaus wants you to pair up with a civilian consultant, Eleanor Clay. She's helping the detectives and needs a uniform. I nominated you. You're welcome."

"Uh, Sir? What about my bike?"

"The tour's cut short, for now, DePeña. Get your land legs

ready for duty. It's time to let the bottom of those shiny shoes touch the pavement."

The sergeant directed Elan to report immediately to Detective Gordon Stanislaus. Elan had not met the department's chief detective one-on-one, but he knew enough from the other patrol cops to start sweating through his spandex. If Stanislaus had been an instructor at Colorado Mountain, he would've taken pains to register for someone else's class, study under someone who Elan thought might be more amenable to his natural good humor. It wasn't that he tried to skate on his charm. He was a sufficiently dedicated student, at least for the length of a term. He just liked being able to make an impression and control it, and from what he understood about Stanislaus, the detective was about as impressionable as petrified wood.

Elan made his way to Stanislaus' office at the rear of the building. The detective was on the phone with his back to the open door. Elan knocked twice on the glass and stood at ease, holding his bike helmet in front of his crotch with both hands.

Stanislaus swiveled and gave Elan a quick down-and-up look, then said into the receiver, "Yeah, thanks for letting me know," and hung up. "Sunglasses, officer."

"Yes, sir. Excuse me, sir." Elan slid the arm of his Smith sunglasses into the front of his jersey, then quickly removed it and folded them into his helmet.

"You're bicycle patrol...?"

"DePeña, sir. Elan DePeña. And yes, sir, I've been riding bike patrol since I joined the department three months ago."

"Three months. CLETA grad?" The Colorado Law Enforcement Training Academy sat a few miles to the south. Bristlecone Springs held onto a few newly minted cops after graduation, but the ambitious among them generally set their caps for bigger departments.

"Yes, sir."

"Hm." Stanislaus looked down to read what Elan assumed was his profile, a single page.

"Okay, DePeña, I'll tell you what I need. I need a uniform to protect and assist a civilian consultant with an ongoing investigation. Do you own an actual uniform, DePeña?"

"I do, sir."

"We'll provide a patrol car and, when necessary, a dog, plus an officer handler."

"Sir? I had some experience at the academy with the canine patrol, and earned six hours at Colorado Mountain toward a veterinarian assistant certificate. I could manage a dog, sir."

"Hm, well, I'm not sure what our dog handler would think of that, but Eleanor likes to work lean. It's Eleanor Clay you'll be working with. She's due in at one. I'd like to brief you on your duties asap, including how to comport yourself with a civilian on the job."

"All due respect, sir, I'm pretty good with people."

"I don't doubt it, DePeña, but this isn't a meet and greet. It's an investigation. And Eleanor—Ms. Clay—is an unusual civilian. Find some long pants, get dressed, and report back to me."

"Yes, sir." Elan went to his locker trying to place the name, repeating it in his head until he remembered: Eleanor Clay, the woman who found the corpses, a ghost story from the academy. The day had taken a serious turn for the worse, he thought. Off the bike and now babysitter to the Grim Reaper. As Elan pulled on long pants and knotted his tie, he felt as though he were dressing for a funeral, maybe his own. He went outside, returned his bicycle to the shed and patted the seat fondly before heading in to hear his marching orders.

CHAPTER
4

Althea Giordano was sick of salad. She forked one last balsamic glazed micro green into her mouth before walking to the edge of the fenced courtyard and dumping the remains of her lunch into the compost bin. Wasteful, she thought.

Today she would have eaten the last crumb of a drive-thru double cheeseburger, licked the fat from her fingers, chased it with chocolate shake thick as acrylic paint, wiped the cup clean with a broom of french fries, and savored the fumes for hours after. Those were the days.

She washed her hands and went back inside to her slides. As a professor of botany at the community college and forensic botanist for CorpsPursuit, Althea spent a lot of time with nature under glass, in the operating room lighting of a lab. Which is not to say she was removed from nature. Her work-space was more greenhouse than laboratory. And she lived alongside her partner, Cal, deep amidst the local flora and fauna in a western fairytale of a house on a plot of land that bloomed a universe away from her shallow roots in urban

Ontario. The aspens of the Rockies were her wallpaper, the grasses of Genesee Park her living room rug, the land her library, and often enough, her kitchen and her bedroom. A good thing it was, too, as you couldn't slide a snakeskin between her and Cal in the tiny construction they shared on their little parcel of paradise. It was an excellent plant-based life. She only wished her aging gut would allow her some separation between the stuff of her vocation and her foodstuffs. Thank god for wine.

Althea was currently without a project, which, she surmised, accounted for her heightened obsession with food and beverages. She was in the lab today to organize, a task that loomed and cast its shadow over the end of every spring term and one that invariably had her poring over cold cases for CorpsPursuit, the volunteer forensics team that lured her out west nearly a decade ago. It was always the one case, her first, that yanked her back. That particular body was not the only body that had eluded the team over the years. And of course, with her help, they'd recovered another dozen and more, but her first lost case was the one that clung to her. All the subsequent successes would only underscore that initial failure. A teenaged boy had gone missing, circumstantial evidence indicated a family member, but it was as though the earth had swallowed the boy up. Ten years ago, she'd been confident, even cocky, about the skills she brought from her work with the London police. On days like today, when nothing filled the gap, she went back to the files to supplement her alien ignorance with what she now considered hard-won local expertise. His name was Charlie, Charlie Montenegro.

Althea turned at a rap on the open door. It was Nina, and behind her, a stranger, a woman. "Hi, Nina. Come in, please, I was just attempting a little spring cleaning. Save me."

"Ally, Ally, come. I want you to meet Eleanor Clay. She's been working with Bristlecone Springs PD, on her own, for almost the same time you've been one of us. Eleanor, Althea Giordano, Lead Forensic Botanist for CorpsPursuit."

"Lead? Very diplomatic, Nina. Lone, how about. It's a pleasure, Eleanor." Althea moved to extend a hand, but pulled it back and raked it through her hair when she saw this big-eyed stranger flinch at even that small advance.

"I just finished lunch, or I'd say we should get some. We could still, if you're hungry?"

"We're fine. We had a good breakfast at my house, but I'll make some tea, yes? Where's your kettle? Never mind, I'll get mine." Nina exited the room and crossed the hallway in quick steps. Althea was reminded of the busy black squirrels she watched from her second-floor bedroom window as a child. Eleanor turned to watch Nina leave the room.

Althea talked to Eleanor's back. "You must be a very esteemed guest, Eleanor, to have seen the inside of Nina's alleged home. Not that Nina is not the most gracious individual I know. We all just assumed she lived here, with the skeletons."

"She told me as much," Eleanor said, without turning around.

Nina came back with two mugs and the electric kettle. "We'll have some of that lovely loose tea you keep, Ally, mint and sage, I think? I'll use the cup you got there for you already."

"Just stay out of the cannabis, Nina, or I'll never get cleaned up here, and we'll have to go in search of food for sure. I will, at least."

"Now you joke. But someday I will have to know what the fuss is about. Maybe when I retire and just want to eat and sleep."

"I'll weave you a little hemp basket at fill it with salad dressing and brownies. Cal will whittle you a pipe."

"Wunderbar, I can't wait. But now, to our business: Eleanor, here, has answered our call. You should maybe tell it yourself, Eleanor."

Eleanor had seated herself on the edge of a stool, and now sat up straight, surprised at being asked to do more than observe. She'd been watching and listening to the two women speak as if they were inside, and she outside, a circle of warm air. She flushed.

"Well, I'm not sure about being called, exactly." She met Althea's eyes. "I'm embarrassed to say I didn't know anything about you and your work, and I still know very little. You find the bodies of the missing. That's what I do, have been doing for ten years. It's only by accident that I found a letter, an inquiry, sent to Bristlecone Springs PD awhile back looking for people to volunteer their skills. I don't know about volunteering, seems like this group has a level of expertise that's over my head. But I came here thinking you might be able to help me understand what I've been doing all these years, and then maybe I'd have some where to start, you know, some way to figure out why it's changed." She looked down into her cup, watched stray tea leaves and herbs sink to the bottom. "Pretty vague motivation, really."

"Althea, you might have seen Eleanor in the news. You see, she used to do what we do, but more recently Eleanor has been finding living people, not bodies already dead."

"Yes," said Althea, "the girl in the sewer pipe, the little one in the cave. Amazing work, Eleanor, heroic. I can imagine how grateful those families are."

"Indeed," said Nina, "and very unlike the gratitude we receive, sincere though it is. At CorpsPursuit, we strive for closure. You have been able to keep the door open."

"Yes, well, I don't know. Maybe. Mostly I'm confused. Kind of terrified, too."

"What do you mean?" Althea noted Eleanor's translucent complexion, shadowed in the hollows under her cheekbones and eye sockets, catalogued the furrows in her forehead. Indoor skin, she thought, but not pampered. More like preserved in a jar, like a specimen. Ghostly. Except for the eyes—those were wildly alive, and captive.

Eleanor looked down into her tea mug, which she held in both hands, fingers interlaced. "When my daughter drowned, her body was not recovered. Her body had been mine to care for, and I couldn't. Not even to bury it. When I found each of the dead children, dead being the only state I found them in, I was grateful to end something for the family, to cap their suffering, but I never spoke to them, and they didn't know me or my role. Then there was Lizzie. Alive, but barely. So, so damaged. And not one bit more protected from the next horror. I found the other girl, and I thought this child, these babies, have looked at death and know it's over their shoulder all the time, this darkness. And the mothers and the fathers and the rest are exposed for what they are: helpless. I'm terrified of the life they're all open to. I'm terrified that I might have wanted the certainty of my daughter, Freya's, death more than I wanted her to be alive without me, or alive and needing more courage than I had."

"You're not saying you'd rather these families weren't reunited with their children, or that the children had been dead when you discovered them?" Althea realized it didn't sound like a question.

"No. Of course, no. I just can't bear the weight of their hope."

Nina covered Eleanor's hand with hers. "Nein, nein. That is why we have our little crew, right, Althea?"

"Hmm," said Althea. *But our little old crew isn't desperate enough to take on this albatross*, she thought.

"Ally, would you treat Eleanor and me to a tour of your magical forest?" Nina gestured in the direction of the Corps-Pursuit nurseries, a covered compound of plants and fungi, regional and exotic, and Althea's masterwork.

"Sure, Nina, I'm happy for the break from all these piles

and files. I know my keys are around here somewhere ..."

"Are these them?" Eleanor drew a finger through a ring and pulled a set of keys from behind a green vinyl binder labeled *Montenegro, C.*

"Uh, yeah. Thanks." Althea held out her hand and let Eleanor drop the set into her open palm.

CHAPTER
5

Eleanor stayed in Boulder as Nina's guest for three nights, spending days at the CorpsPursuit offices and labs learning about their process, meeting the other volunteer members of the forensics team that were in town and available. She was surprised at what a cheerful crowd they were, on the whole, for people who did such grim work. On the fourth day, Eleanor told Nina she would be leaving to see some people she knew in Denver.

"Oh! of course, I should have guessed you'd have people in the city. You lived so long in Colorado."

"Actually, I'll be visiting my husband and son."

"They live in Denver?"

"They do, since about eight years ago."

"Ah, well, I wish you a good visit. It's been my pleasure to meet you, Eleanor. I'll be in touch. You, too ja? I think we still have much more to say to one another."

"Thank you, Nina. You're not who I expected, by the way."

"In science we do not expect, that is for people with no

curiosity. We inspect, maybe. We discover."

Levi Clay lay his violin on his lap and looked at the six-year-old boy in the chair opposite him.

"Martin, what's the matter? Why'd you stop playing? We sound awesome, dude."

"I don't wanna play anymore. I don't like violin."

"Aw, c'mon, Martin, that's a little hard to believe, considering how you've been killing it lately. Didn't we just learn two new pieces? This new one we're doing's a little different, a little harder, sure, but you can do it, man. I know you can."

The boy looked down at his sneakered feet, inches above the linoleum tile, banging heel-first into the chrome legs of the plastic chair.

"What do you say we wrap for today, and you don't quit playing, and we'll see how you feel in the big group on Thursday, okay?"

"Okay. Do the thing."

"What thing? Oh, you mean this?" Levi held his violin low behind his back and played a few bars of Swallowtail Jig, ending with a flourish of farty low notes.

Martin giggled. "I want to do that, Levi."

"Practice, young Jedi, practice. You'll get there. Pack it up. I'll see you in a couple of days." Levi waved to Martin's brother, a young man older than himself by a couple of years, waiting in the hallway outside the rehearsal room door. "Tell your mom I'll let her know soon what time the recital's going to be."

"Okay. Bye, Levi."

"See you, Martin, my man."

Levi put his own instrument in its case, picked up another case holding his mandolin, and walked up the hall to the community center offices, where his father, Emmett Clay, sat bent over his laptop. "Dad? You about ready? We're going to want to swing by the store for dinner stuff. There's not much at home."

"Sure, son, just want to get a foothold on this grant that's due next week. It'd sure be easier if your mother would agree to go to a restaurant."

"Well, that's just not how it is, Dad. Besides, you know I like to cook. If you've got more to do, I can shop and come back for you."

Emmett closed his computer and looked up. "No, no, I can stop where I am. Didn't mean to make you the grown-up, though you're about there anyway, huh? What do you think she'd like tonight? What do you want?"

"I don't know. I was thinking of doing a version of that corn cake and kholowa relish we had last month in Zomba. I think catfish would be a good sub for the kampango. It was so good, and Annabelle and I talked about trying it out soon, so I figured, why not tonight?"

Emmett thought Eleanor wasn't likely to register whatever was on her plate, but he understood it was important to Levi to share something of himself with Eleanor.

"Annabelle won't be home tonight. It's just going to be the three of us."

Emmett met Annabelle Gibson when she applied for a job in project development at DRINK—Denver Resources for Investing in New Knowledge—the not-for-profit Emmett joined as Chief Programs Officer six years ago. They'd lived together—Emmett, Annabelle, and Levi—for the past five and a half years. Emmett loved her, and she him, and together they loved Levi. Emmett and Annabelle hadn't married for two reasons: one, she had been badly married and had no interest in another legal union; and two, Emmett and Eleanor never divorced. Although the four of them had shared many dinners over the years, and each had accepted, if not embraced, a sort of fragile devotion to their situation. There were times, as tonight, when one of them felt the need, or was asked, to step back. Annabelle's absence on this occasion was her own choice. She let Emmett know her plans as they got ready to go to bed the night before.

"Emmett, I just think a night for just the three of you is a good idea—it's been a while. Eleanor must be so tender right now, what with all this exposure. All the more reason to cut our numbers."

"But don't you think it'll feel more stable, more normal, with you there?"

"I think that you sound a little too trepidatious about dinner with your wife. Look, I'm not abandoning you or Eleanor. She and I have already made a date to meet and talk before she leaves town again."

"What about Levi?"

"That's not fair. Levi doesn't need me in between him and his mother."

"You're right, I'm sorry, it's me, being scared of my wife." Emmett snugged himself behind Annabelle and slid his arm under her t-shirt, gliding upwards across her belly to cup a breast. Into the soft ridge where her hairline met the supple skin behind her ear he murmured, "I wonder how different this conversation would have gone if I had been one of those guys who shacked up with a woman twenty years my junior, instead of falling under the spell of your sexual maturity?"

"It would never have gone anywhere, 'cuz it would never have happened. Especially if I hadn't repressed my fantasies of thirty-year old diet cola-swilling construction workers. Wait, is that a hammer in your pajamas ...?"

"Hmm, or some kind of tool."

Emmett emerged from his reverie to find Levi looking at him like he'd just asked a question and was waiting on an answer.

"Dad? Want me to drive? You look kind of spacey."

"Hm? Oh, thanks, Levi, why don't you? I am a little tired, now that you mention it."

Eleanor was sitting on the couch when Emmett and Levi got home. She rose as they maneuvered themselves and several bags of groceries through the front door.

"Mom! I didn't think you'd be here till after six!" He set the groceries on the floor of the entryway, took two big strides toward his mother and folded her in a hug. The top of Eleanor's head tucked right under Levi's chin. When he angled his face to kiss her, a patch of stubble from yesterday's shave rasped her cheek.

Emmett helped Levi put the food away while Eleanor settled onto a stool, then he joined her at the kitchen island and the two watched Levi at the cutting board, chopping and gesticulating with a ten-inch chef's knife, telling stories about his adventures with his young students from the junior orchestra he directed at the community center.

"I wonder if you wouldn't hold their attention even more sharply if you traded in your baton for that blade," joked Emmett.

"They're going to miss you next year," said Eleanor.

"Yeah. Me, too, them."

Eleanor smiled at the reference. "Me, too, you" was a phrase they'd volleyed back and forth over the years, mostly over the phone. Early on Emmett had made an effort to bring Levi to Bristlecone Springs as often as he could—a weekend a month, a school break. After they sold the house in Bristlecone Springs and Eleanor moved into her little apartment, Emmett suggested it should be Eleanor who came to see them. Levi had made new friends in Denver. His life was there, and, after Annabelle entered the picture, Emmett and she bought a comfortable house with plenty of room. Eleanor wanted to do what was asked of her, felt obliged and genuinely wished to support Emmett's visionary family schema, but as time progressed, weeks became months between trips.

Now here before her was her son, so grown. She wondered, as she did every time she saw and held him again after another long interval, how she could have failed him so miserably, been so absent. And yet, he was still as beautiful and kind as any human she'd ever known. She owed so much to Emmett, and to Annabelle, for holding her a spot in this kid's—this man's—life, yet it gnawed on her to realize she still didn't know what to do with it, how to fill it. If she even should. What use had she been to him? What would she ever be able to offer him?

Levi was headed in the fall to CU Boulder on a music scholarship, having declined offers to both Oberlin and Berklee. Eleanor was pained to consider her influence, direct or not, on his choice to stay so close to home. It hadn't been just Emmett and Annabelle who held a space for her. Levi had left himself open, always ready to receive her. She suspected her son's reluctance to fly too far from home had something to do with that hollow. She accepted her own mix of regret and guilt as an inarguable condition of her existence. She often thought, but would never say aloud, that Levi should be free of her, free of the heavy darkness of his phantom mother. She was yet too selfish to say it, to let him go, even if she did him no good.

They ate and talked, and then Levi prepared to leave to practice with his band, Pop the Chute.

"You're staying tonight, right?" he asked his mother. "I made sourdough waffle batter, and Dad and I bought blueberries."

"I am. I'll be here in the morning for sure."

Levi bent to kiss Eleanor, grabbed his case, and left.

Emmett and Eleanor watched the headlights back out of the driveway through the kitchen window.

"He feels it, the separation coming up."

"Well, of course he does, Eleanor."

"I think I'm keeping him here."

"Eleanor, it's his choice. Besides, you're forgetting about Trista. Love is a powerful magnet. Look, Eleanor, Levi is one well-traveled kid. He knows there's a whole world out there, and I, for one, think it's okay he feels like he has the time to see it. The music will happen wherever he goes."

"You're right. It doesn't have to be about me."

"Speaking of that."

"What? Oh, yeah...about me...I wish I knew what to tell you, Emmett. I don't know what's happening. You know I came here from a place called CorpsPursuit, a bunch of forensic scientists in Boulder who look for bodies in cold cases. I don't know. I figured maybe one of them could tell me something about myself."

"How could I know something like that unless you told me, Eleanor?" Emmett knew only what he'd read online about the recovered children. He was used to Eleanor being quiet about her work. When he'd called her the week before, she said only that she'd talk about it when she came up to Denver. He felt a stab of jealousy that she'd been to Boulder, or anywhere, and talked about her life with someone else.

"These recent kids, Eleanor, they're alive when you find them. Don't you think that's a change for the good?"

"Emmett, this sounds crazy, but I feel like I have something to do with the fact that they're in danger to begin with."

The screen on Eleanor's phone lit up across the room on the kitchen counter. She stared at the device for a moment before rising to answer the call.

"Detective Stanislaus." Eleanor stood still with the phone to her ear for ten long seconds. "I'll be there."

She stared at the screen for another second, and then sent Levi a text: *Got to get back early. Raincheck on the waffles?*

"What's happened?"

"There's another missing child reported. They don't want to wait to bring me in. Gordon thinks the disappearances are connected."

"This is the third?"

"Yes, the third in two months. This time a boy. He'll be suffering right now, if he's alive."

"My god, these poor families." Emmett went to Eleanor, who was leaning with both hands on the counter as if to push it through the wall. He stood next to her and echoed her stance, covering her right hand with his left and matching her stare out the kitchen window into the lightless night.

CHAPTER
6

Lizzie, Maybelline, and now Jesse. For each case pinned to the storyboard on the wall in the basement office, there was a photo of a child smiling at the viewer, a portrait taken at a recent birthday party or on Christmas morning, snapped in a moment of unapologetic happiness. For the first two, there was another photo. Lizzie looked down and past the viewer, her gaze trying to escape her own body, to divert attention from the new shame of injury; the other captured the limp body of Maybelline, the body's animation lost to coma. For Jesse Meyers there was just one image, a small boy standing on a patch of turf in a yellow and black striped soccer jersey, number nine, baggy black nylon shorts, tight black socks pulled up to dimpled knees, hands posed on hips, one leg bent, and the foot resting on the black and white pentagonal and hexagonal geometries of a Spaulding soccer ball. A broad cowlick pushes the long dirty blond bangs up before they cascade over his left eye. Both front teeth are missing from his smile. A single deep comma in the right cheek punctuates the smooth, round face.

Stanislaus watched Eleanor as she stood in front of the wall, moving in close, backing up, telescoping in again. From the back, she might have been an art lover or critic absorbed in a painting in a gallery, studying and experimenting with perspective. He thought, that's where she belongs, this intense woman coming on to middle age, mild and opaque: a university, a gallery, a library. But he knew there was nothing academic about how Eleanor studied the photographs of these kids. While he didn't understand her strange methods, or how she came by her intuition, he was clear on the terror that drove her research. This was a bad-smelling, foul-tasting business they partnered in, visceral, no pleasure in theory, relief only in resolution.

Bringing Eleanor in early like this was new. There was no reason to assume she'd be able to help, as her success at finding bodies had had to do with her own on-the-ground search, her own methods. He'd never before discussed a case in progress with her. In fact, her arrival meant the case was over. Put to rest. But she'd found these last two kids alive. He thought maybe, in his discomfort, he—the department—had underutilized her. Still, he wasn't about to fold her in with the investigative team. He doubted Eleanor was a team player—his own intuition. Hence, the storyboard on the wall of a hastily converted storeroom. He had a desk and chair moved in and plugged in an old Mr. Coffee that had never made it out of the packing box in his garage after the last downsize.

"Officer DePeña is assigned to you for as long as you need him."

Eleanor looked away from the wall and blinked at Elan. The crown of his uniform cap nearly met with a stained panel of the dropped ceiling. His face shone a little green in the florescent lighting.

"Oh," said Eleanor.

"Honored to work with you, ma'am."

Stanislaus broke the ensuing silence.

"Yeah, so, we're looking at water, seeing if there's a connection between the river and the hot springs, anything that might expose a pattern between these abductions. And we're keeping a close eye on transit hubs, of course, the bus and the train, given the sweater at the station. We need to fall into step with whatever this bastard is doing."

"You think it's one person, Gordon? I mean, um, Detective Stanislaus. Has anyone talked to Maybelline? Is she awake?" Maybelline had been unconscious at the scene, and remained in a coma at Bristlecone Springs General. Eleanor had left for Boulder hours after recovering the child from the cave by the springs and had had no contact with either the mother or the father.

"No. The toxicology reports on both kids showed a cocktail of THC and valerian root, administered intravenously. The doctors don't know yet if Maybelline's state is more attributable to the drugs or to exposure." Lizzie Barrett had regained consciousness shortly after arriving at the hospital, but had remembered nothing, or could say nothing, of her ordeal.

"Listen, Eleanor, I thought you could talk with the families, Jesse's as well as the others. Maybe you'd have insight we don't."

God help her, he thought, maybe Eleanor's pain is her way in. As many shitty missing child cases as Stanislaus had investigated over the years, here and in Chicago, he'd never suffered the loss of his own child, not by someone else's hand, so long as they'd been children. Even now, he knew just where his children were, even if they couldn't care less where he was. Reflexively, his right hand rose to lay flat on the spot where a gold crucifix lay against his chest under his button down and Hanes beefy tee.

Elan drove west on I-70, Eleanor quiet in the passenger seat. She intended to speak with Maybelline's mother before meeting with Jesse's mother and father. She'd talk to Maybelline's father, Nestor Dodge, later at the hospital in Bristlecone Springs, where Maybelline's condition remained critical but stable, and where he'd sat vigil since she was admitted.

Eleanor read the case file again while Elan ducked into a Kum & Go for coffee.

Elan slipped back behind the wheel and handed her a to-go cup. "Ever wonder if the people who named these quickie marts had any idea what they were doing?"

"What?"

"'Kum & Go'. Like, that's a nickname for a truck stop in a porn flick."

"Huh, I never thought about it." Eleanor stared out the windshield, thinking about what she was going to say to Maybelline's mother. Despite her aversion to contact, she agreed with Stanislaus, after all, that she should meet the families of the children. The detective had Isla and Jeff Meyers at the squad, looking at photos of people with criminal histories, people who the police thought could reasonably be suspected of abducting a child, their Jesse. While Eleanor felt the process was a blind alley—more busywork than anything else—she decided it afforded her sufficient time to drive to Silt to meet Maybelline's mom, Justine Dodge. Eleanor had no idea what she was going to ask her, what she could ask of any of these grieving people. She understood, however, against the boiling resistance in her stomach, that she needed to look into their eyes and hear their voices.

"I don't guess it's worth that much thought."

"What? Oh, no. I was just thinking about Justine Dodge,

what I can say to her."

"Well, I can't claim a whole lot of experience with investigations, but in my intro to non-violent communications class, active listening was always stressed as being much more valuable than anything you actually said."

"'Non-violent communication'? Emmett and I went to a seminar about that once, some event for his work. Moderator used a pair of puppets, a giraffe and a ...I think it was a weasel? Maybe a badger. They were headbands, giraffe and weasel puppet headbands. You wore them while you spoke to each other. The whole thing made me feel kind of violent, actually."

"Maybe you should just forget about classes and seminars, then, and just let her tell you what she wants to tell you."

"Yes. Yes, I can do that. Thank you, Officer DePeña."

The files sat closed in Eleanor's lap as she took in the passing landscape. When she drove by herself to Denver, she kept her eyes on the road in front of her; the highway peripherals rarely registered. She'd assumed there was little to see beyond industrial parks, abandoned barns, dilapidated attractions long rotted to splinters. And in fact, there wasn't much on this stretch they were on, besides the generic roadside scrub, and the giant billboards. The first one they passed read,

Cheers to All God's Creatures!
Enjoy Genesis 1:28

A few miles down the road, another billboard loomed in the same style:

Be Fruitful & Multiply & Fill the Earth
...and your cup with Genesis 1:28!

"Officer DePeña, what is Genesis 1:28?"

"The verse, ma'am?"

"The billboards, DePeña."

"Beer, ma'am. It's a beer."

"Beer? Seems an odd pairing, doesn't it? Beer and the Bible?"

"Yes, ma'am, you'd think so, except in my fermentation essentials class, we learned that beer is as old as the Old Testament, at least. Course, so's the devil, if you were to ask some. Genesis 1:28 is a pretty popular beer, though, if a little too hoppy for my taste. I'm more of a cider enthusiast myself."

"Genesis 1:28. Isn't that the part that talks about 'dominion over every living thing' or something like that?"

"'And God blessed them, and God said unto them, Be fruitful, and multiply, and replenish the earth, and subdue it: and have dominion over the fish of the sea, and over the fowl of the air, and over every living thing that moveth upon the earth.' King James."

"And what class was that, Officer DePeña, or did you grow up in the faith?"

"Intro to world religions and fundamentals of Christian theory. I took the second one for my nana. She thought I'd make a good priest. Can't say I heard the calling, but it got me three credits toward my social science requirements."

"How many credits did you need to become a cop?"

"Not as many as many as I got. I guess it took me a while to settle on a direction."

"Huh."

Justine Dodge met them at the door of the family's duplex in Silt. A baby slept on her shoulder, seven or eight months old, Eleanor guessed. She and Elan stood in the small living room and waited while Justine lay the baby down in a bedroom down the short hallway. When the young mother returned, she gestured to the couch.

"Please, sit down."

Eleanor sat on the couch. Elan positioned himself off a few steps by the dinette set, hat in hand. Justine stood a second before she settled lightly on the edge of the cushion. Eleanor shifted to face her. "Mrs. Dodge, Justine, you may already know that I am the person who found Maybelline in the cave."

"And you found that Lizzie girl."

"Yes."

"You used to find just the dead ones."

"Yes, that's true, too."

"Are you psychic or something? Can you talk to my Maybelline now? Or does she have to be dead?"

"No, I'm sorry. I'm here to ask you if you can remember something else about the day your daughter disappeared, something maybe you didn't think was important at the time."

"I told all I know already. Nestor took Maybelline to the springs on his day off, to spend some time together just the two of them. Nestor's real sweet that way. Understanding the baby takes up so much of my time, wanting to make sure Maybelline gets the attention she needs, too. He was like that even when we were dating, listened to her, got on the floor to play Barbies, never complained about having her around, about sharing our time together. They just went to the pool, like they do all the time in summer. They don't go near the caves. She doesn't like the caves. Nestor neither. They just go to the pool. They go all summer, every week, on Nestor's day off."

"Nestor is not Maybelline's birth father?"

"No, I had Maybelline two years before I met Nestor, but he's her father now, legal. When we got pregnant with Oscar, we agreed to make our family official. Nestor adopted Maybelline as his own. He's a strong and decent man, my Nestor, the best thing ever happened to me and Maybelline, and I'm praying, praying hard every day, but I'm afraid he won't hold up through this...and... I can't lose them both."

"Maybelline is alive and stable, Justine. There's every reason to believe she'll come out of this okay."

"Doctor said the longer she's in that coma, the less chance she has of being right again ..."

Eleanor stared at the woman's hand as it clawed the cushion. Then, as if she'd remembered something long forgotten, she took Justine Dodge's hand in her own, where it spasmed before gripping back hard.

"Justine, please think as best you can about what happened that day. Your daughter disappeared from the parking lot at the pool. Do you remember Maybelline mentioning anyone, an adult she met, any person who had talked to her, maybe a relative of a friend? Someone who might have known her about her and her father's plans? Maybe someone Nestor talked to, a work associate?"

"No, I can't remember her talking about anyone, and Nestor didn't say anything about anybody, but you already know he works at the pool. Everybody there knew how often they come. It was just the two of them, and then she was gone. Mrs ...?"

"Eleanor. Eleanor Clay."

"Eleanor, I'm sorry if I don't sound grateful to you for finding my Maybelline. I only wish whatever sight Jesus blessed you with had shown her to you sooner."

On the drive back to Bristlecone Springs, Eleanor re-read the case file on Maybelline. The adoptive father had no motive and was able to account for his time since the girl's disappearance. All indicators pointed to a loving parent. Eleanor knew from her long history with finding dead and abused children that beneath a veneer of dedication the truth could be ugly, but this guy looked solid.

"Ma'am?"

"Officer DePeña, I prefer you call me Eleanor when it's just us. And I'll call you Elan, if that's okay? I'll be careful to use your correct title at the station. It's hard enough to think without having to be polite in the car."

"Elan is fine, thank you. I still snap my head around looking for 'Officer DePeña' half the time, anyway. Eleanor, did you feel there was anything odd about Justine Dodge, I mean, besides her understandable distress over the circumstances?"

"What did you pick up?"

"I don't know. It just seems to me she's thinking and talking like Maybelline's dead already."

"Hm, yes. I can see where you get that." Eleanor thought, it could very well be how she's surviving the moment, digging the hole in herself before fate gouges it out for her.

Holes, Eleanor thought. Holes. There was something about these spaces. Lizzie was found sealed in a cement box dug into the banks of a river within two miles of the bus station. Maybelline was wrapped in a nylon sleeping bag and wedged into a seam of a cave closed for maintenance less than a mile from the hot springs pool. There was the water connection, and the similar proximities to the abduction sites. She opened Jesse's file. Jeff Meyers was a lawyer for the county, Isla Meyers was a real estate agent. Jesse had been taken from the business park where his mother's office was located.

Eleanor looked up and out the passenger window as they were approaching another bright billboard:

> Cheers to every living creature that moves in the seas, in the sky, on the ground!
> Enjoy Genesis 1:28

She had an idea, not perfectly logical, but it tugged on her. She thought back to her visit to CorpsPursuit. One of the forensic tools they used was aerial maps. The survey maps helped them locate variations in geographical patterns, see where a patch of ground might be inconsistent with its surrounding terra. On her cell she called the number she had for the CorpsPursuit offices. She got voicemail, disconnected, and called Nina directly. When the older woman offered her personal number, Eleanor didn't think she'd ever use it, and she did not reciprocate with her own cell number. Now she was glad one of them had been open-hearted. Nina answered on the third ring.

"Ja? Nina Steuben."

"Nina, it's Eleanor."

"Eleanor! What is it?"

"There's another child, a boy. I need your help." Eleanor briefly outlined her theory.

"Nina, can someone who's looking for them distinguish things like wells or tanks on a property?

"We've had good experiences with the maps in locating places where the ground has been disturbed, for construction, and ja, for systems installations—wells and such. The county offices should be able to help. If you're very lucky the maps will be digitalized and recent. But even if they aren't, they are a good place to look. Good luck, Eleanor."

Eleanor stared at the dash, letting her thoughts drop like tetra blocks into their compartments.

"Elan, radio Detective Stanislaus. We need a list of water tanks in the area, and someone who knows their way around a geographical survey database."

Under her breath she whispered, "Hold on, Jesse, we're coming."

CHAPTER

7

Detective Stanislaus met Eleanor and Elan as they pulled the Ford Escape into the lot at the Bristlecone Springs Police Department.

"DePeña, give the keys to Officer Morgan. I've got cars headed to investigate registered properties within a radius of two miles. We'll widen the circle as we go. You two can ride with me. Eleanor, I'm following your thinking, I think, but you know there are dozens of registered water tanks in the area. I've put all available personnel on this. If you're onto something, we might get lucky and get to the boy in time. No telling, though, how many tanks we've got no paperwork on. Even with a volunteer crew, it's a broad search, and I'm not one hundred percent convinced it's the right one."

Eleanor knew she hadn't offered more than a hunch to Stanislaus, but he'd jumped right in, splitting the territory up and dispatching search teams. Equally moved and frightened by his faith in her impulse, she nonetheless understood that they needed to narrow the field if they were going to find Jesse alive.

"Gordon, when I went to the CorpsPursuit labs, I was told that one of the tools they use to find people—bodies—is aerial survey maps. They don't make them, they already exist as government documents. If we have those, we can see where all the local tanks are, registered or not. At least we would know we haven't overlooked any."

"That's good, Eleanor, it's something. DePeña!" Stanislaus barked, throwing Elan his keys. "You drive. I'll get on the cell and get the county to dig out some of these aerial maps, if they got them."

Their crew of three were on their second tank, on a residential property about a mile west of town, when Stanislaus got the call that there were, indeed, USGS maps which would show where tanks for irrigation and livestock had been installed. A clerk would download the maps from the federal site and get the locations catalogued, then send digital versions of the list and maps to the officers in the field.

Radios hissed like turkey vultures throughout the day as searchers ticked off each marked spot in a macabre scavenger hunt everyone wanted to finish, and no one was going to win.

Officers Morgan and Harris got to the site first, hours into the search, but with daylight to spare. This time, when Stanislaus' radio squawked, it was Morgan with news.

"We got a boy here, sir. Wrapped up like the others. Ambulance is en route. He's alive, sir."

On a derelict ranch for sale about three-and-a-half miles northwest of downtown Bristlecone Springs, Jesse Meyers floated in several inches of rank water in a half-covered aboveground tank, laid out in a homemade dugout constructed from a sawed-off plastic cistern wrapped densely and symmetrically in catgut. Only the boy's face was exposed, his mouth slack, revealing the jagged edge of a front incisor poking through the upper gum line.

Eleanor, Stanislaus, and Elan arrived at the same time as

the ambulance. Jesse was quickly cut out of the cistern and carefully transferred onto a gurney as the EMTs worked to assess bruises and infected skin, take the boy's blood pressure, administer oxygen, and get him in the vehicle. Eleanor watched the team's swift and confident protocols, mesmerized by the juxtaposition of confidence in their movements and terror in their expressions, until the doors shut and the ambulance pulled away, red light whipping, siren screaming.

Stanislaus stood at her back. "The Meyers will meet us at the hospital." He put a hand on her shoulder. "He's going to be okay, Eleanor. That was good detective work, the best outcome for a terrible situation. How about you? You going to be all right?"

Eleanor turned her face to his, her gaze unfocused. "Um, yeah, I think so. Gordon, do you need me at the hospital just yet?"

"I guess not, no. Why don't I get DePeña to take you home? I'll ride over with Morgan. Jesse's where someone can help him, God willing, and you can do your part of the paperwork tomorrow. You deserve a rest."

"Gordon?"

"Yeah?"

"I don't think we're done with this business. I don't think Jesse's the last one."

His hand recoiled as if bit. He walked quickly and officiously toward the patrol car to cover his reaction.He couldn't help it. This quiet, damaged woman spooked the hell out of him. Shame and fear flushed his neck and ears as he growled over his shoulder, "Let's pray you're wrong this time, Eleanor."

When Eleanor got back to her apartment, she found a small basket waiting on the cracked rubber welcome mat at the front door. She pulled a handwritten note from under a pile of young garlic, wild onion, oregano, and a few springs of blooming prickly rose, and read, *Didn't have your number, hope it's not too creepy to have found out your address. In town with my partner, Cal, for a few days. Thought we could chat. I make a very delicious wild herb pasta if I do say so myself.* The note was signed, *Althea,* with a cell number below.

Eleanor hadn't thought she and Althea had particularly hit it off, but then, she hadn't been trying to make a friend when they met at CorpsPursuit. She wants something, Eleanor thought. But what? Motive wasn't her strong suit.

A rush of garlic and herbs wafted up from the basket and filled her nose, which reminded her, painfully, that she hadn't eaten since the day before. Levi's fish. She let herself into the dim space and called the cell number.

"Hi, this is Althea Giordano."

"Althea, it's Eleanor."

"Eleanor, thank you for calling! I hope you don't feel my stopping by was obnoxious."

"You know, it's been a long day and a plate of pasta sounds good, if the offer's still good. Just you, though. I don't want to offend, but I don't think I can meet anybody new right now."

"No, it's fine. Cal is off doing his thing, anyway. And yes, I am always up for pasta. See you in thirty?"

"So, I was hanging off the embankment next to the El, scraping mold onto a slide while Freddy, our geologist, held me by the ankles in the freezing rain. Every forensic botanist's dream scenario. We made that case, though."

"Amazing what you, what you all do at that place. And in your free time. Not typical volunteer work."

Althea split the remainder of the bottle of Barolo she'd brought between their glasses.

"It's not typical work under any circumstances. I think we're all a little about the lost cause, and very much about helping the living get past the disappearance of a loved one. And also, we're a bunch of nerds who can't get enough of the stuff we geek out on. For me, it's the language and lexicon of plants."

Althea fished into the bottom of the little basket and produced a slender, neat joint.

"Dessert! Along with a hunk of this." From the bottom of her grocery bag, she brought out a bar of dark chocolate with cherries.

"Oh, the wine's plenty for me, I think ..."

A sharp knock on the door froze Eleanor in place. No one came to the apartment. Pappardelle squirmed in her stomach.

Althea saw Eleanor blanch and rose. "Let me get it."

Elan DePeña stood on the step, dressed in jeans and a t-shirt and a short leather jacket. A bicycle helmet hung from his wrist. In his hand was a pink bakery box.

"Yes?"

"Um, is Mrs. Clay...is Eleanor here?"

"I don't know. Hold on a minute." She turned her face slightly away from Elan, her classic profile a flirty echo of a modern Aphrodite. "Eleanor, are you expecting a nice-looking young man bearing sweets, name of ...?"

"Officer DePeña, ma'am. Elan DePeña. I work with Mrs. Clay."

"Name of Elan, he says."

Eleanor came to the door. "Elan, what's happened?"

"No, nothing! I'm sorry. I only thought after today maybe you'd need a little pick-me-up." He opened the lid to reveal a slab of tiramisu.

"Oh, my God, Eleanor, let's get this fine young man in here. Only no more of this 'ma'am' business."

After Althea introduced herself to Elan, she slid a plate of food in front of him and plucked from somewhere another bottle of red wine, a chianti this time. An hour and a half later, the joint was smoked, and the pastry demolished.

"Oh, my god, Althea, that pasta...let's see, I got the baby onion and the rosemary...what was that other thing? A pinch of sumac?"

"You're good, young sous chef. Very, very good."

As it happened, the two new people in Eleanor's life had much in common. Althea delighted in what she discovered to be Elan's amateur love of botany; Elan was duly wowed when it was revealed that Althea had a cousin who'd won several stages of the Giro D'Italia. Eleanor watched and listened as her two surprise visitors behaved like old friends long separated and joyously reunited, rather than strangers just met. She couldn't remember the last time she'd been in a room with this much human volume. In the time she'd lived in this space, the decibel level never rose above the shuffle of a slipper, the scrape of a spoon. She was a bit dazzled, and also uncomfortable—the exhaustion of the day settled heavily in her limbs. Her body responded, however, to the chatter of these two new people as to a piece of music she'd forgotten she'd known and now missed.

She realized, suddenly, that Althea was taking to her.

"Eleanor, I'll clean up here. Why don't you get some rest? Elan will help me, and we'll let ourselves out."

"Yes, I could go to bed, thank you. But why don't you take the couch, Althea? It's late. Elan can find his way, I'm sure, and he can't exactly give you a lift on that bike of his."

"Unless you rode the handlebars. No, kidding, they're touring handlebars. You couldn't anyway." He cleared his throat and straightened his posture. "Eleanor, I'll be back with the car to pick you up at 09:00. We've got our reports to write, and Detective Stanislaus wants you to interview Jesse's parents." He added, "I'll bring coffee."

"Large latte, two percent, squeeze of honey, per favore.

Thank you, Elan, and thank *you,* Eleanor, I accept. With Cal combing the countryside and a headful of wine, I'd be grateful for the couch and the company."

CHAPTER
8

Eleanor was pinning Jesse's post-recovery photo to the board when Stanislaus entered the basement office.

"Turns out that parcel of land we found the boy on isn't so neglected, after all. Two separate parties have made offers on the property very recently, neither yet accepted. That tells me there have been more people than we might have thought tromping through that ranch in the past week. We canvased as much as we could yesterday, but we didn't walk away with much—no prints, no blood. I put a detective on tracking down sources for the cistern and the cord."

"Who's been there? Who are these potential buyers?"

"Well, it's interesting, if not surprising in these modern times. One is Genesis 1:28, the beer company. They're looking, apparently, to grow hops. The other is a company called Cannabis Cumulus. They're a big name in the pot business, want to expand production."

Elan piped up. "Sir, excuse me, Cannabis Cumulus is not a company. It's more of a consortium—you know, made up of a

lot of different companies and parties with a common interest."

"Let me guess, DePeña, you're working on your MBA, as
well?"

"No, sir. Just intro to market concepts, sir. Plus, I've got an
uncle that grows for one of the medical marijuana outfits."

"Well. Okay, I guess we have our work cut out for us. My
people upstairs will contact whoever may have visited the
property lately. Eleanor, I want you to check the site, see if you
can get anything off it."

"Gordon, when do you want me to talk to Jesse's parents?"

"We're going to put that off—your part, that is. The boy's
conscious, but not communicating, and the mother and father
are still pretty upset, understandably. We got a preliminary
interview already, and I'm going to have a detective circle
back."

"Is there something wrong? I mean, besides the fact their
child was abducted and nearly died?"

"Well, yes, and no. They're freaked out. I'm going to
restrict their interaction to official personnel for the time
being."

"Meaning I'm the freak that's freaking them out."

"Eleanor—*Mrs. Clay*—just please head to the site."

"Yes, sir."

In the late morning sun, the only thing indicating a crime
scene was the police tape enclosing the area around the water
tank, which looked like any water tank, particularly one which
had not been used to any purpose recently, let alone a kidnapping. The sparse Kentucky Bluegrass shot with red clover
was flattened in spots, but to Eleanor, the landscape was
unrevealing. This wasn't the way it normally worked for her.

In order for her to find something, it had to be actively lost. She found the thing, or the being, not the reason it got lost in the first place. She found the object because it somehow disturbed the landscape, caused a break in the pattern. It was the boy who'd suffered the scarring. If she were to locate the missing thing at all, find this child stealer, it would be through the breached bodies of Jesse, Maybelline, and Lizzie.

Despite her lack of confidence in the process, she and Elan spent a diligent hour at the site. She took notes, or more precisely, doodled and scratched out whatever associations came to her, which weren't many. Her flip phone vibrated in her jacket pocket.

It was Althea. "Cal won't be back through town for a day or two. I've been to the hot springs, no huge interest in the tram. What are your dinner plans?"

"Uh, none. No dinner plans. But you know what? I could use some lunch. I've got something I want to ask you about, if you don't mind. There's a diner on Main, Bea's Place. Meet you in an hour?"

"Diner is one of my favorite words. Put a tuna melt in front of me and ask away." Althea thought, *I may just have a couple of questions of my own.*

"Botanical evidence is not often perceived by the initial police canvas, even a careful one. I'm not surprised nothing stands out for you at the ranch. Might be something there, though. The beauty of a piece of land used primarily for grazing, from a search perspective, is that what grows and does not grow on the property is clear, and usually limited. Pollen and such dragged in from elsewhere can point to something. Cops can generally discern when a body has been moved after death. At CorpsPursuit, we've been able to identify the scene of the crime, and link a suspect, by comparing the flora from the dump spot and/or the scene of the crime."

The server, the titular Bea's daughter, came to the table

with a pot of coffee. "Don't you worry about rushing out. I got to clean the bathrooms and set up before I'm out of here, least a half hour."

Althea had paid the bill after she and Eleanor had eaten their soup and sandwiches. She'd bought two take-away pies out of the case, chocolate silk and fresh peach, which sat boxed and tied on the counter, and had left a generous tip.

Eleanor smiled into her coffee. "I don't think Dottie's said more than ten words to me in as many years."

Althea laughed. "I find people respond very warmly when you show interest in their pies. Eleanor, I'm interested in your case and I'd like to help, but for one thing, it's probably not kosher that you're discussing it with me, even unofficially, and for another, I don't know what I can offer. CorpsPursuit takes on cases by consensus, and we do cold case recovery. We don't investigate kidnappings."

"But I thought, since you said you're on break from the college, and your partner is traveling ..."

"I don't have a lab." Eleanor watched Althea pour sugar onto her spoon, tip it into her cup, and stir, all the while staring at a chip on the Formica. "Maybe, *maybe*, I could interest some students at the college in a summer internship, if I can convince the school to give them some lab hours. They could run a few tests, check the data systems ...we could try to trace the source of the intravenous THC and valerian ...but you've got to okay this with your PD, Eleanor. In my experience, police departments do not love working with strangers, especially out-of-town forensic experts. Be sure and tell them I'll work for free—it helps. That is, if I can plant myself on your couch."

"Althea, thank you. I'll admit, I'm pretty lost. If you can help me put a picture together of what's happening, then maybe we can find the person, or people, taking these children, make it stop."

In Althea's experience, this brand of terrible event never stopped, seemed only to gain and lose momentum. She was excited, however, to play a part in an investigation with living, breathing subjects, for a change.

She couldn't put a name on what motivated Eleanor. Althea had walked into lunch determined to get to the root of Eleanor's agenda, discover why this strange woman had visited CorpsPursuit, what had sustained her in her grisly, solitary work in the last ten years, how she could persist as the dark anomaly she was in this little resort town. Althea was beginning to believe, however, that Eleanor had no agenda whatsoever, not the vaguest plan, couldn't even imagine what she would be having for dinner, didn't care. Like some members of the families that benefited, if they did, from CorpsPursuit's efforts, the people who had lost someone to the world with no trace of departure, with no letting go, with no opportunity to anoint and mourn a body, Eleanor was the embodiment of perpetual grief—a howling, shapeless loss silenced and contained, reverberating from within and against a corporeal form.

"Let's grab our pies and go. I don't want to lose favor with Dottie, now that I may be hanging around for a while."

CHAPTER

9

"Free? Who works for free?" Elan and Eleanor were on the highway headed to the VOLT campus, the large central headquarters for Value Our Loving Traditions.

"Althea has agreed to contribute her expertise to the case, and yes, she's doing it without financial compensation."

"But, why?"

"Elan, why do you take so many courses at the community college? You've said so yourself: not every course is a potential career path. Seems to me you are a naturally curious person."

"I guess. Or, as Terrance says, I'm just *unable to focus and loathe to commit.* He uses my school transcript as evidence that I'm not serious about a relationship. Sometimes I really hate that he's a lawyer. But yeah, you're right. Some things I want to know just to know."

"If you don't mind me asking, why did you become a cop?" Before he could answer, she thought better of it. "No, you know what? Forget it, it's really none of my business."

"No, I don't mind, I guess, but the thing is, I don't have a good answer. I don't come from real law and order kind of people. My father would've died before owning a gun. Although technically, I don't own my gun, the department does."

"I've never fired a gun."

"You're not missing much, in my opinion. It's my least favorite piece of equipment."

"Well, for what's it's worth, I appreciate Gordon assigning you to me, and I hope you can get back on the bike soon."

"It's cool, for now. You know, people make jokes, but I was super lucky to get bike patrol straight out of the academy...and I couldn't stay in school forever, could I? Hey, you want a coffee? The next Kum and Go's coming up."

He was in the convenience store five minutes when Eleanor decided she had to pee. Elan faced the wall perpendicular to the rest room door, balancing two cups of coffee in one hand while holding his phone to his ear with the other.

"Have to use the restroom."

"Yeah, sure," said Elan. "I'm just calling my mom. She worries, you know, since I became a cop."

"So you call her."

"Yeah."

Eleanor looked past him to the restroom door.

"Oh, sorry, you need to get in there..." He held out one of the coffees. "You want this? Oh, wait, probably not why you're ...I'll meet you in the car."

Within a few miles of the campus, which had its own exit, billboards sponsored by VOLT appeared every half mile. The first one read:

> *...as the sound of your greeting reached my ears, the baby in my womb leaped for joy ~ Luke 1:41*
> *Choose Life!*
> *Value Our Loving Traditions*

Eleanor commented, "They don't vary their marketing strategy much from product to product, do they?"

The next two read,

> *I have set before you life and death, blessing and cursing: therefore choose life, that both thou and thy seed may live*
> *~Deuteronomy 30:19*
> *Choose Life!*
> *Value Our Loving Traditions*

and

> *You shall not murder ~ Exodus 20:1 Choose Life!*
> *Value Our Loving Traditions*

"Or maybe they do at that," she muttered.

They were on their way to talk to John Yearling, CEO of Genesis 1:28, who also happened to be, since the year previous, president of Value Our Loving Traditions. He was on the VOLT campus all week to prepare for a big in-training for programs the conservative Christian organization operated in fourteen countries across the globe.

Elan said, "I still think it's weird we're going straight to the top when all I asked was could we talk to someone involved in the real estate offer. You'd think they'd have a PR rep or department head or someone deal with us, not the chief."

"Lucky us."

They took the exit and followed the signs to Calgary Fire, a vast parking area ringed in quaking aspen, then followed New Covenant Road on foot to First Hope, a long building with a steeply pitched roof which housed the VOLT administration. Inside, a receptionist greeted them through a golden dry mist of pine-redolent sawdust, the buzz of a circular saw, and the staccato punch of a nail gun.

"Blessings. How may I serve you?"

Eleanor stepped forward. "I'm Eleanor Clay and this is

Officer DePeña from the Bristlecone Springs Police Department. We're here to talk to John Yearling about a piece of land his company Genesis 1:28 put an offer on."

"Yes, Pastor Yearling is expecting you! I'll just see he's in his office."

Eleanor raised her eyebrow and turned to Elan. "Pastor?"

"Makes sense, I guess. VOLT got tax identification to call itself a church this year."

John Yearling strode into the lobby, teeth bared, hand extended and aimed at Eleanor like a guided missile. She stared at it while the man's other hand grasped hers and locked it in place.

"Pastor John Yearling, blessings! Mrs. Clay and Officer DePeña, I understand? Greetings and welcome to our humble campus! But you're here to talk about Genesis 1:28, so let me put on my CEO hat and we'll take a walk, get a little distance from the noise." He swept an arm toward the south end of the building, as if to unveil a spectacular extravaganza. "We are fortunate to be expanding our daycare center this year."

Outside they followed a paved walking path tightly edged with tall cylinders of arborvitae alternating with spheres of crimson red-berried viburnum, to a water feature minimally ornamented with a sculpture of a dove taking flight from the crossbar of a crucifix.

Yearling took a seat on a bench, leaned back, and crossed an ankle over a knee. "There, now we can hear ourselves think! How may I help you?"

Eleanor remained standing. "Mr. Yearling, our investigation shows your company made an offer recently to purchase the Walstan Ranch in Bristlecone Springs."

"Yes, indeed we did. R&D has us convinced we can grow our own hops on that site, and we're eager to produce a brew with deeper regional roots. What is your interest in our plans, Mrs. Clay?"

"My interest, Mr. Yearling, is in service to a police investigation involving the child who was abducted and restrained on the property."

"Mrs. Clay, are you a police officer?"

"I am an official police consultant, assigned to this case, along with Officer DePeña, by Chief Detective Gordon Stanislaus."

Yearling looked from Eleanor to Elan as if he'd forgotten about him. "Yes. But not just this case, or this boy. You are the hero, or heroine, who found the other missing children, as well. Isn't that right?"

"Mr. Yearling, if you would please focus on who visited the property from your company in the last two weeks."

"Certainly. All the senior officers visited the site, myself included, plus our chief brewer. We toured the acreage with the broker."

"Who, as it happens, is Jesse's mother. Were you aware that the real estate broker is the mother of the boy we found in the water tank?"

"Terrible thing, having a child go missing, then turn up hurt. We've been praying for the family. Unfortunate coincidence."

"Were there multiple visits to the property?"

"I've been to the ranch a couple of times, yes."

"Alone?"

Yearling planted his feet and leaned forward. "Genesis 1:28 has significant distribution in Bristlecone Springs. I'm in town quite often, sometimes by myself, more often with a member of our sales team. If I stopped by the ranch to take another look or two at a potential investment, it was well in keeping with my usual itinerary. I want to help the authorities with what they need to bring justice to a tragic situation, but I don't know what you're fishing for here, Mrs. Clay."

"The police are trying to ascertain who was on the property and when, Mr. Yearling, as well as who might have noticed anything or anyone out of the ordinary. A boy was drugged and bound in a cistern and left in a water tank to die. On a property you and your associates have been visiting recently."

"You've found all these children close to death, haven't you, Mrs. Clay? I'd say that's a kind of miracle, wouldn't you?"

Eleanor's expression remained neutral. Elan watched, saw her jaw flex and fix itself before she spoke. "Mr. Yearling, we'll need a list of your employees who toured the property, and we'll need you to remember the occasions you returned unaccompanied."

"Of course, anything I can do."

"One last thing. Our records show Genesis 1:28 is competing with a company called Cannabis Cumulus for purchase of the ranch. Have you had any direct contact with the owners or representatives of that organization?"

Yearling rose from the bench and gestured back toward the path. "I have not, no. It's no secret I oppose the use of good land for the production of illegal drugs, especially so close to honest, hard-working communities. I have had no direct contact with those parties."

"You understand, of course, that cannabis production has been legal in Colorado for some time now, do you not, Mr. Yearling?"

"I do, but I side with the federal government on this issue, Mrs. Clay, and will refer to Corinthians 15:33, which tells us, 'Do not be deceived: Bad company corrupts good morals.'"

They had arrived at the parking lot.

"Speaking of the Bible, Mr. Yearling, I'm curious about the name of your brewery."

"Yes! Genesis 1:28! You know, I think of myself as a progressive in many ways, Mrs. Clay. The brewery is part, a very pleasurable part, of my mission to serve Jesus Christ through joy. Was it not Benjamin Franklin who said, 'Beer is proof God loves us and wants us to be happy'? Genesis 1:28 is an exten-sion of that concept of God loving and caring for his flock, and providing the ingredients for a blessed life. We are not a dour ministry, you see. We feel it is our spiritual duty to celebrate the life God has given us. I'll just make that list for you now, Eleanor. Excuse me—Mrs. Clay—if you'll be kind enough to wait a moment."

Eleanor and Elan walked in the direction of the other buildings, centerpieced by an enormous modern tabernacle. "Elan, what do you make of John Yearling?"

"Well, despite the yawn fest of his khakis, polo, and sport coat ensemble, I'd say Pastor John is a bit of a showman. A real change of pace from the guy he replaced here at VOLT. Misquoted Franklin, though he's not the first. A lot of people get it wrong. Franklin was talking about wine. Enology for lovers, non-credit, Valentine's gift from Terrance. Wouldn't have served the good pastor quite as well."

"How long exactly has he been president of VOLT?"

"If I have it right, it was spring of last year. June."

"Do you think it's unusual for the powers that be to choose a brewer for its spiritual leader?"

"The PR at the time said he'd been a key player at VOLT long before he went into the beer business. I did a feature on the transition of power at the school newspaper, The Hawk, for aspects of modern journalism."

"Of course you did. Player sounds about right. He does slide across a little oily, doesn't he? Everything he said seemed to carry some agenda, right from hello."

"Occupational hazard, maybe."

Eleanor looked at Elan and smiled. "Which business, alcohol or Jesus?"

"Yep."

CHAPTER

10

"There's evidence of cannabis pollen around the tank. That's not particularly unusual, as it's wind pollinated. It could probably be sourced to an outdoor grow site, although any outdoor operation around here is likely to be unregulated, illegal, and hidden in someone's backyard."

"Althea, what about the hops?"

"That's a little trickier. Hops are also wind pollinated, but I didn't locate any farms in the vicinity. Interesting, though, the strain we found is the same one Genesis 1:28 is proposing to grow. It's not currently being grown anywhere but their test garden, a long way from here, far as I can tell from the brew forums on the internet. Its presence is harder to justify than the pollen from the weed. Except, of course, that a whole passel of Genesis 1:28 folk have been on the property in the last week."

Eleanor sat on her couch with her elbows on her thighs and her head in her hands, eyes closed. Nothing was coming together for her. She felt no connection between the kidnapped children and the pieces of land that had held them. She spoke into her knees.

"And then there's the injected drug combination, the marijuana plus the valerian."

Althea stirred a pot of Bolognese and lifted the wooden spoon to her mouth for a taste. She scraped chopped oregano and parsley from a small cutting board into the pot, set it to simmer, poured two glasses of red wine, and joined Eleanor on the couch.

"Yes, that. Not meant to kill, it seems, just used to knock the kids out. Maybe. Feels oddly specific." Althea reached into her bag on the floor and pulled out a little glass vial. "You got a headache?"

"Yes....no, not exactly. Just tense."

"I've got just the thing." She unscrewed the vial and held it out to Eleanor. "Give it a good deep sniff."

Eleanor inhaled lavender and rosemary and something like camphor. "Smelling salts?"

"Make 'em myself! How do you feel?"

"Remarkably clear, thank you. Very Victorian of you."

"I am fond of the word apothecary. About that intravenous cocktail, though, I do wonder at the combination. I can't decide whether it was prepared by someone with a lot of pharmaceutical expertise or very little."

"Why's that?"

"There are lots more common choices for anesthetizing someone. This isn't the scientist talking, but it feels like the cannabis, both the pollen and the injectable, are there primarily to draw attention to themselves."

"Or point to someone else," said Eleanor as she sat back and took a sip of her wine.

"Gordon, I'm just saying he's worth watching."

"Eleanor, listen to what you're saying." Stanislaus had a day's growth of beard and was wearing the same shirt he had on the previous shift, but his tie was neatly knotted and his breath carried the tang of medicinal mouthwash. "John Yearling is one of the state's most public figures. It would take more than some seeds at the crime scene to make sense of him being responsible for these kids' disappearances."

"Maybe it's not him, but someone close to him, someone at Genesis 1:28 who wants to discredit the cannabis people, maybe, get the land for the brewery."

"I can't see it, Eleanor. Yearling's got all kinds of pull. Between the beer operation and VOLT, he has friends in every pocket of Colorado, a reach well beyond our little hamlet. He wouldn't need to resort to this kind of sick performance to acquire a piece of land he wanted."

"There's something there, Gordon. How can you dismiss the fact the real estate broker who showed the property to Yearling is Jesse's mother?"

"There's nothing there, Eleanor. I've interviewed the family myself. Isla Meyers has shown that property to dozens of potential buyers in the time it's been on the market. I regret to say, Eleanor, that detective work isn't your thing, whatever your thing is. I appreciate you getting the details from Yearling on his involvement on the ranch, but I want you to take a break."

"Gordon, I'm not a detective, I know that, but for the first time since Lizzie..." She bent forward and leaned into the desk, hands gripping the edge, and looked into the faux wood grain surface as though peering into a dark pool. She lifted her face to meet Gordon's eye. "I feel like there's a pattern forming. Let me stay long enough to see it. Please."

Stanislaus looked down at his desk at the spot at which Eleanor had been staring, his right hand absentmindedly rubbing his chest below his collar bone. *What did this woman see?* Without looking up, he said, "Take a break, Eleanor. Go home."

"Gordon..."

"I said no. You tapped a good resource to find that tank. I won't forget that. It was good work, and likely saved that boy's life. Now, my police need to do their job to catch whoever's responsible."

"I can help."

"Look, it was different before, when..."

"When nobody knew what I did. When it didn't matter."

"It mattered, Eleanor."

"But?"

"I've made my decision. You're on leave. We'll take it from here."

Elan met Eleanor on the way out of the station. "Hey, Eleanor, I have been trying all morning to talk to someone in charge at Cannabis Cumulus. You wouldn't believe how hard it is to reach a human being. Their website says they 'operate on a cooperative model', which is starting to translate to 'nobody works here'. I'm thinking we should just head over to the address on the site, in Carbondale."

"Check in with Detective Stanislaus, Elan. I'm off the case."

"I'm sorry, what? You're off the case? But we just brought Althea on!"

"And now we're both off, Althea and I. You're the only official element among us, Elan. You still have a job. Give Stanislaus what you've got. I'm officially on leave."

Althea let herself into the apartment and jumped at the sight of Eleanor slumped on the couch. "Oh my god, you scared the shit out of me! Why aren't you at work?"

"Sorry. This is my apartment, though, last I checked."

Althea slid the overstuffed bag of groceries she'd nearly dropped onto the counter and sat next to Eleanor. "What happened?"

"Gordon cut me loose. He doesn't like the Yearling link. Says I shouldn't be making a case from a few seeds at the crime scene. Says I'm not a detective."

"Yeah. I'm afraid that happens a lot in my world. Not that I'm alluding to any kind of 'I told you so' despite the fact that I did tell you exactly that."

Eleanor stared at Althea stone-faced a second before she started giggling. She was crying with laughter by the time she could sputter, "You did!"

Althea chuckled and raised her eyebrows as Eleanor convulsed. "This is either the delayed release of a whole week's worth of my wit, or you've gone and lost it, my friend."

Eleanor gasped and daubed her eyes with the cuff of her sweatshirt. "Oh, I've lost it, all right. I've lost all of it, every last bit." As she caught her breath she stood, unsmiling now, hands on hips, staring at the linoleum, a fourth-place runner crossing the finish line, spent and out of the money.

"Here, before you swing too far to the dark side." Althea handed Eleanor a champagne glass of something bubbly scented with summer fruit. "Bellinis! Happy hour just got pushed up. I've got nibbles, too. Let's go out back and drink like tourists in the afternoon and see if we can't turn this day around."

"Althea, you can't really believe all the world's problems can be solved with food and drink."

"Can't I, though?"

On their second glass, the women's conversation turned to crossroads.

Althea said, "I was doing good work in London. I liked the people I worked with; I liked my friends there. One day I discovered I'd got pregnant, and then I miscarried. In between those two events, I considered an abortion, but the choice was made for me before I could take any action. And I was different, suddenly, although I still couldn't tell you precisely how or why. I had plenty of friends who'd experienced the spectrum—abortions, miscarriages, full-term pregnancies, and birth. But none of their experiences spoke to my particular altered state. Anyway, I met Cal in there somewhere, and we woke up one morning finding we meant something to one another. He'd been planning a move to the Great American West and asked me to join him. I figured if the Rockies couldn't overshadow my ennui, nothing could."

Eleanor nodded. "I remember losing myself in the ridiculous beauty of it all, all the time, from running through the blue drama and buffalo grass when I was really little, up to the day, the second, maybe, before Freya died...we were at a picnic for Emmett's work. Sometimes my memory tells me that what I was thinking as Freya slipped into the current was how magnificent the river was. That instead of reaching into the rushing water for my child, I was struck by its merciless *beauty*. I did reach, though, I did: waded in and slipped on a rock, fell to my knees, watched my flip flop follow Freya under the froth, a part of me already cleanly amputated and listening to the Roaring Fork swallow the screams of a woman on her knees."

"A horrible, horrible moment, Eleanor, a terrible loss. I'm so sorry."

"We can be sorry for one another, for all the good it will do us, hm?" Eleanor drained her glass. Wet peach, yeast, and sere pinon from the webby stand that screened the cracked rear patio of the fourplex filled her nose.

"Kindness, though, kindness is powerful. Like a silk thread, binding, if only barely there. I can't say I know how you felt, Althea, but I was pregnant once before Freya. I had an abortion. I was in my early twenties, couldn't imagine a child in my life, my own child. I may never have come to see the possibility, but for Emmett. He was so kind. Not *nice*," Eleanor laughed, "no. Niceness, in the end, wouldn't have been so influential. It was his kindness that opened me up to the idea that having a child could be anything other than terrifying. To be truthful, I was never not scared, but he made it seem like a chasm worth crossing, that if we put one foot in front of the other and kept our hearts about us ...and we did it, we made two people who made me happy that we could make people."

"Well, that's what we humans are built to do, some of us."

"But not you."

"Not an option after the miscarriage. I don't know that I would change anything. Cal and I share no great drive to parent. And, to be truthful, I don't believe the emptiness and anger I felt was about losing a baby or not being able to grow a baby. That's just not accurate. The darkness came more from the perception that as a woman, I was debilitated, fundamentally flawed, had lost some bit of identity I didn't know was critical before I'd lost it. All the time I thought my personhood was in my brain, my ethos. I was dumbstruck to realize how deeply my emancipated, modern social circle believed it to be in my womb, how deeply I believed it. But, ugh, the worst thing, the very worst thing, was the pity. The pity was brutal."

"Pity, oh yeah. Agreed—the pity is the worst. Worse, even, when it thinly veils the curiosity. I prefer to be ignored."

"Well, I can't ignore my stomach much longer. What do you say we head into the kitchen and I make something starchy and garlicky to chase those bubbles?"

CHAPTER

11

Elan rolled his bike up to a one-story home on Twelfth. He'd received a radio call that a woman had reported her child missing from their home, gone less than an hour. The address had a history of calls for domestic disturbance.He climbed a plywood ramp to what looked like a new porch, running the width of the front and painted a shiny marine white, in contrast to the chipped and graying planks of the house. He tugged on his cap and knocked.

The door opened and a man—early thirties, stocky, in Carhartt's and a green plaid shirt—yelled back into the shadows, "Sarah, it's the goddamn police! How far you gonna take this?"

"James Thorenson? I'm Officer DePeña. Your wife called to report a missing child?"

"I'm Jimmy Thorenson, yeah. Paulie's dad. Look, I don't know. We need you guys here. I think my wife—my ex—is pulling some kind of stupid joke. I'm about to get in the truck and take apart my ex-sister-in-law's place. I've got a pretty good idea that's where she's stashed him."

"Mr. Thorenson, it didn't sound like a joke to dispatch down at the station. I need to ask you and your, uh, ex-wife a few questions, then we can take steps to locate your son."

"Are you really a cop? I don't see no car."

"I'm bicycle patrol, Mr. Thorenson."

"Huh." Thorenson stepped back to let Elan into the living room. "Sarah! Get your ass out here! There's a bike cop who wants to ask you some questions about where you're hiding Paulie!"

Sarah Schmidt ran from the back of the small house to Elan and grabbed his arm with both hands. "Oh, thank god! Officer, my son is missing, someone took my Paulie!"

"Her drunken sister has him, I'm telling you!"

"He's gone, you son of a bitch, like those other kids, and you don't care one shit!"

"I care that you're trying to fuck me out of a visit with my own kid!"

Elan shook his arm loose from the woman's grip and held a hand up before each of the couple's faces.

"Please! I can't help you if you're fighting. Now, when did you both last see your son? Mrs. Thorenson, you first."

"It's Sarah. He was here, this morning, about eight thirty. We'd just had breakfast, and I told him his dad was coming for him so he should get ready. I never left the kitchen. I heard the front door slam and when I got there to open it and look out, all I could hear was a loud-ass truck like Jimmy's got turning the corner. I figured Jimmy had picked up Paulie and just taken off without saying anything to me. Pretty typical these days. Wasn't til I stepped outside and saw his little backpack leaning up against the house that I knew something was wrong." Sarah bent over and clutched her stomach as if punched, then turned her distorted, tear-streaked face to Elan. "Officer, someone just stole my baby right off the porch!"

"Mr. Thorenson, when did you last see Paulie?"

"Last visit's when I saw him. This past Wednesday, when I brought him home. Brought him here."

"You haven't seen your son today?"

"For fuck's sake, didn't you hear the kid was gone before I got here?"

"I'll need to get a description of what Paulie was wearing. I'll need a recent picture, too, and your sister's address, Sarah. Is there anyone else Paulie may have gone off with willingly? Grandparents, other relatives, family friends?"

Sarah answered, "No. We're all he's got."

Stanislaus looked at the picture of Paulie Thorenson, a seven-year-old boy wearing a Spiderman hoodie and an ear-to-ear grin, sitting in a wheelchair in front of a lineup of rainbow-colored Chevy Camaros and Pontiac GTOs, under a banner that read Grand Junction Downtown Car Show.

"Kid's in a chair. Jesus."

"Sir, the mother puts his disappearance a little after eight thirty, so Paulie's been missing for under ninety minutes. Should we call Mrs. Clay, Detective?"

"We've got the alert out DePeña, we're on this. I'm not convinced the parents aren't up to something here, but our search won't stop with them. State Police are tracking the roads. We're going wide and hard this round. I think we can get on top of this one and leave Mrs. Clay in peace."

"Yes, sir."

"Eleanor! Eleanor!" Elan pounded on the door of the apartment.

Althea came around from the backyard, caked in potting soil up to her forearms, carrying a hand spade. "What the hell, Elan? She's sleeping, late night. What's the matter?"

"There's another missing kid, Althea. Stanislaus thinks

we've got it covered, but if my sensitive stomach and tight throat are telling me anything, he's wrong. We need Eleanor."

Eleanor opened the front door dressed in a big t-shirt and stained terrycloth slippers. She squinted at the sunlight. "What is it, Elan?"

"A boy went missing from his mother's house this morning. He was taken in a truck off his front porch, in his wheelchair. It's been about two hours, now. The alert's gone out."

"What do you want me to do, Elan? That's awful news, but Gordon sent me packing, remember?"

Althea shook her head and spat on the ground. "Fucking monster."

"Just come down to the station. I don't think he'll turn you away."

"Intro to police psychology, or divination 101? No, forget it, Elan. The last time I interfered with protocol it didn't pan out too well. If Detective Stanislaus wants me on this case, he'll have to be the one to ask me."

"Really, Eleanor? What's this kid supposed to do, wait until you both finish spraying lines in the sand and put your egos back in your pants?"

"Don't be disgusting. It's not pride. Gordon may be right to keep me away after all. I can't explain it, Elan. I don't think I save these children, I think I...imperil them."

"That's bullshit and you know it, ma'am." Elan dropped an envelope at Eleanor's feet, hopped on his bike, and sped away, high in the saddle as he entered traffic.

Althea picked up the envelope and withdrew a slip of paper with Paulie's Twelfth Street address written on it, plus the names of his mother and father, and held it out to Eleanor, who looked at the dirt-smudged note as if it might bite her.

"I know who you are. You're the one that's found those other kids."

On the porch, dressed in an eyelet sundress with the morning light glinting through her hair, Sarah Schmidt looked younger than her twenty-four years. Inside the living room, with the blinds shut, Eleanor could see the creases around the young woman's eyes, striping her brow. Anger, worry, and other hard intimacies had bled the vitality out of her face.

"That's right, Mrs. Thorenson, I am."

"It's Sarah Schmidt. There's no Mrs. Thorenson anymore, not since my dead ex-mother-in-law. How're you going to find my Paulie?"

"I was hoping I could meet you, see Paulie's home, understand better who your son is, then maybe I can get a feel for where he is."

"'Get a feel?' I don't understand. How are you going to find my boy from here, where he got took? By feeling?"

"Sarah, all I can tell you is this is how I do it. I can't tell you why, because I don't understand it myself, how I find what's lost. Please, can I see Paulie's room? Maybe you can tell me what you can about his routine, what his day looked like, what he liked to do?"

"Since the police say they got everyone out looking anyway, I guess I won't say no. Just in case you do got some kind of magic."

Paulie's room held a twin bed set in the middle of the room, covered in a red, white, and blue chevron quilt. Bookshelves lined the walls and rose midway between floor and ceiling, end to end with dozens of model cars and trucks. A fold out desktop held a computer screen and mouse. On a waist-high hook on the back of the door hung a child-sized chef's apron. Eleanor focused on it.

"Paulie likes to help me shape and bake the rolls down at work. My boss at the bakery gave him that apron for his own.

See, I'll show you. It even has his name done up on the front."
Sarah took the white bib front apron from the hook and held
it up for Eleanor to see the embroidery, *Paulie T., Asst. Baker.*
Then she crumpled the fabric, pressed it to her face and
sobbed.

Eleanor put one hand on the woman's shoulder, and with
the other, lifted a trailing fold to meet the clench of fabric in
Sarah's grip, as a veil, or a sacred cloth. She spoke softly.

"Sarah, will you let me take this for a while? Just for a bit.
I'll bring it back. I'll bring it back for Paulie." Eleanor gently
took the apron from Sarah's grip, feeling the tears still warm
in the fabric.

"I brought this on, you know? His being taken away is my
doing."

"What do you mean, it's your doing? Sarah, do you know
who took Paulie?"

"I do. I've known it since the minute he was gone. It's God
Himself took my boy as retribution for my taking the lives of
those other babies."

"What are you saying?"

"I'm saying I killed my babies, I *murdered* my babies,
aborted two before Paulie. This is a message from God, telling
me I don't deserve a living child."

Eleanor felt the air leave her lungs, chased by a stream of
some hot and heavy mineral. She pushed to the surface to take
a breath and found her voice.

"You listen to me, Sarah. Whatever happened in the past,
or did not happen, today you are Paulie's mother. And when,
when, we find your child, he's going to need a mother to hold
him and love him and hope for him. He's going to need you.
Don't you let go of your boy before he's gone."

Althea sat parked in the rental car at the curb. Eleanor slid
into the passenger seat, clutching the apron.

"We need Gordon."

Stanislaus was not happy to see Eleanor, but he did not refuse to hear her out. They had no leads on Paulie Thorenson's disappearance, and every minute that passed dimmed their chances of finding him alive and safe.

"What if you're right, Gordon? What if Jesse's location had nothing to do with a land deal? What if it has everything to do with his mother? Maybe what she does for a living?"

"Revenge on a real estate broker? How does that translate to finding Paulie?"

"The crimes are not about what the mother does, but the crime scenes may be. What if the location says something about the mother? Paulie's mom is a baker at Freidman's. It's a busy commercial bakery, open everyday, so I don't see trying to hide a child there. But there're the baking soda plant and the trona mine, just a few minutes from here. I did a search on Althea's phone, and they're shut down right now for renovations. I'm thinking there won't be a construction crew around on the weekends. Long enough to drug a child, hide him, and let him die."

The clap and echo of a dozen pair of police boots filled the empty plant and rang off the dormant metal as officers scattered to cover the factory floor. Eleanor reached the giant centrifuge tank first. She climbed the ladder and leaned over the open container. Wedged into a bank of silt along the outer wall was four feet of drainage pipe, cut in half lengthwise and wrapped around its circumference with rope.

"Over here!"

Paramedics descended like aerialists to lift the borehole collar and cut through the concentric hemp cording. Exposed, the body looked like an infant, Eleanor thought, cradled and curled, the thin-limbed baby his mother would have laid eyes on for the first time outside of her own body. The child's eyes were lightly shut, with just a hairsbreadth gap between the long dark lashes and the tender hollow above the cheekbone. The slender neck tilted back, pulling the pale lips open as if to receive a breast. The skin was a milky blue, deepening indigo as she watched. Eleanor felt a scream travel up through her trunk, lodge in her throat.

The chief paramedic called out, "Pulse is faint, but he's with us!" In seconds the grim and efficient medics had rigged Paulie up and were speeding toward the hospital.

Eleanor felt herself pull away with the ambulance and its flashing light, dragged by all of her senses onto a highway of panic, every cell on alert, and yet unable to stem the momentum, steer the catastrophe to safety. Her legs, unable to run; her voice, unable to shout. Ears and eyes alone performed their functions, amplifying the agony of a whimper to a scream, intensifying the color of blood and its loss. Frozen, Eleanor thought, *I am here, I am here, I am not enough.*

Around her she could sense the hard hum of the men and women who had arrived at the scene to help, whose job it was to arrive at these scenes. Never business as usual, this business of responding; with chilling regularity, people were caught up in and mangled by the machinations of the world. More incomprehensible when it is a child, least so when that child is a target.

Elan appeared next to her. "Eleanor, that was amazing! How you found him, just amazing! Who would've thought to look in the mine?"

"At least one other someone besides me. That boy's nearer to dying than any of the others, Elan. We almost didn't make it."

"*Pour estimer le doux, il faut goûter de l'amer.* Taste the sweet with the bitter, *comme ca.*"

"What the hell, Elan?"

"I just mean, you know, you did something good, something extraordinary, in the face of something horrible, and you should feel that for a moment. Paulie's in bad shape—I won't be the only one seeing that pale, limp kid in my nightmares, I'm sure. These are the cases they told us at the academy would make us reconsider our career choice or else roll up our sleeves. He's alive, Eleanor. Alive. That's everything, and you're the one to thank for it. Plus all these other folks. I'm sorry, I'm only trying to help. Also, I hardly ever get to use my language requirement. Twenty-four credits of French."

"Elan, where's Stanislaus?"

"He's headed to the hospital, wants to meet the parents there. No telling what that scene is going to be like, but you never know. Maybe those two will find peace in adversity."

"We should go, too."

"Actually, Eleanor, Stanislaus directed me to take you to the station for paperwork, then drive you home. He says he'll meet you at the station tomorrow morning, ten o'clock, unless he's at the hospital."

"What else did he say?"

"Nothing. He was in a hurry to follow the ambulance out."

For the first time ever since she began working cases with the police department, Eleanor wanted to debrief. She wanted to hear what other people thought and felt, wanted to drink a cup of coffee, or a beer, with people who understood what it was like to show up like this, to a scene like this, with no certainty, doing your best, trusting the next link in the human chain to do their best, all the while attempting to keep the cannibalistic horror of the thing at the edges.

"Yeah, okay, I guess I can wait to see him tomorrow. Hey, Elan? You want to come to the apartment, have dinner with me and Althea?"

"I'd love that, Eleanor. I would love to chill with you and Althea, but Terrance and I have a thing tonight. For real, some kind of benefit, his boss at the law office, all the senior partners will be there. I cancel on him I'm in the shit for a week. Sorry." Elan watched Eleanor shrink. "I'm really sorry."

He reached out to touch her arm. Eleanor cringed and began to twist away before she stopped herself and let his hand rest. She lifted her face and softened at the steady, liquid compassion in the young man's eyes.

She sighed. "No, it's fine. I'm fine, and I totally get it. I'll just take that ride, then."

CHAPTER

12

Paulie respirated in the rhythmic quiet of the ICU. Outside, in the hallway and in the lobby and on the sidewalk beyond the automatic doors, a dissonance of human voices pressed upon the singular pinging persistence of the machines that tethered the boy to life. His silent companions in the ICU were an eighty-six-year-old stroke victim, a woman who had survived a car accident and lay in an induced coma due to the swelling of her brain, and a three-year-old child who had fallen from a window and had had to undergo surgery to set the pelvis, a femur and an elbow.

The gossamer cord that tied Paulie to the living was stretched and weak. Kidney function was low, an infection escalated his white blood cell count, and his lungs could not operate on their own. The sterile hum and fluorescence of the ward held Paulie and his three quiet companions in an uneasy suspension.

When the RN on duty left the room, a slice of human noise fell like an ax through the crack in the door.

Sarah Schmidt sat in the waiting area beyond the nurse station surrounded by people simultaneously staring at her and typing into phones and tablets, or, in the case of a couple of old schoolers, bobbing their heads as they took notes in pencil on spiral top notepads. The young mother was no longer crying, but the tears had carved their dry red riverbeds in her geography.

She spoke mostly to herself, occasionally grabbing the hand of the closest reporter and holding their attention in her wild eye. "It's me that's to blame, me that's put my child here. I never deserved him. God just gave him to me to take him away, take him for himself. Oh, my Paulie ...my angel..."

Jimmy Thorenson had abandoned the waiting area for the cafeteria, where he sat with a cold cup of coffee, brow squeezed tight, working his phone as fast as his thumbs could tap.

Stanislaus arrived at the police station at 8:04 a.m. Eleanor rose from her seat on a wooden bench to greet him.

"Gordon."

"Eleanor, DePeña tell you I said good work yesterday?"

"He did, thanks."

"I also told him I'd see you at ten."

"Gordon, what's going on?"

"I don't suppose you look at your phone much?"

"I answer your calls, Gordon. I talk to my family."

"Well, the airwaves or sound waves or whatever the magical wireless highway is made out of is bumper-to-bumper with traffic from yesterday's events."

"I don't understand."

"No, of course you don't, you existing only in your own dark little world. Let's get into my office."

Stanislaus opened up the Bristlecone Springs Police Department Chitter account on his desktop.

@MadDad: Why is nobody asking how she's finding these kids?

@MadDad: She's no cop. What's wrong with this picture, Bristlecone PD?

@MadDad: Bristlecone PD Hires Kid Thief

"That's Jimmy Thorenson. Not a big surprise, considering his grief and the fact he's got a phone in his pocket like everybody else. But now there's this."

@valueourfamilytraditions: Feats of Clay - Child saving or criminal neglect? Christian parents deserve answers.

@valueourfamilytraditions: With the count at 4, it seems the safest place for a child is out of Eleanor Clay's occult radar.

"That's Mr. John Yearling himself, bringing his considerable weight to bear on the situation."

"Gordon, I don't understand. How does this affect us? We're the police, doing a dirty job. Of course everybody's emotional—there are children involved. This is just an outlet, right? A way for people to ease the pressure ..."

"I didn't get to the worst posts about you, Eleanor." Stanislaus scrolled and stopped. He dulled the edge of his tone. "Brace yourself."

Eleanor read,

@valueourfamilytraditions: Is a mother who watched her own child drown the person to be saving our children?

Eleanor stared at the screen, her features perfectly inanimate. Stanislaus could read nothing from her stock-still expression.

"This is already a circus, Eleanor. I don't want a war. I can't have you involved on the ground anymore."

"Gordon, you don't believe any of this, do you?"

"Eleanor, I'm asking you to step back, maybe get out of town for a bit."

"But what if there's another child? You can't deny it's me that's found them. Me. Every time."

"That's a problem for both of us at this point."

"Gordon, for god's sake! What about Lizzie and Maybelline? They're home now, and Jesse, back with his parents? Are we in contact? Have they remembered anything about who took them?"

"Lizzie's with a grandmother in Wyoming. Jesse's folks have put up a barricade, and Maybelline has yet to utter a damn word. And I'm afraid to say, as of this morning, Paulie is still deep in the woods. Chances are he won't make it. These kids have been found, yes, but no one's living their happy ending. And Yearling, clearly, has his high-powered sights fixed on you. Nobody needs or benefits from that kind of attention—not you, and certainly not this department.

"And hey, now that you've seen this stuff, do yourself a favor. Don't start in reading all of this poison when you go home. I do believe it's garbage, Eleanor. I know it's crap, but I can't ignore it."

For the second time in a week, Eleanor left Stanislaus' office in a fog, and for the second time, she met Elan in the lobby on her way out.

"Good morning, Mrs. Clay." He was wearing his bike shorts and helmet.

"Elan, hey. Judging by the change of uniform, I'm guessing you know. I'm out. Again."

"Yeah, I'm sorry about all of it. Let me get the keys to a car, and I'll drive you home. You don't want to go out there alone. There's a half-dozen people from the press on the sidewalk—a crew from Denver, even. They look hungry."

Althea was zipping up a suitcase on the couch when Eleanor walked through the door.

"You know, I sort of forgot you don't really live here. Weird, huh, for someone who has lived alone for as long as I have. Is Cal back? Or are you just wanting to get out ahead of the firestorm?"

"It's terrible, Eleanor, what that man is saying. Both of them, all of them. I hope just because you know it's there, you won't feel like you need to read it. I saw a couple of posts this morning and shut it down. So-called Christians. Vile, even for that group." Althea walked to where Eleanor stood, slump-shouldered, and wrapped both arms around her. Eleanor softened, allowed herself to be held in the embrace for a long moment before she stepped back.

"Althea, I won't read any of it. I can't. I have a flip phone and a land line."

"Oh! That's actually why I'm packed up! Levi is all over your answering machine. I couldn't help but hear. He's coming to the apartment. I figured you'd want your couch back. Cal's swinging back through Bristlecone Springs and homeward bound in a day or two, anyway."

Eleanor pressed the button on the plastic box with the blinking light. She heard "Hi, Mom," pressed the stop button and entered his phone number into the handset.

"Mom, hi!"

"Levi! You're coming here?"

He laughed. "I knew you wouldn't listen to my messages. Yeah, I'm on my way west now. The band's going to play Keystone tonight, and I figured I'd drive over to your place after the show, if that's okay."

"Sure, it's okay, it's so much better than okay. Listen, Levi, have you heard anything about what's been happening here?"

"Chitter is bullshit, Mom."

"You've seen then. Thanks, honey. And Levi? I'm sorry."

"For what?"

"I don't know. Hey, I can't wait to see you."

"Me too, you."

Eleanor hung up and felt a hot press of tears rush her face, push on her eyeballs.

Althea waited for a moment and said, "There's a message from someone else on the machine, too. Hannah, Anna, maybe?"

"Oh, that's Annabelle, most likely. Emmett's partner. She always calls when they're back in the country and home."

"You have a very modern family, there, Eleanor. I'll give you that."

The phone rang out, making Eleanor jump. She let it ring again and picked up. "Hello?"

"Eleanor, it's Annabelle."

"Speak of the devil. You're home, then?"

"What? Yes, we're home. Listen, are you all right? This Chitter mess is crazy. Levi messaged us before we boarded out of Cape Town to say he was headed out to see you. Do you think that's the best idea, Eleanor?"

"It wasn't my idea at all. I just talked to Levi. He says he's coming here after a show tonight in Keystone. What, do you think he's not safe here?"

"I don't think *you're* safe in Bristlecone Springs right now, Eleanor, maybe not even in the state of Colorado. I think you should call Levi; he's not answering our texts. And I strongly suggest you make plans to leave town for a while yourself. Come here, come home. We'll figure this out together."

"Annabelle, I'll call you back. I have to think."

"You'll think plenty, I know, Eleanor, but you won't call me back. Get to Levi. If you can't and he shows up at your place, let him drive you back with him to Denver. Best thing in my opinion right now is to pull this family to one spot. See you soon. Please."

Eleanor moved Althea's suitcase from the couch and sat down. "Annabelle wants to call the chickens home, tuck us all away from danger. No doubt her instincts are good." She turned to face Althea. "Push comes to shove. You and I don't know each other very well, not nearly well enough for me to ask this, but would you consider staying here with me one more night? I've got a rollaway for Levi, and I really think I'd like you two to meet."

Althea took both of Eleanor's hands in hers. "Let's get Elan to wear his uniform and bring something over in a pink box. It'll be more pleasant to batten down the hatches with a police guard and a nice cheesecake."

Levi sat up in the back of the van, wiped his eyes on his sleeve, and crawled to the passenger seat, sweeping energy bar wrappers and a few stray rolling papers to the floor.

"You shredded it tonight, Levi! The crowd was *lost* on that solo in the last set!" Bash took a swig of his Rockstar and took a quick sideways look at his friend. "Dude, you okay? You kinda look like shit right now."

"I'm tired, bro. I think a bunch of stuff is catching up to me." He fished under the seat, brought up a battered stainless-steel water bottle, and shook it.

"What do you mean, like, the show? Or leaving for college, or the Chitter war on your mom, or your car breaking down, or Trista being pregnant?"

"Yeah, Bash, that stuff."

"It is a lot, dude."

"Helpful."

"Hey, Levi, you know anything I can do, man."

"I know. Giving me this ride out of your way helps. I just really want to see my mom.

CHAPTER
13

Levi arrived a little after one. Elan stayed at Eleanor's for another hour, asking Levi about his band, laughing at funny anecdotes about things the orchestra kids said, entertaining Levi with his adventures riding a bike for the Bristlecone PD. The two young men chatted easily and with energy. Eleanor watched their bright, smooth faces, observed a not-much-older Elan make space for Levi, like a generous brother. It occurred to her that neither one of them attempted to draw her into the conversation. They did not ignore her, but accepted her presence without asking anything of it. She wondered how the two of them could fall into that sort of tacit agreement, as if she'd trained them, somehow, to behave identically; or, if it involved no agency on her part, how they, incredibly, organically, could share the same instinct toward her. She wondered at her sudden awareness, however slim, of her own presence. She'd thought herself invisible, but in her tiny late-night kitchen, sitting alongside, yet outside, the warm exchange between these two men, she understood her mistake. The only person she'd become invisible to was herself. In a group, people simply, and mostly kindly, but cautiously, moved around her like an open manhole.

One-on-one, Levi couldn't get enough of Eleanor, drank in his mother as though she were the last puddle in a desert, looked at her as though by the sheer act of seeing her, he could fix her to the spot, feed and flush her with his affection. Mother and son stayed up talking until the wee hours as Althea snored lightly on the couch in the other room, until he fell asleep on the rollaway they'd set up next to her double bed. Eleanor finally dropped off in the dense silence before dawn, watching the last light of a full moon marble her child's face.

She woke to the sound of two male voices in her kitchen, one of them markedly different from the late adolescent warblings of Levi and Elan the night before.

"Levi!" she called from the bedroom. "Would you come in here for a minute?"

"Morning, Mom! You want a cup of coffee? Althea buys excellent coffee."

"What I want right now is to know who's in the kitchen with you? And how do you know I didn't buy it?"

"Mom, please. It's Cal, Althea's partner. He got into town early this morning. Hey, it turns out he saw the band's show in Keystone last night. Isn't that insane? Did you know he makes mandolins and fiddles? He was just showing me a picture of an electric violin he made for Dewey Jacobs, maple overlaid with the art from his first album, *incredibly* cool."

"I bet. Levi, where's Althea?"

"She'll be right back. Went to get some stuff for breakfast and pick up a package at the post office. You feel okay to come out? I could ask Cal to take a walk, come back when Althea's here, let her introduce you two. She didn't want you to be uncomfortable. I was the one who wanted him to hang out and talk about fiddles once I knew what he did."

"It's fine, Levi. I'm fine." She tried to smile a little. "I think

I'll get dressed, though, before I say hello. And I'll take that coffee. Bla ..."

"Black, plus all the sugar that will melt, got it."

Eleanor showered and dressed, taking as long as she could, willing Althea to return to the apartment. When at last she heard her friend's voice in the mix, she stepped out of her bedroom to meet the crowd in her kitchen. Althea squeezed Eleanor's hand and gestured to a man in his early sixties, medium build, modest gut, crowned with a thick pile of white hair, and a full beard to match.

"Eleanor, this is my partner, Cal Abrams. Cal, Eleanor Clay."

Eleanor stared.

"Yeah, I know. Every year someone from the Genesee Chamber of Commerce asks me to put on the Santa suit for the parade, and every year I tell them I'm Jewish. Ho, ho, ho. Pleased to meet you, Eleanor! Althea's been much happier, I'm sure, sharing your home than she would have been in the quaint flea and tick motels I've been touring."

"Um, it's good to meet you, too. Will you and Althea be leaving town soon, then?"

"Ha, ha, ha—here's your hat, what's your hurry, eh?"

"No, excuse me, I didn't mean it like that ..."

Althea said, "Part of Cal's disarming charm, I'm afraid, is his aggressive humor. You know, I always wondered how that played as a bedside manner, Dr. Abrams ...anyhow, Cal, honey, Eleanor's used to my subtle WASP repartee, not your Catskill schtick. "

"You're a doctor?"

Cal bowed a little. "Retired. It's only the fiddles I care for now. And, of course, my lovely partner in crime." He slid an arm around Althea's waist and leaned in to kiss her cheek. "But yes, I used to work in family health. Mine was an itinerant medical career."

"Doctors Without Borders kind of thing?"

"Something like that, but another organization. I've worked in southeast Asia, Africa. Most recently I was in private practice in Toronto. Last stop for me, as far as professional health care goes."

Levi said, "My dad and his partner Annabelle work a lot in Africa, with DRINK, a not-for-profit, financing and building water infrastructure. I've gone with them to Malawi a few times. They just got back from a trip, in fact."

"From Cape Town, though, this time. Annabelle said you texted them as they were boarding in Cape Town."

Levi shrugged. "I think maybe you might've heard that wrong, Mom. Dad said before they left, they were meeting with a group in Lilongwe. That was the contact info he sent me, anyway. Cape Town's not exactly close, if they were taking a side trip. He usually makes sure I know where they are."

"Huh. Annabelle gave me the impression you might have been a little spotty in your communication this time."

"Sorry, Mom, but you're not exactly the person to talk to me about consistent communication. Whatever, they could have been somewhere else, I guess. We can ask them when we get to Denver."

Althea cleared her throat. "Hey! Speaking of getting on the road! Before we head out, I want to take a few minutes to go over what my protégées at the lab sent me. Might be something in there for Stanislaus that you, or maybe Elan, could pass his way. No use wasting good research. What's your time frame for getting out of dodge?"

"I don't know. Levi needs to get back to Denver soon."

"Yeah, I do, and I need the company, too. Don't go backing out on me, Mom. We talked about this last night. We're headed to Denver together as soon as Mom can get a rental car."

Althea poured cream into a cup, then coffee. "I say we take today to line up our ducks. Clean up, pack, avoid the media as best we can. Eleanor, we'll find you a suitcase or a garbage bag or a few paper grocery sacks and empty your closet. Cal, you can show Levi your wares and pick up some lunch. I'll sift through this package and pass off anything of interest. Yes? Is that a plan? Are we a go?"

Eleanor laughed. "Gee, Althea, I'd be insulted if I weren't so impressed by your military precision."

Cal nodded. "My thoughts exactly, Eleanor. I thought maybe I was hearing Nina there for a minute." He clapped Levi on the shoulder. "Young man, I believe we've been given our walking papers. Let's say you and I go find our own fun, leave the women to their strategies. And for the record, my love? With a name like Giordano, you and your repartee are about as WASP-y as my great aunt Rose."

Eleanor did as she'd been instructed, packed some things, albeit randomly, and rented a car for her and Levi. It occurred to her she wouldn't be returning to her apartment anytime soon, if at all, if she was no longer welcome at—or of use to— the Bristlecone PD. Nothing else claimed her. As dark as her life had been in these rooms, a weight jittered her limbs as she thought of leaving.

She walked to the station to drop off the notes Althea made and left for her regarding her students' findings on the drugs used on the kids. It was still before noon, but the sweat from Eleanor's armpit was profuse enough to saturate a crescent of moisture onto the manila envelope.

The sergeant's desk sat empty, along with what seemed like the rest of the first-floor rooms, disarmingly silent. Clarissa, the records clerk on duty, clicked around the corner from the restrooms.

"Clarissa, what's going on? There's nobody here."

"Oh, hello, Eleanor. Weren't you getting out of town? Gordon said you'd be leaving to visit family, or do some visiting, anyway. Something. You're still here."

"I am still here. We were just running a few last-minute errands. Where is everyone?"

Clarissa stood in silence for a moment, making eye contact, or trying to as Eleanor fidgeted.

"You know, Eleanor, it's probably not my place to discuss this with you ...but it was you who found those other kids, sad shape or no ...okay, well, here it is: Gordon's got the whole department out looking after another girl gone missing now, this one from Grand Junction." She added, "We thought you were headed out of town, Eleanor. But you're here, and now you know."

Clarissa watched Eleanor turn away from her without acknowledgement or comment, watched her as she seemed literally to spiral away. Eleanor tore her flip phone from her purse, punched the number for Gordon Stanislaus, and snapped the phone shut when she got his service. Then she opened it and dialed again.

"Elan! What's going on?"

"Eleanor, I can't use my personal device while I'm in uniform." He said, "Meet me at the train station," and hung up.

Clarissa caught Eleanor by the elbow as she turned to leave. Eleanor looked down as though an animal taken her arm in its maw, then looked with blind terror at the records clerk, who stood cool and calm and firm.

"You got something there for Detective Stanislaus, Eleanor?" Clarissa asked, meeting Eleanor's wild eye.

Eleanor pulled away and took a deep breath. She stood tall and looked again at Clarissa, this time in an effort to mirror the woman's professional composure, take some of it for her own. She tightened her clamp on the envelope, made an attempt to control her features, and managed what she hoped was a polite smile.

"Thanks just the same, Clarissa. I'd just as soon give it to him myself. And, um, thank you."

Clarissa shook her head very slightly, almost involuntarily, as she watched Eleanor hurry from the building and disappear into the street. Then she turned and walked back to the records desk, the tap of her heels echoing off the epoxy floor.

Elan met Eleanor at the entrance of the historic depot building. Without a word, he ushered her swiftly to a long bench of polished wood at the far west end of the station, under a sign with old-fashioned lettering that read, Men's Waiting Area. The California Zephyr wasn't scheduled for hours. There were no passengers waiting, nor any tourists come to inspect the art deco ceiling fans, artifacts of an older, slower west. Eleanor's voice whistled through the brass fixtures.

"Elan, what the hell is going on? If there's another child missing, why wasn't I called in? How long is she gone?"

"Shh, Eleanor, keep it down, huh?"

"There's no one here, Elan."

"Except the ghosts. This place gives me the creeps ... look, Stanislaus wants you far away from this one, Eleanor. He was hoping you'd be in Denver, or farther, by now."

"I don't understand! Isn't it me who's found these kids? Didn't you yourself tell me I was being stupid for thinking it was me who put them in danger?"

"Yeah, look, if it were up to me, you'd be working this, but I'm just bike patrol, remember? The whole department's out hunting, plus a team from Grand Junction. You know I think it's you who should be on this. I don't know the why of it any more than you do. Stanislaus knows it, too, but he's getting killed by the media. According to mob rule, Eleanor, you're not police, you're a witch."

"Where's Stanislaus, Elan?"

"Listen, for the moment, maybe it's better we leave the detective to his business. I cornered Drubbs. He filled me in for a mocha and a bag of Bea's donut holes.

"Inez Escalante's mother reported her missing at approximately 5:30 p.m., after the grandmother went to pick her up from a school bus drop site and she wasn't there. The kid'd been on a youth camp fishing trip to Porter reservoir, twenty miles west. Someone inside Grand Junction Police connected Inez's disappearance to the other children and contacted the department early this morning."

"Was she on the bus?"

"She got on the bus at the reservoir, according to the counselors. No one remembers seeing her at the drop-off site. The bus driver says they made one bathroom stop in Parachute."

"And what am I supposed to do with this information? Work it on my own?"

"The department is going to concentrate on the reservoir area and river, the water spots. My shift is ending. Let me drive you to Grand Junction and you can talk to Inez's mother, like you did with Paulie's mom."

"Why would she want to see me, Elan, if, like you say, I'm now the face of evil?"

"She's the mother of a missing kid, and you find kids. She'll see you. I'll make the call."

Elan and Eleanor drove I-70 with the sun in their eyes.

"My uncle keeps saying he's going to tint these windows, but nothing says Drugs Onboard like blackout windows on a Cadillac Escalade, so here we are."

"I thought you said he worked legal?"

"He does. Doesn't prevent him from being stopped on his way to Costco."

Outside of Chacra, they passed a new billboard for VOLT. It broadcast a split screen-style picture of what looked like a mugshot of Sarah Schmidt on the left, and an image of Paulie Thorenson in his wheelchair on the right,younger by a couple of years and hooked up to an IV. The caption read,

> *Choose life, that both thou and thy seed may live ~ Deuteronomy 30:19*
> *Value Our Loving Traditions*

"Enough to make you want to skip church, huh?" said Elan.

"That poor woman," said Eleanor. She wondered at Sarah's choice to allow her pain to be plastered on a forty-foot billboard, and then considered that it was no choice at all, that she might feel she's been offered penance, an exorcism, a homeopathy of pain.

Eleanor felt her focus pixelate. A picture of her own mother took shape in her head, her mother in a sunny shirt-waist, kneeling next to a small boy, five, in Prince of Wales plaid shorts and a short-sleeved shirt buttoned to the collar. Her hands, fingers forward, clamshell the boy's waist. She smiles, toothy, toward a something or someone to the side. The boy squints into the bright lens. There is a flash, and the picture changes to another boy, the same boy, ten years on, her brother, reedy in a white t-shirt and another pair of shorts, Bermudas, their mother's long calves, their father's eyes, but bluer, and slightly sunken, set above indigo half-moons tattooed by the exhaustion of trying to survive the cancer which would kill him, and with the permission of his own, young body. Her mother is there again, too, gripping, this time, his thin arm, locking her gaze on him, as if to fix him there.

Eleanor shook her head, squeezed her eyes shut, and opened them to see the Welcome to Rifle sign, and a few dozen yards beyond that, the next billboard, which showed only

Paulie in his hospital bed, and read,

> *Behold,*
> *I was brought forth in iniquity, and in sin did my*
> *mother conceive me ~ Psalm 51:5*
> *Choose Life!*
> *Value Our Loving Traditions*

They drove in silence until they got to Grand Junction. Catalina Escalante met them in a Starbuck's close to the interstate.

"Ms. Escalante, thank you for meeting us. I'm Eleanor Clay. You already know Officer Elan DePeña, I believe."

"By phone, yes. Thanks for driving out. Now tell me, why aren't you working with the police to find Inez?"

"There's been some backlash to non-police involvement in these cases."

"No shit. My Chitter feed practically has you tried and guilty for taking those kids yourself."

"Why are we here, Ms. Escalante? What do you want from me?"

"My Inez is missing, and you're the only one, looks like, been doing the finding. Besides, mostly it's these men mouthing off on the internet. I've been talking to police all day, and don't feel any closer to my daughter. What do I want from you? I want you to do what you do, okay? Fuck those haters. Look, I got a picture here, different from the school picture I gave the police. It's from last summer, so she's bigger now, but it's from when Inez went on a trip with the same camp. The clothes are the same, her smile's the same, holding up that fish." She pushed the photo across the table.

The picture showed a girl, about six, on a rocky lakefront beach, squinting and beaming into the camera, wearing a too-big mustard yellow t-shirt that read Camp Goldenrod, reedy legs poking out of neon green jersey shorts, a band-aid plastered across a knee, a few inches of bass dangling from a fishing pole gripped in a small fist.

"That was at another lake, closer to home. I forget the name."

"Ms. Escalante, what do you do for a living?"

"I work at Evergreen Lodge, an assisted living place out-side of town. Been there since Inez was two, since her father left."

"And your mother helps out?"

"Yes, I couldn't do it without Yaya, but she's not my mother, she's my grandmother. Also, my brother Samuel, he does a lot for us. You do what you can, Ms. Clay. I don't care if you're police or not. Officer DePeña's got my cell number, you need anything from me. Money, too, if you want it. You go find my baby."

Elan and Eleanor drove into the darkening pool of the eastern sky, toward Bristlecone Springs. They were quiet as the last tendrils of orange and pink plumed and faded behind them. She watched the Colorado run in and out of view, felt her body lean into its devastating westward current. Once again, the river took her under and back.

"Eleanor, for god's sake, it's a picnic. Get a beer, talk to someone. We don't have to be joined at the hip. I'll be on the volleyball court. Go have some fun."

Eleanor watched Emmett walk away. She thought about something a friend once told her, that they'd never known anyone who required as much privacy as she did. That was before kids, before she abandoned the notion of privacy as she'd known it. Now, if she couldn't hope for solitude, she felt like she could ask for a little solidarity. She wanted Emmett to stay with her, to be her buffer against all this social aimlessness. She disliked needing him this way, about as much as he clearly disliked being needed. She disliked him, too, for chalking an outline around her clinginess, making a crime of it.

Levi wrapped his warm, wiry body around her legs.

"Mama? Come, do the ropes course with me! I've done it three—no, wait—two and a half times already. I'm really good."

"What, Honey? Oh, yeah, I bet you're terrific."

She spotted Freya walking by herself toward the river. Eleanor and Emmett had talked to the kids about not swimming alone, a rule rigorously reinforced at swim lessons, which both children attended like church since they were toddlers. Freya was always one to push the envelope a bit.

"Freya! Wait for Levi and me!"

"Mama, I don't want to go swimming. MAMA, I want to show you the ropes course!"

"Levi! We'll go, I promise, but let's get Freya first. Besides, it's hot. We could cool off a bit before you show me your stuff."

"Ugh! We ALWAYS do what Freya wants! How come we never do what I want to do?"

"Just a quick dip, honey, I promise, and we'll ropes course it up."

He glared, angry and tearful, but took her hand and walked with her to a half moon of rocky bank tucked beyond a wall of bog birch, where Freya perched on a rock like a snowy egret, wings extended, leg bent, toe-tip poised over the frothy commute of river.

Elan's voice, then.

"What are you going to do, Eleanor?"

"Well, Elan, the first thing I'm going to do is disappoint my son. After that, we'll just have to see."

CHAPTER
14

Cal Abrams was happy to volunteer. "No worries, Eleanor! I'd be delighted to drive with Levi back to Denver. Be a nice change of pace for me, traveling the territories by my lonesome, as I have, all summer. If we don't have ourselves a grand adventure, maybe we'll manage some good car talk."

Levi looked away from his mother's face. He hadn't said a word since Eleanor told him she was staying instead of driving back with him to Denver.

"I'm so sorry, Levi, but I can't leave just yet." Her son's expression mirrored the one Eleanor saw in her nightmares, when the world was on fire and her limbs were poured lead and her boy was kept just out of her reach. She rarely thought after she woke from those dreams what she would do, who they would be, if she actually could get to him, if they could, by some miracle, escape her nightmare.

Levi cleared his throat, looked past his mother. "It's okay, Mom. I'll see you after this is over. Unless I'm in school by then. Cal, I don't mind driving at night if you want to head out now."

"Let's wait till sunup, how about? I'm better company in the daylight."

"Sure, whatever. Maybe I'll just get some sleep, then. You're probably not going to bed soon, anyway, are you, Mom?"

"No, I think I'll be up a while yet, Levi."

"Right. See you in the morning, unless I don't. Good night. Goodbye, if I'm gone when you get up."

"I love you, son."

"Yeah."

Light leaked from under Eleanor's bedroom door long into the night. From the couch, Eleanor could hear her son's low hum, likely talking with Trista, his girlfriend, but maybe with his dad or Annabelle. Cal slept in the camper of his truck outside the apartment while Eleanor and Althea talked, Eleanor cradling a cup of instant coffee, Althea twisting the stem of a glass of syrah.

"I don't know how you drink that swill. If you're going to intake caffeine this late, you could at least let me brew you a decent cup."

"This is fine. I like it. It has texture, helps me focus... so, let me get this straight: you're telling me you might see a connection to an old case? Do you think you've uncovered anything that would help me find Inez right now?"

"No, I don't have anything specific to this case, nothing to help Inez. But if I've learned anything in the field and at CorpsPursuit, it's that history often reveals a pattern, and a pattern can be interrupted. I may find nothing in the old files, I don't know, but I feel it's worth a look. Honestly, Eleanor, I wonder if I'm just looking for an excuse to leave. I forgot how hard it is, working with live cases. I wish you would come back with me to the lab while I check the records. Nina would love to see you." She sipped, looking over the rim of her glass at Eleanor, who was milk-pale at the apex of a sunny summer in a resort town. "But you won't leave, now, will you?"

"No." The sliver of light between the floorboards and the bedroom door went dark. "I can't leave now."

Eleanor dreamt of rivers. The rivers of her dreams rushed like derelict mine carts through dark, sheet-faced canyons, carrying every loosed entity, not toward deeper water, but to a bottomless darkness, gravity only, no salt. Awake and slick with sweat, Eleanor pushed herself upright on the couch. Althea was gone. It was still more night than day. She pulled on shoes, grabbed her jacket and the rental keys, and left.

The three twinkling points of the Summer Triangle were fading with the climbing sun as she drove through town. She pulled into a park on the creek on the northwest side of the city and rifled through the glove box for the flashlight she'd tossed in. She walked up the creek trail a half mile and back, scanning small, individual grids of bank and bush. It was full daylight when she called Elan.

"Elan! I'm at the park on Winchel Creek. Inez isn't here, but ..."

"Eleanor? Eleanor Clay? I'm sorry, this isn't Elan. I'm Terrance, Elan's boyfriend. He's in the shower. Excuse me, but I saw your name on the screen and I thought it best I picked up."

"Oh, um, Terrance! ...Listen, Terrance, I need Elan to call me back...no, I need him to just meet me...wait...shit, I don't mean to sound so...I'm sorry..."

"Eleanor, Elan will be out in a second. You can talk to him

directly. In the meantime, I'd like to ask you a question."

"Uh, yes, okay. You're, um, you're a lawyer, right?"

"I am, but I'm not asking as a lawyer right now. Not entirely. Are you aware that Elan can lose his job for helping you investigate a case without authority?"

"Terrance, I ..."

"I'm not necessarily complaining, not officially. My opinion is, Elan can do anything he wants, be anyone he wants. I'm not sure that means being a cop, but I'm not sure it doesn't, either. All I'm suggesting is it would be a terrible irony if Elan finally finds his passion only to get shit-canned for embarking on an unsanctioned *Mission: Impossible* with you."

"Terrance, I don't want to ruin Elan's career or upset his life. But I know he wants to save these kids, and he believes I can help, has from the start. I don't know what to say, Terrance. I need him."

"Well, I need him, too."

"You need who now?" Elan walked into the bedroom with a towel wrapped around his waist and a Q-Tip hanging out of one ear.

"Here, it's Eleanor Clay. I picked up in case it was an emergency."

Elan pulled the Q-tip from his ear and grabbed the phone. "Eleanor! You okay? What's going on?"

"I'm at Charleston Park. Inez isn't here, but I don't think she's far. How soon can you meet me?"

"I'll bike to the mall. You can pick me up. There's that coffee shop next to the bus station. I'll see you in twenty." Elan looked at Terrance, who was still sitting on the bed. "Since when do you pick up my phone?"

"Since I'm worried you think you're some kind of Dr. Watson to BSPD's own Mrs. Holmes. You're aware of the fire she's taking on social media, accusations of child endangerment?"

"Eleanor hasn't hurt any children. She's the one who's finding them, for Christ's sake!"

"Yeah, I know. But that fire can easily burn you too, you know. Look, Elan, I believe you. Or, I believe you believe."

"What the fuck does that mean?" Elan pulled on bike shorts, grabbed a Bristlecone PD jersey from the back of a chair.

"It means I'm excited to see you involved in something that moves you, and that I'm worried it's dangerous—professionally, bodily, emotionally." Terrance rose to face Elan and took both of his hands in his own. "I'm saying I'm sorry for the insensitive comments I've made about what I formally and mistakenly labeled your lack of ambition and am happy to have a boyfriend who rides a fancy bike in a sexy uniform."

"And if I get fired?"

Terrance ran his hand over Elan's left cheek down the back of a nylon thigh and said into his ear, "We'll keep the uniform for special occasions." Then he stepped away, grabbed a rainbow-colored Can't Think Straight t-shirt from the dresser and tossed it to Elan. "In the meantime, if you're going to go rogue, cover it up."

"Yes, Counselor."

"Jesus, Eleanor, when's the last time you ate?"

Eleanor stuffed the last section of the bagel Elan brought her into her mouth and gulped her coffee. Then she leaned back with her eyes closed in the passenger seat of the rented Jeep Liberty. "Dunno. Althea made something last night, I think. Thanks for breakfast."

"Sure. Maybe we'll even wolf down a sandwich later, upend a vat of soup. I'm not scheduled for duty until four. I checked in at the station. Inez's search is in full force, still concentrated on natural waterways and bodies of water, mostly, between here and Grand Junction. They've been all over the creek already, Eleanor. What exactly brought you here?"

"Elan, I ..." She turned to look him in the eye. Took a deep breath. "I had a dream."

"Like, Einstein's dream of relativity, or Lincoln's dream he's flying in a coffin?"

Eleanor smiled. Elan lifted an index finger to his teeth to indicate a wedged seed between her incisor and bicuspid. She laughed. Fished it out and flicked it at him.

"So, Colorado Mountain College teaches dream theory?"

"Nah, that's HuffPost. And my abuelita, she was into dreams. What did your dream tell you? What did you see?"

"Steep canyon walls, really flat, and a river, but it wasn't headed to the ocean. It rushed toward nothing, or anyway, nothing I could see. What did you say earlier about water-ways?"

"I said the search team was searching the waterways be-tween here and Grand Junction."

"No, no, what about the waterways? They were concen-trating on natural waterways ..."

"Yeah, so? Probably not exclusively, though, given that Jesse was found in a ranch tank."

"Right, of course. But in the dream the water was moving, like a river but not a river."

"A canal? The old ditch in town was filled in long ago. No telling how many canals from here to Grand Junction. Another culvert?"

Eleanor stared at the picture of Inez that Catalina Esca-lante had given her, at the lake, at the shoreline. At the fish.

"Emmett and I used to take the kids to a hatchery a few miles from here."

A handful of tourists, seniors, and parents with small

children pitched pellets at the kokanee salmon and cutthroat trout in the long, straight raceways at Bristlecone Hatchery. Eleanor and Elan ran the lengths of the channels searching for an obstruction, but there was nothing. Elan asked the Parks & Wildlife technician on duty if there were any outbuildings or storage sheds onsite, and if she'd seen anything or anyone unusual lately.

"We keep the live transport boxes and bags with the oxygen in the shed over there. You're welcome to look. As we told the other officers, none of the staff has seen anything unusual, just parents looking for something to do with the kids besides the springs, the RV crowd, you know. This time of year, we mostly just keep the pellets stocked and run the video on a loop."

Elan found nothing in the shed or in the nearby woods, but Eleanor kept staring at the raceways, the concrete straits squirming with young brown trout and Arctic grayling.

"Well, Eleanor, even my abuela used to say about her dreams, sometimes a cigarillo is just a cigarillo."

"No, Elan, there's something here, just not here." She looked at a carved and painted forest service-style map, like a child's rendition of a map, in wood. "There are two more hatcheries within thirty miles of here, one north at Rifle Falls, the other south at Crystal River...let's go north."

Rifle Falls had dozens more visitors than Bristlecone Hatchery. It was a popular birding site, as well as a favorite summer-day hike destination, with a view of the seventy-foot limestone cliffs and a cool mist from the waterfalls spritzing hot tourists coming off the paths. Elan thought it unlikely they'd find a living girl hidden on the property among the traffic.

They spoke to the hatchery tech, Phil, who climbed in his golf cart and drove ahead of them on a gravel road past the falls and a series of breeding ponds to the storage building which housed their inventory of live transport boxes and polypropylene bags.

"Bristlecone PD was here just yesterday afternoon. Seemed to me they looked around pretty good. Nobody said anything about anybody coming back out. You two don't look exactly official, either."

Elan pulled his badge out of the stretch waistband of his shorts. "This official enough for you, Phil?"

The two men faced off for a moment before the technician shook his head and huffed. Phil put the key in the lock and pushed. "That's odd," he said.

"Is something missing?" asked Eleanor.

"Well, I can't say anything's missing, for sure, but we counted these vessels just last week getting ready for a transport, and they're not stacked the way we left them. Could be one of our staff reorganized, though, maybe an intern trying to be useful. Or your people moved stuff when they were here yesterday. All I know is, the door was locked, all right."

"So, okay, Phil, the door was locked, but what about that window over there, wide open?" Elan scanned the ground below the window, looking for evidence—a boot mark, a dropped thing.

Phil tugged on the bill of his P&W cap. "Don't know what anybody'd want with some plastic bins, and we keep the oxygen in the office. Probably kids messing around, seeing what they can get into."

"Two police visits in two days, Phil—think about it. We're not about to dismiss potential evidence as 'kids messing around' when, in fact, we're after a perpetrator who's been stealing kids, wrapping them up in all sorts of materials and leaving them for dead. Material like you got here. You been watching the news, Phil?"

Phil squinted. "Oh, yeah, I've been watching all right. I've been watching enough to know all about your woman friend. Hey, if you're here with her, does that mean you're not official police after all? I don't want to stir any trouble with my agency if that badge you pulled out of your pants is a fake. Where'd she go, anyway?"

Elan pointed at Phil. "Don't touch anything in this room, Phil, until an investigative squad gets here." He turned and bolted from the storage shed. "Eleanor!"

He caught sight of her at the second in a chain of four ponds, enclosed by drawn curtains of rushes and cattails, tall and sturdy in the noontime stillness, swaying only when a red winged blackbird swooped between green blades to land and balance on a tight brown spike. Elan trotted to catch up, ignoring clusters of red mites flowering and dispersing in the dust, currents of swallows chasing damselflies in a low-altitude ballet.

"Where are you going? Shouldn't we take the SUV?" Eleanor stopped and stared at the third pond. "Eleanor, those ponds have been checked. They're too shallow to conceal a ...the kinds of things we've been finding." Elan tried to see what Eleanor was looking at. A small, man-made body of water, still but for a modest cascade at one end, rolling oxygen into the shallow depths. They stood there, watching the water fall and gently disrupt the surface, before Eleanor bolted down the path toward the main park, toward the roar of Rifle Falls.

"Eleanor!" Elan ran after, watching as Eleanor cut a clean swath through the vacationers up the trail toward the falls, disappearing around a rocky turn. He ran through the channel of stunned hikers until she came back into view, scrambling over an outcropping of limestone as she raced toward three colossal columns of water. The only sound was the sound of water pouring unimpeded through the air, crashing green and foamy into a boiling pool of itself. When Elan caught up to Eleanor and grabbed her shoulder, she twisted and swung her free arm like a bludgeon at his head. Elan caught it, but was hit powerfully just the same by her feral glare.

With the same force she used to swing at him, Eleanor pulled Elan through the brush and around the edge of the pool. He understood they were headed behind the falls. The noise pushed everything but the fact of it out of his brain. As they approached the nearest column, he held his hands over his ears, but his elbow edged into the path of the water and the force pushed down into the pool, pummeling him under sheets of water bearing down on the surface, exploding into millions of stinging molecules upon contact. He scrambled out and made his way behind the wall, where Eleanor stood in a kind of hollow, too shallow for a shelter. She pulled him toward the next column, again protecting a little concave space, again showing no sign of Inez or any human. As they waded to the third and final column, Elan felt his brain convert the relentless pounding to something like white noise, if white noise could contain the tenor of violence. In the enormity of the sound, he felt a kind of helplessness, almost like peace. His heartbeat slowed as they slipped behind the wall of water, then surged when he saw that in place of the shallow niche of the previous two pockets, the space fissured and broke into a cavern. Eleanor lunged ahead of him. He ducked into the dark recess and could just make her out, on her knees, ripping at something pliable, shaking her head, mouth agape, emitting what would surely have been a blistering scream if he could hear anything besides the rush of water.

"Drubbs, who the fuck is Teddy Davis?"

Gordon Stanislaus rarely cursed aloud, tried to be mindful of his language, but found the limits of his civility breached by the chaos of this case.

"He's the father, sir, though the mother says, quote, 'he can go fuck himself and his papa, too.' Apparently, he's been an absentee dad. The records show he's been delinquent on child support since it was set, over five years ago."

"So why are we giving this prick any more attention than he's due?"

"He's causing some disturbance at the hospital, sir. Ms. Escalante would like us to arrest him, but we don't have cause for that, not yet anyway."

"Okay, tell him I'll talk to him at the station."

"Sir? He won't leave the hospital. I think he likes the, uh, media presence."

"Oh, for Christ's sake." The last place Stanislaus wanted to be was the hospital. He'd been there all day, fending off reporters, trying to establish an appropriate environment for the mother, god help her. Now this asshole. "All right, Drubbs, let's go."

Teddy Davis was a large man, fair, still on this side of thirty, clearly fit, likely steroidal, with a buzz cut and a twitchy way of scanning the room as he talked.

"You Edward Davis?"

"Yeah, I am. Inez's father, too, though nobody gives a shit about that. You the police chief?"

"Chief Detective Stanislaus. Mr. Davis, I'm sure you can understand that your *daughter*, as well as Ms. Escalante and her family have suffered serious trauma in the last days, and we'd like to make sure they have a quiet space to have some peace in this difficult time. Your little press conference here is not conducive to that goal."

"Her family? *Her* family? I'm Inez's goddamn family, and I'm not going anywhere. And another thing, nobody will talk to me, but since you're the top cop, I'm gonna guess you'd be likely to know: is my daughter's hymen intact?"

"What?"

"Is her hymen intact? Was she, you know, violated by

whatever sicko is doing this to these kids? I want to know if my kid is broken like that. I want to know if I have to kill the bastard."

"There's nothing I can tell you, Mr. Davis, exceptyou don't have a right to that information, as far as I can tell. And if you do, somehow, have any rights to information regarding your biological daughter, you should not, in my professional opinion, be permitted to exercise them in this way, in this moment. Now, you'd do well to shut up and disperse the media party before I take you in for disturbing the peace."

"Bullshit, you can't do anything to me. I have rights, plenty of them. And I will *exercise* them. You can't touch me."

Stanislaus stared Davis down for a moment, then turned and moved away. "Drubbs, move these reporters outside a perimeter. Father of the Year over there can hold court in the parking lot."

Eleanor was asleep, sitting up and leaning into a corner of the couch when Elan came by the apartment that night. She wore the clothes she'd had on all day, even the shoes, everything still damp, all edges caked in mud. Two fingernails on one hand and three on the other were torn and dark red with dried blood. She looked to Elan like she'd crawled out of a wet grave, which, he thought, was close to the truth.

He set the to-go boxes on the counter and went back out to the car, Terrance's Volvo, which he'd borrowed to make a grocery run and pick up dinner for Eleanor. He grabbed the Ralph Lauren micro-mink blanket thatTerrance's mother had bought them the year before, went back into the apartment, and draped it over Eleanor's shoulders. She stirred but kept her eyes closed as he tugged at her wet shoelaces, replaced the soggy socks with an unpacked pair from the bedroom, and rose to put the kettle on. While he waited for the water to boil, he put tea, coffee, filters, sugar, Cup Noodles, peanut butter, raspberry jam, bread, and a container of trail mix in the cupboard. Sliced cheese, deli turkey, bagged salad, two apples, a bag of clementines, a bottle of balsamic dressing, a quart of milk, a dozen eggs, and a tub of whipped butter went into the fridge.

"Elan," Eleanor croaked, "I'm okay. You don't need to do all this."

"Oh, please. Please, please, please, Eleanor. Stop it. Althea was here for how long? How can you still not understand the people in your life do for you because they care, because they can, and they want to? I want to."

The microwave dinged. Elan removed a to-go container of chili and put it in front of Eleanor with a little package of oyster crackers, a paper napkin, and a spork.

"Thank you."

"Don't mention it."

"Elan."

"Yes?"

"I can't survive this."

"Eat your chili. You'll be fine after food and a few hours of real sleep. Maybe a bath."

"No, Elan."

"No bath? Oh, Eleanor ..."

"Elan. I've been living in the dark in this empty apartment for ten years. My life had already ended, except for Levi. There have been times I only knew I was alive by the pain I felt when I let him down, which was often, and still I seem to do it every chance I get. You know, when I was trying to tear that bag off of Inez's face, I had a moment, just like with Freya, when I thought I'd give up and let her go. Only with Freya I did let go, and no amount of holding onto these other children will bring her back. I'll never recover her. I'll never recover."

"I don't know about that, Eleanor. It didn't look to me like you showed any hesitation saving Inez. I don't know much about recovery, either, except that I imagine it's far less likely in wet smelly clothes. I'm going to run a bath. Eat chili. Drink tea. I told Terrance I was going to hang around here tonight. I can listen if you want to talk, and I can sit quietly, too, if you don't. Again, Eleanor, you did something amazing today—kept the future open for a family, once again. I'm sorry this job falls on you, but I'm glad as hell you're here to do the work."

"Elan, how is this going to end? Are we just going to continue to pull children back from the brink? I mean, what are we even dealing with? Not a natural disaster, these aren't tragedies. A human being is planning and carrying out this horror over and over. Maybe more than one of them. And what happens when—if—we get them? Is it over, then? Or do we cycle into some new nightmare?"

"I don't know, Eleanor. I can see where it would feel like all the weight is on your shoulders. Remember, though, there's a whole team of us on this. Special as you are, this case is more than you doing your special thing. We'll catch the lowlife, and we'll do it together. What I'm saying is, you've got to stay in the game. We need you, but also, I got you." Elan adjusted the blanket, pulled it a little tighter.

He sighed. "As to what happens after we hunt down the evil bastard, or, as you so pessimistically suggest, bastards... the system will do its thing. Or, some relative reeling from grief takes them out with a licensed and perfectly legal assault rifle. Want to control the outcome? Vote your conscience and pray for good luck. Now please, oh please, take a bath."

Eleanor laughed. "Okay, fine." And then she crumpled again and choked, "Oh, Elan."

"I'm here. I'm right here."

CHAPTER
15

Cal and Levi left Bristlecone Springs at first light. Cal stopped at Bea's to pick up a bag of donuts and a couple of coffees before heading east out of town. Levi watched the Eagle River come and go from view out the passenger window. They were in Gypsum before Cal broke their silence. Levi turned his head and noted, somewhere beneath the surface of his consciousness, the way the porous chalky hills moved like a glacier behind the older man's snowy head, in contrast to the speeding river.

"I tell you, Levi, I love living out here in the Rockies! It's not only the mountains, unfailingly inspiring and humbling as they are. It's the whole of Colorado. Glorious state! The eastern plains, the front range—this land is the home I never knew. Of course, as a young man who comes from these parts, I'm sure you feel a mighty impulse to get out and see what the rest of the world has to offer, no matter how spectacular the home territory may be."

Levi sat up and tried to clear his throat of the salty misery that had lodged there since the day before, when Eleanor told him she wasn't coming home with him. "I guess so. I mean, I've already done a fair bit of traveling with my dad and Annabelle, been to Africa twice a year since I was twelve, been through most of Europe. I'd like to get to India one of these days, Japan. I don't know much about South or Central America yet, except for a few trips to Mexico. Truth is, my next big move is barely an hour from home. I'm going to CU Boulder in the fall, for music."

"You want to teach, then?"

"Maybe. I teach now, in a way, and I like it. I run the junior orchestra at The Center in Denver. But I want to play, too. I want to perform. And I want to compose. That's really what school's about for me, I think."

"Gotta say I enjoyed the show in Keystone the other night. You got chops. And style. I guess you'll have your summers and holidays to play the venues."

"I'm getting the feeling you don't think much of school for musicians."

"No, no, not at all. I'm all for higher education, got a bunch of it under my own expanding belt. That's how I got to see the world, by being a doctor. But unlike medicine, you can practice music without a degree. I was just wondering, CU Boulder has a fine reputation, but if you're interested in composing, why not one of the big east coast schools? Julliard? Berklee? Why not Europe? Seems you're not casting your net very far, is all."

"Yeah, well, it's complicated. What about you? I see the white beard, but you don't seem old enough to be in full retirement mode. I know enough to know itinerant custom fiddle making, awesome though it is, is more of a labor of love than a living. You independently wealthy, Cal? Some kind of trust fund baby?"

Cal laughed. "Once you find your voice you don't fool around, do you, kid? I get it, I'll stop sticking my nose in where it hasn't been invited. I'll bet, though, in the drive we have left, we can entertain each other with a story or two of our adventures, and skip the land mines. Maybe you can tell me a little about Africa? I spent some time working at a clinic in what's now KwaZulu-Natal, you know. I always wished I'd seen more of the continent."

They took the long way up CO-131, abandoning the big resort towns to run parallel to the Colorado, eventually dropping into Heeney and Silverthorne before reconnecting with I-70 for the last leg to Denver.

While they hadn't even remotely crossed paths in Africa—Emmett's and Annabelle's work with DRINK was concentrated in Malawi, long after the period Cal said he led a medical team at a women's health clinic in South Africa—they shared similar impressions of and appreciation for the people they'd met, their warmth, and what they both interpreted as a deep commitment to family and community.

"I liked my time in New Zealand for the same reason—strong community bonds, a sense of civic unity. The beaches, of course, are breathtaking. But for me, again, it's the mountains, the terrible volcanic splendor of Mount Tarawera, the majesty of Aoraki/Mt Cook. New Zealand's where I took up the fiddle. And fiddle making, for which, it turns out, I have a far greater aptitude."

"What got you to Colorado? To stay, I mean."

"Well, I came to the American West from eastern Canada, which turned out to be the last stop for me in my clinical career. I might have moved on still, except for Althea. I didn't realize it at the time, but as soon as she agreed to come with me to Colorado, I felt myself begin to, or begin to want to, you know, *root*. Botanical sorceress, my Althea. It's good magic, however she comes by it."

Levi went quiet. He'd spent the better part of the previous night talking and crying with Trista. He'd wanted to tell

Eleanor about the pregnancy on this drive— they'd have taken the long route, too, gone an hour or two out of their way, slowed the journey down long enough for them to be themselves with one another, no plans, no obligations, no expectations, except that they would love and listen to one another through the noise and disharmony of the world. Suspended on this brush-rimmed road, they'd have tripped like an earnest creek through the rocky landscape that held them so lightly. So Levi had imagined.

"Something on your mind, Levi? I can see it was a disappointment to not make the trip with your mom."

"Yeah, I guess I should be used to it. I miss my girlfriend, and I guess I'm thinking about everything that's coming up."

"School?"

"Sure, yeah, school. And other stuff. Hey, I got a download of Tim Crouch. Want to listen to some music for a while?"

"Wouldn't mind at all."

Bluegrass filled the space until they pulled up in front of Levi's home.

"Thanks for the ride, Cal. I'm sorry if I wasn't great company."

"You were fine company. Ordinarily it's just me and my tools, a fiddle or two. They don't provide much chit chat."

Emmett came out to the curb as Levi was unloading his backpack and fiddle case from the truck. He shook Cal's hand. "Emmett Clay. Thanks, Mr. Abrams. We appreciate you helping Levi out."

Levi said, "It's Dr. Abrams, Dad."

"Just Cal, please."

"Dad, I'd like to invite Cal to sit in on an orchestra practice, if that's cool. We were talking about playing something together for the kids. They always like it when I show off a little, and you can't beat Santa for a guest spot."

"Your call, Levi, it's your show. No doubt the kids would love it."

"It's opportunities like these when the Ol' St. Nick schtick really pays off. Covers up for some of my weaker skills on the fiddle."

"Hey, Cal, you're welcome to stay and have some lunch or something, right, Dad? Annabelle won't mind."

"Oh, thanks but no thanks, Levi. I got some re-entry organizing to do, now that I'm home. And I understand you two just returned from a long trip, yourselves—I'll leave you to your family. Let me know when you want me to show up for the kids. You got my number. Nice to meet you, sir. Levi's a great young man and a fine fiddler."

They turned toward the house. Annabelle leaned out the front door and watched Cal's truck until it disappeared around the corner.

Emmett said, "Dr. Cal Abrams seems more Moses than Santa, wouldn't you say, Annabelle?"

"What?"

"I was just remarking that Levi's driver gave off a kind of Biblical vibe ...hey, you okay? You look really pale all of a sudden. Still shaking off the jet lag?"

She stood tall and met Emmett's concern with a little smirk, kissed his cheek, and looped an arm around Levi's elbow, pulling him close as they walked inside. "I'm fantastic, thank you. And so very happy to have you home, honey."

"Thanks, Annabelle. I'm glad you're home, too. Mom had it that you were coming from South Africa. She's got her head full of all that trouble in Bristlecone. I'm not surprised she got mixed up. I wish she'd come with. I'm pretty pissed at her, actually."

"I know," she said. Me, too, she thought.

Annabelle lay in the warm water of the bathtub with the lights off, submerged but for her eyes and nose. A full moon edged its way into the skylight, casting a blue tint over the white-tiled room. A shaft of gold fell through the cracked door. She could hear Emmett puttering in the bedroom, the baritone voiceover of a nature documentary on the television.

She'd managed, she thought, to keep it together through the afternoon until after an early dinner, when Levi left to see Trisha. She couldn't eat, but she fussed with putting together a salad and interjected the occasional comment as Emmett retold the story of their latest Africa trip. Levi had very little to say, and while that was unusual—after a separation from his dad, especially—it was easy to chalk up his silence to a long day, and to yet another let down from Eleanor.

She felt relieved, in that shaky way that the body registers near-disaster, that Emmett had gone out alone to meet Levi when he arrived home that afternoon. She'd been two or three beats behind him when she saw Abrams's face appear from the driver side of the truck. She'd felt her own cheeks flush, her chest contract, her breath tighten in her throat. She'd stepped back from the sunny threshold into the cool house and made an effort to compose herself. What forces of the universe could have combined to put that man on her front lawn? She sank into the hot water and thought, if there was a takeaway worth keeping from her first faithless marriage, it's the certainty that no secret can be kept indefinitely. Everything is revealed, eventually. She should have known better.

Yet the fact remained, she wasn't ready to discuss South Africa with Emmett. She hadn't intended to lie, and she hadn't had to yet, not really. Emmett was perfectly satisfied that she'd left Malawi for Pretoria to consult on sustainable water practices for local hops crops. It would not have been the first side trip she'd made to communities outside of DRINK's project docket. She knew she couldn't keep her true purpose from Emmett forever. She justthought she'd have more time. But now with this Abrams showing up, *and at their home...*all her plans would blow up in her face.

She wasn't about to allow this man, any man, to sabotage her life simply because he thought he had something on her. He wanted something, she was sure, maybe some brand of revenge. It was possible...unless Santa-slash-Moses really had appeared by coincidence. But Annabelle Gibson did not believe in coincidence, and would leave nothing to chance, not when it came to looking out for her own. She'd seen him first—that was good, an advantage, she thought. She'd be proactive, eliminate the threat, diffuse it, before it undid her.

CHAPTER
16

Gordon Stanislaus knocked on the door of Eleanor Clay's apartment. He'd never before seen where Eleanor lived. Despite a pot of fuchsia geraniums under the broken doorbell, or maybe because of them, the shabbiness of the place tamped down the rage he meant to direct toward this incomprehensible woman. He deflated still more at the sight of her.

"Jesus Christ, Eleanor, what a shit show."

"Wow, Gordon, is the colorful language a new thing? Some sort of coping mechanism? Come in. Please. Thanks to Elan, I can offer you some tea."

In the dark room Eleanor's skin was a flat taupe, offset by charcoal-blue bags under her eyes.

"I came here to ream you for screwing with an official investigation and dragging a police officer into the mess, but now that I'm here, I don't know what I want to say to you."

He picked up the single memento in the room, a framed photograph of a man and a woman flanking a boy somewhere between fourteen and sixteen, all smiling big for the camera.

Gordon noted the strong resemblance between the man and the boy, but could just as clearly see something of Eleanor in his expression.

"How's Inez? How's her mother?"

He set the picture back. "Both alive, neither great. The brother is a good soul. He's stuck right by his sister since Inez came in with the EMTs. The grandmother looks like she's aged about twenty years in a day, but she's rallied, bringing food, saying the rosary in a chair in the waiting room. There's a lunatic ex I've managed to beat back from the family, got no legal connection to the girl."

"Inez's father is at the hospital?"

"Sperm donor would be generous. But yes. Talking crap about Inez's quantifiable virginity, of all things."

"What the hell?"

"He was badgering the hospital staff and me to tell him whether or not Inez's hymen was broken, for Christ's sake, like that gets to mean something to him. Now he wants to go kill someone. Get in line, I say. This one's the worst yet, Eleanor, and they're all bad. VOLT has not let up on Chitter, still putting in overtime casting you as a menace and a curse. And now, *now*, the Economic Development Commission is on me about the bad press. That pot company, Cannabis Cumulus? They were ready to buy up a huge parcel of land near town. Now they're talking about backing out, due to the *bad vibes*. Jesus." He rubbed his chest absently, then noticed the steaming cup in front of him. "Thanks."

"Chamomile. Althea swears by it. Helps you sleep."

"Not working for you, apparently."

"Yeah, no. What about Inez?"

Stanislaus sighed into his mug, sending a rush of hot moisture into his already ruddy and sweating face. "It's bad. Skin rot, lung damage, almost certainly brain damage from oxygen deprivation and trauma, though the doctors won't commit to a diagnosis just yet."

They sat in silence for a moment. "Gordon ..."

"Listen, Eleanor, I'm out to sea here. I should arrest you and fire DePeña. How the fu ...how did you manage to find her? We'd been all over that area, you know. *We'd been there.*"

"I know. I don't know what to tell you. It's not going to help if I tell you I had a dream."

"Dear god that's all I need. No, don't tell me that.I feel like all we're doing in this case is crisis management. I've got no motive, barely a pattern, no idea how to protect the next kid. I wish you could tune your powers into the perpetrator, find the monster that's to blame, instead of finding these half dead babies."

"Me, too, Gordon."

"Well, I can't have you leave town now, which is another thing I came here to tell you, but from the looks of it you're not going anywhere. Unlike the tourist trade, according to the Chamber, which is evacuating in droves."

"I'm sorry."

"Yeah. Drink some fucking tea, get some sleep, and see if you can dream us up a serial kidnapper."

"You're not going to fire Elan, are you Gordon?"

"No, ma'am, I am not. Officer DePeña will henceforth resume special duty in support of our police consultant. You've got yourself a houseman, Mrs. Clay. I'd like to keep you both where I can find you."

CHAPTER
17

Althea had the CorpsPursuit facilities to herself, but there was clear evidence of others having been there in her absence. Her greenhouse plants were flourishing, and while she had them on an automatic watering system, she could tell Nina had been talking to them. Paw prints in the drive meant that Jason and the dogs recently cavorted through the property. Tonight, however, she was alone.

Alone. She'd missed it, she realized. Alone with her thoughts, alone with her fears. She took comfort in the quiet. She was a loving person, a social creature, but there was a keen freedom in this solitude and silence, in being alone with her work.

Althea made this trip to Boulder with a case in mind. She could have had Nina send the files, but she did not want to review the data in company. It was the case that brought her to CorpsPursuit, if not to Colorado. Not Charlie Montenegro's case, in which she'd had an active part, but another unsolved crime that the CorpsPursuit team ultimately passed on.

Several children went missing in the London, Ontario, area over a period of months. Canadian officials arrested a suspect who was subsequently convicted, then murdered in prison. Nina had interviewed Althea in a preliminary investigation designed to help the special forensics team from Colorado decide whether or not they thought they could be successful in recovering the bodies of the children. While Althea had not been a member of the original investigative team, she was tapped to weigh in with her expertise in forensic botany. In the end, CorpsPursuit passed on the case, but the results of the investigation remained on file.

Nina had been moved by the mission of CorpsPursuit, and by Nina's intensity specifically. The fact that they headquartered in Boulder played a part in saying yes to a move out west with Cal, although she'd never shared as much with him. Part of the draw was how the CorpsPursuit team accepted failure. They learned something and moved on. Or they learned nothing and moved on, kept moving.

Although the information was available in digital form, Althea was glad to have a physical file to workwith. It made it easy to spread the documents out on a lab table and see everything at once.

Much of the data was outside of her direct expertise, except for the toxicology report, but she was comfortable enough with their multi-tiered process to understand the whole of the investigation. The bodies of the children were deemed unrecoverable (at least with the available resources at the time) due to the death of the suspect and a lack of witnesses. A confession from the suspect stated he drugged up to six children with injections of heroin before killing them and disposing of their bodies. The motive was said to be drug related, as in, the children were hostages taken to weaken a competing narcotics operation: they were casualties in a turf war. It was broadly assumed by Canadian authorities that the suspect was a martyr to a wider cause. They considered the probability that he had not acted alone and did not rule out the possibility that it was not he, after all, who was directly responsible for the children's deaths. After he was killed, however, all further investigation went dark. It was two family members of the lost children—not the police—that contacted CorpsPursuit. Cops weren't generally inclined to call upon the organization, as Althea had warned Eleanor.

As she looked at the pictures of the missing children, photos of gap-toothed and reedy kids just like the before shots of the kids Eleanor found in Bristlecone Springs. Althea recalled with some unpleasant wonder how resolute she'd felt, quite suddenly it seemed now, about leaving a city and a job she'd loved. She and Cal had been packed up and on the road in no time at all. She remembered Eleanor's comment about military precision. If crisp planning and organization were, in fact, tools in her skill set, she was highly selective about when she employed them. There was little precision in how she'd lived her life since Ontario, outside of work. And now it was ten years past, and her head and heart were back in London, staring at these young, lost faces, remembering sharply, almost painfully, how desperately she'd wanted to find them.

There were similarities, she thought. The abductions, the drugging. But the motive in the Canada kidnappings seemed so particular, while the motive for these current cases was unknown. There's some messaging involved, she thought, but what is the message? No one's seeking ransom. Most perplexing of all, the kidnapper leaves them alive, at least long enough for them to be found. The suspect in London admitted to six abductions. The count in Bristlecone Springs is five. Clearly there wasn't enough data to make a connection, but it didn't stop Althea from believing there might yet be a tie between the two sets of serial crimes.

She wouldn't go back to Genesee tonight, she decided. She

wanted to keep her thoughts and hours free for a little longer, let the information settle. No doubt Cal will have made a lovely dinner, she thought, maybe even chicken and dumplings, but he'd understand.

She texted: *Gonna warm the cot in the lab tonight, be home early tomorrow. I'll wake you up. <3.*

A minute later the screen on her phone lit up with Cal's response: *I'll take that as a promise. Bring something I can eat in bed.*

Althea was famished, suddenly. Her mini fridge held an expired yogurt and a wizened Granny Smith. She opened Nina's and helped herself to a wedge of English cheddar, fig jam, and several slices from a cocktail pumpernickel loaf. She made a cup of peppermint tea, dumped the manila envelope that contained her student's recent research, and arranged those papers adjacent to the old, cold case.

Different drugs. Different outcomes. Still. Althea threw a pillow and a blanket from the storage closet onto the cot and set her phone for four a.m. She'd talk to someone at London Police Service first thing in the morning, before heading home to Cal. She wondered if anyone she knew would be there, in London, if anybody remembered her.

Cal woke when the sun hit the pillow on Althea's empty side of the bed.

"Hrmph, so much for promises," he said out loud. He made coffee, squeezed some cannabis-infused honey on a slice of toast, and placed a record on the faux-vintage phonograph Althea bought him a few birthdays ago. He chewed and gazed out into the field of blooming sunset hyssop as Alma Mahler's violin sifted through the scratches on the brittle 78.

His phone buzzed with an incoming call from Levi Clay. He

smiled and wondered again about coincidence.

"Levi! Didn't expect a call quite so quick! I was just playing an old record, thinking how much I'd like to share it with you. Your ears must be burning."

"Hi, Cal. I don't know about that, but I did call to ask if you still wanted to sit in with me at orchestra practice. We've got one today, 3:30, at the Center on South Emerson Street. I know it's short notice, so if you can't, no worries. It's just that after this week I'm going to be pretty busy getting ready for school and training somebody else to take over the orchestra. Today it'd just be us and the kids."

"I'd be delighted, absolutely. I'll bring a few fancy fiddles and maybe come by a little early? You know, to talk about something we can play together for the kids?"

"That sounds great, Cal, thanks. I'll meet you at three in the activity room, first floor. You can sign in at the window inside the front door."

Cal finished his toast, rinsed his cup, and turned the volume up on the record player. He sat back, eyes closed, fingers knitted low across his rounded belly, letting the strains of the violin flood the small room, threading the morning peace with Mahler's taut beauty, saturating the air with someone else's loss.

CHAPTER
18

Elan sat on Eleanor's couch dressed for a shift on his bike, helmet in his lap.

"I don't know why you're all suited up, Elan. We're not going anywhere."

"The detective didn't authorize a car for me, Eleanor, and Terrance needs the Volvo today to visit clients, so I rode my bike. I thought I might peddle over to the hospital to check on Inez and her mom, ask about Paulie."

"Gordon doesn't want us anywhere near them, you know that."

"Well, I can swing by on my way to get lunch real quick. Truth is, Catalina's been calling and texting. She wants to talk to you."

"Talk? Or scream? I can understand her wanting to rage at someone. Who wouldn't? But I don't think I can bear it. And don't you think you ought to stick to calling her Ms. Escalante? Keep a little professional distance?"

"Seriously? This is you telling me this? All I've got at the moment is professional distance, marooned to this apartment with you. Besides, it's not my impression Catalina wants to rage at you."

"You know, you really are a very sensitive and caring cop, Elan. I'm sure your mother is very proud."

"My mother is not proud of me, Eleanor. I think she's probably the opposite of proud."

"What? Why?"

"Forget it. Truth is, I don't know how my mother feels. I haven't been able to tell her about being a cop, about completing the program at the academy. I can never get her on the phone, and let's say I'm not welcome at the house."

Elan sat on the couch next to her.

"I'm sorry. It's none of my business. What do I know, anyway? About family, about anything except what's lost. And not much about that."

Elan kept quiet, eyes in his lap. Eleanor reached over and lay her arm across his rounded shoulders.

When she spoke, her voice was hoarse, as if forced to travel through a channel of sharp rocks to reach the surface. "Hey, for what it's worth, any parent would be lucky to have a kid turn out like you. I'm happy you're here and very grateful. You know, you'll get to talk to your mom, yet."

Elan looked up. Eleanor's face was turned to the side. She looked off to the middle distance of the kitchenette and kept her hand on his back, sliding it up and down as though she were settling a child for sleep.

Elan opened his mouth to speak as Eleanor abruptly rose from the couch, stepped over to the kitchen, and buried her head in the refrigerator.

"You know what? I *am* hungry. Starving. Looks like there's nothing much here ...a sandwich would be great. Go get some bugs in your teeth or whatever, get me a sandwich. And go ahead and give Inez's mom my number."

Elan looked at Eleanor's backside sticking out of the fridge, thinking that she would probably stand there, chilling, until he left and she could hear the click of the door closing after him. Still, he took his time adjusting his helmet and fastening the strap.

"Will do, Mrs. Clay, ma'am. And by the way, I ride a bicycle, not a Harley. Turkey on wheat or egg salad?"

"I don't care."

"You do."

"Ugh. Egg salad. On dark rye. Salt and vinegar chips."

"See? Okay, I'll be back in an hour."

Thirty-five minutes later, Eleanor got a call from Catalina Escalante.

"Mrs. Clay?

"Yes, this is Eleanor. How are you, Ms. Escalante? How is Inez?"

"Eleanor ..."

"Listen, Catalina—Ms. Escalante—I'm so, so sorry. About Inez, about everything...If I could have found your daughter sooner, even an hour sooner ..."

"Eleanor, please listen. My ex is all over Chitter and everywhere saying how you know where these children are the whole time and wait until they are near death to recover them, after the damage is done, after they're broken ..."

Eleanor sputtered, "I...I wanted to find Inez sooner! I'm so, so sorry, so sorry...I wish I could tell you..."

"You don't have to tell me anything, Eleanor. Not one thing, that's what I'm saying. I called to tell you something I think you need to hear. Maybe, for your own good, you need to shut up for a minute about being so sorry. What, do you think I have one single thing in common with that evil shitbag ex-husband of mine, other than he was there when Inez got made? No, no, no—for every nosy bastard's information, there isn't anything broken about my daughter. *My* daughter. My baby is whole, and she is perfect, and the motherfucker who says different deals with me. You brought her back to me alive. The rest is noise, my friend."

"How is she doing?"

"She's doing. We got a road ahead of us to figure out, but trust me, me and mine will figure it out. The old folks from Evergreen sent handmade gift cards, and, oh my god, so much fruit. One of the old soldiers gave me his Purple Heart, for me and Inez and all of mine, said it would remind us how tough we are. Not everybody's an asshole."

"Yes, good to know." They sat silent for a few seconds. "Catalina, have you heard anything about the other children? About Paulie?"

"The boy is hanging on, I hear, but goddamn, what a horror show that is. That poor woman is out of her mind."

"You mean Sarah?"

"Yes, Sarah. It's like a public stoning, only she's throwing the rocks at herself."

"I saw some of those billboards. She's got plenty of help."

"True. Those VOLT bastards are killing her with her own guilt. Asked me, she should've kept her mouth shut about the abortions. Isn't anybody's business except her and her god's, if she really has one. I never even told Yaya when I had mine. Went to confession and moved on. Not that it was easy. What it *was,* was *private.*"

They were quiet for a couple of seconds, then Catalina said, "Hey, Elan told me you can't be here, and I wouldn't ask even if you could, there're too many jackals prowling around. But after this is over, you come see me and Samuel and Yaya and Inez at our house. My brother and my grandmother, they can *cook.*"

They hung up, leaving Eleanor to wonder how it could be that a woman in Catalina Escalante's position would call offering comfort and support, at a time when the young mother needed so much for herself.

The phone lit up again, this time from Althea. "Hey! Are you okay?"

"Sure I'm okay, just under house arrest with Elan."

"Not really?"

"No, not really. But Gordon wants me to lay low."

"Inez is still alive, though, right? Jesus, Eleanor, I can't believe you found her breathing, not with the way the news described the scene."

"She was very close to not breathing. That much is true, and it looks like the damage is deep. Good news is, she's got all the support she'll need. Where are you? Home?"

"No, I'm in Boulder, at the lab, about to leave. Eleanor, I spoke with the London Police Service this morning about that cold case I told you about."

"You haven't told me anything yet."

"Well, I didn't have more than a feeling, so I didn't think it was useful to share too much, but I've been poring over the files and revisiting with my old team, and now we've got more to go on than feeling, I think. The Ontario case involved the disappearance of six children. No bodies were ever recovered, but the suspect confessed to drugging the children with heroin and killing them as part of a local drug war. The suspect was convicted, even without the bodies, by virtue of his confession. He was murdered in prison less than a month after being locked up."

"I see some parallels, but I'm not getting the connection."

"No, I wasn't, either, which is why I called the LPS. Turns out the crew isn't much changed since I was there—it was weird to just pick right up where we left off ten years ago— anyway, I met Nina when two of the families of the missing children appealed to CorpsPursuit to help them find the bodies after the suspect was dead. She and the team rejected the case, and Cal and I moved to Colorado right after that. I got the job at the college, and then applied to join Nina's team."

"Althea."

"I'm getting to it. This morning I happened to talk to a detective who worked the kids' case ten years ago. Days before the suspect in the Canadian abductions was arrested, he'd come across a similar scenario that occurred in Los Angeles a few years before. Six victims, all young kids. In the L.A. cases, the kids were drugged with curare, thought to be a message from enemies of the local Ecuadorian gangs. The detective dropped the lead after the Ontario suspect was arrested and gave it up."

"And the bodies of the L.A. victims?"

"None found. No arrests, either. I don't know what, if anything, this means, Eleanor, but I think you should tell Gordon about these other cases."

"I will."

"Elan taking good care of you?"

"He is, although I don't imagine it's the police work he envisioned when he was at the academy. He's out getting me a sandwich."

"I'm not worried about Elan. He's someone who'll always do what needs doing. All right, then, I'm going to head home. Stay in touch, eh?"

"On the phone to Canada for twenty minutes and already with the 'eh'?"

"What can I say? I'm suggestible. Love you, eh?"

"Love you, too."

Elan charged through the door like a rodeo bull. "Eleanor, we have to leave!"

"What the hell, Elan?"

"Grab your phone, no wait ...yes, your phone, it's better you have it ...c'mon, Eleanor, move it! I got an SUV from the station."

"You didn't steal it?"

"No, no, Stanislaus okay'd it ...Eleanor! Let's go!"

They left the apartment in the black Ford and Elan made for I-70, eastbound, checking the rearview mirror every few seconds.

"Elan, what the hell is going on?"

"It's crazy, Eleanor, what's happening."

"What IS happening?"

"There was a mob at the hospital, and another one at the station, all yelling for you."

"You mean we're at 'burn the witch' for real?"

"No, not even. The town is overrun with families who want you to find their kids, kids gone missing. There are hundreds of people in town wanting to see you, to ask for your help. Hundreds. The station is swamped, people are camping in the hospital parking lot. Stanislaus thought it was only a matter of time before they found the apartment."

"Jesus."

"Nobody's talking about hurting you, but the mood is pretty desperate, and the detective told me to get you out of Bristlecone Springs ASAP."

"Where are we going?"

"I don't know. I thought you'd tell me."

"We can't take this mess anywhere near Levi and Emmet and Annabelle. East feels right, though. I'll make a call."

Nina Steuben read the note left under a tidy bundle of lavender on top of her little refrigerator: *I ate all your cheese and fig jam. You really shouldn't stock all my favorite things if you want to keep any snacks around. Love, Althea.*

Her phone buzzed. Nina was pleased to pick up when she saw Eleanor's name on the screen, though she thought good news unlikely. So little of what came over the lines of telecommunication was good news in her experience.

"Eleanor! What a delight."

"Hello, Nina. I was hoping I could ask a favor."

"Like you should have to ask. Will I be lucky enough to have the pleasure of your company?"

"If you'll have us. Officer Elan DePeña is currently escorting me out of town, and we need a quiet place to stay for a bit. Also, if you can spare the time and are willing, I would be grateful to talk with you about a few things, some developments."

"Ja. I have time. Maybe you and your officer should come to the house. I can give you the address in case you don't remember where to find me. When may I expect you?"

"We should be there around four or so. Thank you, Nina."

"Bitte, bitte."

Nina had kept abreast of the case in Bristlecone via news channels, and could see by Althea's detritus that she'd visited the lab to look at the cold case files. So, she thought, Althea is trying to find a system. From where Nina stood, the only discernible pattern was the missing children, the bodies of children, bodies piling up, discovered and no.

Emmett was sitting with his second cup of coffee when Levi came into the kitchen. "Your mother found that child hidden at Rifle Falls Hatchery."

"I know. I read it online. I'm glad the little girl's alive."

"Levi, is there something you want to talk about?"

"I'm fine, Dad. There's nothing I want to talk about."

"Well, if you change your mind, you know where to find me."

"Sure, Dad, thanks."

Late the previous night, Trista told Levi she'd made the decision to have an abortion. She was going to let him know when she had an appointment, and they'd go together to the clinic. If he wanted.

Emmett said, "I've got a meeting at ten. You want to grab some breakfast downtown? You could drop me off and take the car."

"Bash is picking me up in a bit." Levi checked the window. "And look at that, there he is now. I'll see you later, okay?"

Levi popped the door to the van and slid into the passenger seat. "Hey. Got any weed?"

"Good morning to you, too, dude. What's up? I've never known you to partake before sundown. And then hardly ever."

"Got any fucking weed or no?"

"Hey, now! That's a lot of language coming from you, my friend, so early in the a.m. Or ever. Ironically, as much as I'd like to share the pleasure of a pipe with you, bro, I'm taking a break."

"You're kidding me."

"Nope. I'm doing a cleanse, too. Just gonna eat a soup I made with lentils and kale, drink nettle tea, plus these energy drinks, for a few days, recalibrate my system."

"Those drinks are the closest sugar gets to cocaine, Bash, you know that."

"I'm just human, Levi, imperfect. This is how it looks for me today. Speaking of which, once again, you look like yesterday's shit."

"Trista's getting an abortion."

"Oh, man. Are you guys okay?"

"I don't know. It was much easier to know how I feel about stuff like this before I was in it. Really twists the whole concept of choice, you know? Like, yesterday I could make a choice, there were actions I had power over ...today it feels like we've just spun the carnival wheel, hoping it lands on something we can live with."

"But you and Trista having a kid now would be compli- cated, right?"

"Like everything else in life, yeah. People have kids all the time, Bash. And give kids up for adoption, every day. It's Trista's body, it's her call. I support her all the way. Let's just say I got feelings I was unaware of till now."

"I hear you. I'm a day into this cleanse, and I get it. Vulnerability. Manhood, dude. Who knew?"

They drove several blocks in silence. At a red light, Bash turned to Elan. "Hey, Kyle checked in wanting to know if we were practicing this afternoon."

"Absolutely, yes, let's just play some fu ...let's just play some music. Orchestra practice goes until 5:30, so, after that. You know Cal Abrams, the fiddle guy? He's dropping in to play something with me and talk with the students. He heard us in Keystone. Turns out he's the boyfriend of a woman my mom met in Bristlecone Springs, lives in Genesee. Come by if you want. He's cool."

"Maybe, yeah. He saw us in Keystone? What did he think?"

Levi laughed, "He said I was awesome."

"Oh, ho!" Bash laughed and took a hand off the wheel to shove Levi into the passenger door. "Fuck you, bro, what are we now, just the wind beneath your fucking wings? It's weird, though, right? How people connect? Small freakin' world after all, I guess."

Levi took a slug from the open can in the cup holder. "I guess."

CHAPTER
19

Gordon Stanislaus picked up the receiver and pressed the blinking button on the phone.

"Ms. Escalante, hello. How are you and your family doing? How's Inez?"

"We're all doing okay, Detective, thanks. Better every day. Well, most days, I won't lie. Listen, something's been bugging me about Paulie Thorenson's mom, Sarah."

"Yeah?"

"Yeah. You know, I knew her from a while ago, when Paulie and my Inez were toddlers. I'd forgot until I kept seeing her on those billboards."

"How'd you know Sarah Thorenson?"

"Well, I didn't *know* her, exactly, but we were in the same parenting class, if you could call it that, at Covenant Crossing when we both had husbands. It was bullshit, what it was, but I guessed we were both talked into being there by our exes. Now that I'm thinking about it, though, she might've been there for her own reasons."

"Why do you think this information might be important, Ms. Escalante?"

"It's a weird feeling. Those classes—god help me I took one about marriage, too, before that penis in a plaid shirt left us— they were a kind of poison, you know? People running them were all nice and friendly, but you'd leave feeling—I'd leave feeling, I don't know—carved out, hollow, you know, like a Halloween pumpkin or something. Not my son-of-a-bitch husband, mind you. He left strutting like a king. And no fucking wonder."

"What do you mean?"

"It was like this: if the baby won't eat, leave her in her highchair until she picks up the cold, slimy broccoli, chews and swallows. Maybe give her a light smack. Don't give in. Your husband wants more blow jobs? Give him the attention he deserves. Your marriage depends on it. Not a fucking word about what I deserved, of course."

"So, Sarah and her husband Jimmy attended these classes?"

"Not the marriage one, not at the same time, anyway. And maybe not all the parenting ones, either. But they must've got under her skin at some point to throw herself and her kid on the altar like she is. Like I told Eleanor, she would have been better off keeping her history to herself, like I did."

"Are you saying you had an abortion, as well, Ms. Escalante?"

"I'm not ashamed of it. I just chose, at the time, to not burden others with my personal business. Now I'm telling you."

"And you told Eleanor. Anybody else know?"

"Not that prick of an ex, no, if that's what you're asking. I almost wish he were mixed up in this, just so you could put him away. But not even the guy I got pregnant with knew. I paid for it myself. The only people had any knowledge was the clinic. And those folks aren't prone to gossip. Seems like a connection, though, which is why I called."

"You sure no one else knew? Not a girlfriend, no one?"

"I told you, no, only the staff at the clinic. You think I don't remember keeping something heavy like that to myself? I made one call when I was going through the directory to some pregnancy advice place, turned out they were God Squad, weren't going to help me the way I wanted. They got my name, more than they should have got. I didn't know any better, then. But that's it. Didn't even tell them on the phone it was me who was pregnant."

"Okay, Ms. Escalante. We appreciate your help. You take care."

"Yeah, sure. I got plenty of help. Those old sweethearts at work can't do enough for us. Listen, tell Eleanor I said hello."

@notgonenotgone: *You have a gift you have to use it don't abandon us Eleanor Clay*

@knowhesouthere: *Do they talk to you Eleanor can you hear the voice of my boy*

@neverthesame: *One last reason to live will try one more time with you Eleanor Clay*

@norestnopeace: *God's not listening and you can't hear me no one can hear me anymore Eleanor I am a ghost*

@brokenfamily: *Eleanor you know what this feels like please help*

@wontgiveup: *VOLT can f*ck off we believe Eleanor Clay can save us find our baby*

@babysalligot: *You're our only chance to find our boy the police are done Eleanor come back*

@fallentopieces: *Selfish woman you can't just disappear with our last hope Eleanor*

@cantbegoneyet: Willing to risk hell to find my child Eleanor

@lostwithouther: Eleanor where are you we need you Eleanor Clay

Elan could have kept reading. There were dozens more posts. He, Eleanor, and Nina sat on a sunporch at the rear of Nina's house in a quiet pocket of South Boulder. It was the sort of golden scene that filled the senses with a sense of everlasting calm, as though nothing terrible could ever happen again, only magnificent achievement and happiness lay ahead, and records of past atrocities were so faded as to have become rumor; or if the wounds were real, they were like the landscape, scarred and healed, reseeded with ethical intention and natural merit. The view from Nina's sunporch lit magnificently the opiate effect of the West, the compulsion to Manifest Destiny, but the view was lost on the threesome, with Elan's head bent over the screen of his phone, and Nina and Eleanor staring inward at their own jagged terrain.

The sun dropped and the shadows lengthened, intensifying the vivid incarnadine of the fairy trumpet and copper mallow, the chalky low clouds of blue flax. In the distance, a mountain lion loped low and quick along a purpling ridge.

Nina spoke. "After my brother and I got out of the camp, we started to hear stories of what happened inside the other camps. At first we whispered our stories, as though speaking them in full voice would invoke the return of those terrible hours. We say, 'Never again' and for so long, so many people, even good people, did not or would not understand what courage it takes, what bile must be swallowed, to tell these unthinkable stories of ours.

"I don't know how much you know about Jewish customs, but, as in many other ancient cultures, how the body is cared for after death is very specific and ritualized. The body is washed, purified, dressed. No embalming, no chemicals. And of course, in the old tradition, there is no cremation. We did not have the solace of our rituals in Buchenwald, in Auschwitz. We were denied our basic human right to honor our dead. And so many dead.

"We were dead ourselves, nearly, but some of us found ways to worship, not a god who would save us, but the godlike in us, what was un-killable. There was music. Beautiful, hopeless music, for our unburied dead, for us all. So we heard."

Eleanor watched the cougar slip behind a crag. Saffron and russet blurred and faded until she was viewing her young and spindly self, folded into a chrome-legged chair under the red tin ceiling of her childhood kitchen, watching and listening as her mother wielded pot against pan to bang out a percussive symphony of rage. Her child body rippled in waves of fear-taut muscle—as natural a state, under her mother's changeable weather, as the shimmer of aspen leaves in spring. The child would not look away. To take her eye off the storm would be to succumb to it. The image flashed vividly, and was gone.

She was once again looking at Nina—calm, kind Nina, who had managed, somehow, not to be rent to shards by her grief, as Eleanor's mother had been, with the death of a son—Nina, who did not topple and sink from the loss of her beloveds, as she herself had, with the loss of Freya.

"How did you live through it? How did you manage to even speak to another human after that horror?"

"My brother lived. I lived. That's all I can say, really. I'm only a scientist. I can't make a poem of it."

"All this hope people are talking about, it's not hope at all, is it? I am not their hope. I can't be their hope."

"Nein. These people who have lost their children, it's too hard for them to accept their loss, singular as it is. No body to bless, to say goodbye to, terrible enough when there is a body."

Elan put his phone down. "I don't get it. They can't actually expect that you can help them find all their missing kids. And what's going to happen when you never show up, when they can't reach you?"

"It doesn't matter, Elan. I'm not the answer. I'm not what they need."

Elan scrolled through his feed. "Tell that to them."

John Yearling sat in the back of the Range Rover, headed for Bristlecone Springs, sipping an apricot LaCroix and checking his phone. It was a very good day. He'd just wrapped up one of the most well-attended and successful trainings for VOLT's ultrasound education program, summer sales of Genesis 1:28 were off the charts, and this morning he received a leaked police report that showed a cannabis cocktail had been used on those kids the woman, Eleanor Clay, was finding through-out the county. He'd get his property yet, at the right price, maybe better than he'd bargained for.

What's more, there were all these people, hundreds of lost souls, who'd made a pilgrimage to Bristlecone Springs in search of a savior. Well, he'd give them one, a real one, not that deranged woman with her occult accidents. The board at VOLT had disagreed with this trip, citing the generally anti-VOLT rhetoric on Chitter from the group at large, but Yearling saw only opportunity, not resistance, and convinced them of it. He'd booked the conference room at the Bristlecone Springs Inn and announced a forum, free to the public, to address VOLT's position and actions regarding the missing children. Amassed in one room, these desperate folks would be a captive audience, fish in a barrel. But he wouldn't shoot to kill, no, quite the opposite—he'd have them in his thrall, show them the light, just as he'd done with the board, as was his sworn mission to do. All the better that Mrs. Clay was nowhere on the radar, though even if she were, Yearling felt confident he'd have her sorely outclassed.

He smiled as the car passed a Value Our Loving Traditions billboard, their latest:

> *Your eyes saw my unformed body; all the days ordained for me*
> *were written in your book before one of them came to be ~ Psalms 139:16*
> *Value Our Loving Traditions*

Yearling thought he couldn't have asked for a better representative than Sarah Schmidt. A true penitent, and pretty enough, if pathetic, next to that crippled boy of hers. Yes, things were really going his way.

Gordon Stanislaus wondered at what point he had lost all control of his town. He stood under the pelt of the shower, hand against the wall, letting the pulse hammer into the double fisherman's knot at the back of his neck, watching the crucifix swing from its chain under his dripping nose. The shower, too hot, was the only place he couldn't hear the buzz and ding of his phone, be subject to the shrill jet stream of angry voices and all-caps rants.

He exited the shower and let himself drip for a minute before he applied the lotion his doctor had prescribed for his flare-ups, which had spread from patches on his arms and legs to canvas most of his body. Despite the summer heat, he pulled on a clean white short-sleeved t-shirt and extra-long boxers, a barrier between his tortured skin and his woolen-blend dress uniform. He had directed all available police in the department to suit up for crowd control. He didn't know what to expect from John Yearling's impromptu public forum today at the inn, but he knew enough to preparefor the worst. Just a few days ago the Chamber was bitching at him because Bristlecone Springs had emptied out like a plague had rolled in and swept all their business to higher ground. Now dispatch was on fire with neighborhood complaints about visitors taking up all the parking and letting their dogs crap wherever they saw fit. The grocery was sold out of water, bread, and milk. The toilets at the public parks were stopped up, the waste bins brimming. Worst of all, he was no closer to solving the case responsible for this chaos, and he'd exiled the one person who had, thus far, managed to limit the damage to catastrophe and stave off complete devastation.

Eleanor hadn't liked Yearling. Stanislaus wasn't prepared to like him, either, but he still couldn't square the beer king's real estate ambitions with the abductions and torture of five young children. While, as a Roman Catholic, he internalized generations of suspicion for Evangelical Protestantism, he had to think, as an officer of the church, Yearling was in some way, in the most essential way, a man of God, that despite his organization's vulgar and insidious billboard ads—which Stanislaus was certain Yearling had personally approved— the president of VOLT had to honor the Lord's commandment to refrain from murder. Or attempted murder, thanks to Eleanor Clay.

The detective shook cornstarch into his dress shoes. As he laced them, he felt a sudden envy of DePeña's shorts and ventilated Reeboks. He sat up on the edge of the bed and found himself out of breath. "Shit, I gotta get more exercise," he said aloud.

CHAPTER
20

Cal was gone when Althea arrived home at the cabin. She marveled, was almost shocked as she sometimes was when she returned from a case for CorpsPursuit or weekend trip, at the fecundity of their little parcel. She had done the plantings and designed the hydration systems, of course, but as she noted the upward splash of new flowering hops on the southern wall of the cabin, the pointillist poppy mallow and bee balm, and the startling purple on the stalk of the Rocky Mountain penstemon, she wondered afresh at the compositional impulse of nature.

A note on the fridge under a magnet shaped like a mandolin—*String Alchemy Custom Builds*—read: *Darling Girl, In the city with Levi to meet some young musicians. Last night's dinner's in the fridge. See you tonight. Love, C.*

She missed him, she realized. This summer they'd spent an unusual amount of time apart, even for their independent habits, with Cal following the festivals, and she moving onto Eleanor's couch in Bristlecone Springs. She hadn't really had the chance to miss him before this. It seemed impossible to her that they had spent the last ten years so entwined, but it was a fact that outside of her colleagues at the college and the CorpsPursuit team, Cal was her whole world. Standing alone in her beautiful, rustic kitchen, looking around at the little western paradise she and he had pulled around themselves, she wondered that she didn't feel more devotion. It was as if the last decade had simply poured out, she thought, with very little effort or investigation on her part. Still, she missed him, and was disappointed to come home to an empty house, had looked forward to the domestic presence of her lover in this place they made and shared, had anticipated folding herself into the bearishness of him, had taken for granted that he would welcome her home, and that he would take great pleasure in doing so. She missed him, but was not wrecked by his absence. *Mild deflation,* she thought, *over-sensitivity due to fatigue*—that's how she chose to diagnose her ennui. She sighed. A little lack of enthusiasm was nothing to focus her weary and overfilled brain on just now.

She scooped some noodles out of the casserole and ate them cold from the serving spoon while standing over the sink. She noticed the lifted lid on the photograph, walked over to see what Cal had been listening to, and saw the old 78. Viennese Waltzes recorded before the second World War.

Cal treasured his collection of 78s. He usually played them when she wasn't around, said he didn't want to bum her out her with his sentimental indulgences. Althea knew very little about why they carried so much sentiment for him, except that they were recorded by a distant relative, a woman, second cousin or something to Mahler. She'd died in a Nazi concentration camp at least ten or twelve years before Cal was born. They'd never had a conversation about his family and the Holocaust. She didn't know if the word *Holocaust* had ever passed between them.

Althea and Cal seemed only to mention his Jewish roots in jest, much like how they referenced her Italian heritage. Neither of them felt particularly tied to their lineage, or so she'd assumed. She grew up with a single mom of Greek descent and never knew her father, though her mother kept his Italian surname and gave it to her. In the time Althea had known him, Cal had never discussed his religious or cultural roots, never went to temple, and, even more than she, defaulted to stereotypes for the easy joke.

She replaced the record in its sheath and closed the lid on the phonograph. She supposed it was a good thing there was still a little mystery to their relationship. She made a vow to herself to be more curious about her partner and maybe a little less snarky. Something in her, she had recently discovered, was ready for deeper waters.

Levi watched as Cal laid out the instruments he'd brought to show the students, a violin with a mother of pearl inlay, a cedar mandolin—the back of which was hand painted to represent Gustav Klimt's The Kiss— and the plain spruce and maple fiddle he played himself.

"These are so beautiful, Cal. Wow," said Levi. "So, what would you like to play? I've got plenty of sheet music, but I'm open to suggestion."

"So happens I brought some music myself, inspired by the streak of sentimentalism you interrupted with your call today. Rose Mahler's interpretation of her uncle's 'Ich bin der Welt abhanden gekommen'—'I've Become Lost To The World.'"

"I don't know it. Or her."

"No, it isn't likely you would. She was a virtuoso in Europe before WWII, played the popular music of the day, mostly waltzes. This piece is a little different."

Cal put a CD into the player. The room was suspended for a moment with a single, honeyed note that stretched and held until it broke and tumbled into an avalanche of feeling. The music was sweet and sad and also masterful in a way that denied passive listening, insisting that the audience agree to withstand whatever was coming, even if what arrived proved to be their undoing.

"What was she saying?" Levi asked when it ended.

"I'm not sure I have the words for it. She recorded that right before she was arrested and transported to the concentration camp. I don't even know if it was an SOS, carries more a of a note of resignation, if you will. You know, her fame, such as it was, was partly due to what she accomplished after she was arrested inside the camp. She took over a women's orchestra in Auschwitz, trained them to be good enough to not be murdered."

"She was a hero."

"I don't know what she was. Maybe a heroine, even if few survived. Not a survivor herself, clearly. An artist, surely... thank you, Levi, for allowing me to share that with you. We should maybe choose a lighter piece for today, something a little more youth orchestra friendly?"

"Probably, yeah. But thank you."

Levi and Cal spent the late afternoon listening, talking, playing, and laughing with the kids, who ranged in age from six to thirteen. For many of them, this 3:30 to 5:30 locally sponsored class was a way to keep them under someone's supervision after school during the academic year, but Levi had volunteered this year and last to hold sessions throughout the summer, and to offer private instruction. As a result, the group had a high retention rate, and the caliber of playing was such that they had been invited to participate in multiple city events.

The end of class rolled around. Parents and siblings started coming around to collect their students. The kids shuffled past him with their customary side hug. Levi found himself over-come.

The room emptied out. Cal put a hand on Levi's shoulder. "That was a rare and amazing afternoon, Levi, thank you. I forget, what with hanging around all the hide-hardened musicians I keep company with, how tender the young shoots can be. But tough, too, right? You really hold them to their routine!"

Levi rubbed his arm across his face. "They're good kids, some of them really good musicians, too, all of them talented. I'm going to miss them." Levi got up and began to move about the room, folding chairs and lining them up against the wall. "Cal, I know we don't know each other very well, but do you think I could tell you something in confidence?"

"Levi, if you feel comfortable, I'd be honored."

"For some reason, I feel like we've met at a weird moment, like you're meeting a version of me I barely know. Look, I haven't told this to anyone but my friend Bash, but my girl-friend and I are pregnant. Since we've known, my emotions are all over the place. I feel like I either want to burst into tears or slam my fist into something. Or else I'm just kind of numb, inside and out."

"Well, sure. All those things seem legitimate. Can't think of a bigger life event than a pregnancy. And, of course, you're still a very young man. A mature one, to be sure."

"I'm sorry. I don't mean to weigh you down like this. I mean, we don't even really know each other. It's just that I wanted to tell my mom in Bristlecone Springs, or on our way to Denver, and well, you saw how that worked out."

"It's no burden, son. Maybe you and your mom weren't in the right space for that conversation. She has a lot going on."

"Yeah, sure. But then, you know, when doesn't she? Dad and Annabelle and she have gone to the moon and back making sure I have everything I need, and I do, and they did that. Absolutely they did. But her grief, her inability or refusal to deal with Freya's death, and then whatever she feels or doesn't feel about me and Dad leaving—I just can't handle her unresolved crap right now. My own shit's blowing up, and my mom is more out there than ever."

Cal packed up his instruments and looked over at Levi, who'd folded himself tight into the last open chair, head hung, chest over thighs, hands clasped behind calves. Levi sat there another few seconds before he stood up, still bent at the waist. With his eyes shut, he took a deep breath, extended his arms like wings, lifted his torso, turned his palms up, lifted his arms above his head, then lowered them slowly, exhaling with an audible whoosh, ending with his hands together positioned for prayer. He opened his eyes and shook it out, jogging a few steps in place and wringing out his hands.

Levi turned to face Cal. "Hey, I'm sorry, this isn't a conversation you need to be having."

"No worries, Levi, really. What would you say to grabbing a bite? I could do with a burger and a Dr. Pepper right about now."

"Thanks, Cal, but I can't. I've got to meet the guys for band practice right after this." He added, "Hey, I think the kids had a really good time today. Thank you."

"The pleasure was mine. You want to put up with my fiddle playing or listen to some more sad old music, just give me a call. That is, if you have time before you take off for Boulder."

"Yeah, sure. That'd be cool."

At nine o'clock that night, Levi sat and stared as Emmett helped himself to a second plate of poached salmon and herb salad. He'd brought dinner home from the fancy neighborhood deli after an offsite meeting had run over and Annabelle called to say she'd be working late.

"Not hungry?" Emmett said as he buttered a slice of baguette.

"No." Levi clenched his back molars and watched Emmet chew and swallow, chew and swallow, until finally, unable to withstand further mastication, he pushed back from the table and let the words spill out of him.

"Dad! For god's sake, can you stop eating for a second? How can you sit there and eat like there's nothing going on, with our family falling apart like it is?" He paced, hunched, like he was trying to hold on to a kick ball with his stomach.

Emmett looked up from his plate, a spear of kokanee hanging on his fork.

"You know, I get that we're *unconventional*, or whatever... but, still... I don't understand how you can calmly gnaw on salmon when shit is hitting the fan all over the place...Mom's in the middle of an investigation of a serial crime spree, with the whole state, it feels like, talking smack about her ...you and Annabelle have hardly said a straight-up word to me since I'm back ...I can't just pretend we're not in trouble here, and I don't have the brain space for our usual *intentional dialogue,* not with Trista pregnant and getting an abortion, and Mom all alone wherever the fuck she is now ...I mean, don't get me wrong, I'm plenty pissed at her, but she's still my mom ..."

Emmett choked on a piece of frisee he'd stopped chewing when Levi let loose. "Hold up there. Trista's pregnant?"

Levi stood still. "Oh. Yeah."

"Wow. Wow, oh my God, Levi...that's...well, that's big! I'm guessing that's not the way you planned to share that information, if you planned to share it at all?"

"Look, Dad...it's not that I didn't think I could share it with you. I don't know what I thought, don't know what to think about it myself. For real, like, I don't have the words for how I think, and I definitely haven't figured out how I feel, except for really confused, and sad ...and angry. I'm scared shitless, Dad. I'm terrified."

"I know."

"C'mon, Dad, seriously? How can you know? You can't know everything, you can't know this. I get that you love me and all, but you just don't, you just can't get where I'm coming from right now."

"I do though, Levi, or I think I do. Believe it or not, I wasn't always your dad, some guy with a job and a Subaru and an answer for everything."

Levi sat, tore at a piece of bread, stuffed it into his mouth. He chewed like he was trying to grind a handful of screws and stared at his father. "You mean you and a girl had an abortion?"

"She had the abortion, but yes, I was there with her."

"Was this before it was legal?"

"Ah, no, we were both kids when the Roe v Wade decision came down in 1973. Which is not to say, just because it was legal, it was easy."

"Can I ask what happened to your relationship with the woman after she had the abortion? Did you stay together, or did you break up?"

"We broke up, but it was long after the abortion. We stayed together through the births two children, Freya and you, and then for several more years, which I remember as being very good, until Freya died."

"Oh, wow. You and Mom."

"Me and your mom, yes. You're right, though. I'm not you, and Trista is her own woman. Who knows what this means for the two of you? Hell, I was thinking leaving for college would be enough of a relationship challenge. Levi, I can share my experience, for what it's worth, but I think all it comes

148

down to is that we—your mother and me— chose to trust each other."

"And you were in love."

"Oh, yeah. Definitely."

Levi cleared the plates. He wrapped the leftovers for Annabelle to have when she got home.

CHAPTER
21

The room capacity of the conference center at Bristlecone Springs Inn was 934. At 8:30 a.m., with the forum starting at 11 a.m., Detective Drubbs reported a count of twelve-hundred-plus people snaking around the building. Stanislaus checked in on his people monitoring the lines before entering the hotel, a modern construction less than five years old. It stood as a sharp and efficient contrast to what used to be the only real hotel in town, a grand old beast across town named The Golden Crescent, more commonly known as The Carrot since an unfortunate paint job in the 1970s, corrected some years later, but not before the nickname took.

Stanislaus stood in the lobby, grateful for the air conditioning. Marvin Breton, the hotel manager, bounced through the reception area carrying several ropes of electrical cording. Pleased at having already booked the room to VOLT at an inflated price, and ecstatic over the potential concession income, Marvin was practically dancing through the recreation and dining rooms, outfitting them to provide remote video of the forum.

"You're going to keep it to code, right, Marvin?"

"Detective Stanislaus, good morning! Don't you worry, sir, we're inviting people to watch the event from multiple viewpoints. It should be very comfortable for everyone and perfectly safe."

"All right. Make your bank, Marvin. I know it's been a hard season. Just mind you keep the aisles open."

"Of course, Detective. May I have someone get you an iced tea or glass of ice water? It's quite warm today."

"I'm okay, thanks." Sweat dripped down the back of Stanislaus' neck. From Marvin's cool solicitude about his hydration, he surmised his face was as red as a stoplight. He had a pang of nostalgia for Chicago winters.

The front lobby doors slid open and John Yearling strode into the open space dressed in jeans, smooth but not creased, a navy blazer, and light blue button-down shirt.

His buffed boots were a shade or two darker than the golf tan that bronzed his face and throat, peeking through his open collar.

Yearling walked directly to Stanislaus and extended a hand. "Detective! A pleasure to see you again."

Stanislaus recoiled slightly at a shock of static as they touched.

The scent of Yearling's woodsy-sweet cologne hung between them. Stanislaus resisted a sneeze. "Mr. Yearling. This is quite a production you've arranged. I'll admit it was all we could do to line up enough staff to police this pop-up event of yours. Our little resort town has had enough trouble this summer— I trust you've come to help these folks, not rile them up. My job, you understand, is to keep the peace."

"As I understand it, Detective, your job has been to catch a serial kidnapper, an effort that doesn't seem to be going all that well for your team, given that the only success you've had has been at the hands of a questionably qualified consultant.

Where is Mrs. Clay, anyway? I would have thought I was creating the perfect opportunity for her, and your department, to defend your incompetence."

"See? That's what I mean, Mr. Yearling. That's my concern right there, that incendiary comment of yours. Let me be clear. I won't have you inciting a riot among these people, and tearing up my town more than it has already been torn up. Eleanor Clay left by my orders, for her own safety, which has been endangered, specifically, by your internet recklessness."

Yearling rested one manicured hand on a bronze belt buckle in the shape of the state of Colorado, and placed the other over his heart. "But that's why I'm here, Detective Stanislaus, to clear the air in person, to clarify my position as an agent of the church, and to offer peace and blessings to these suffering folk, which I would extend to Mrs. Clay, as well, if she were here. If you'll excuse me, I must see the manager about a sound check. I'm sure we'll have the opportunity to speak again, Detective."

At 10:30 a.m., the doors opened. Stanislaus watched as the crowd poured over the brightly patterned carpet through the red ropes to the convention room until it was filled. The overflow was then directed by Marvin and hotel staff to multiple auxiliary viewing areas, all equipped with snack carts and beverage service. The faces were mostly, but not exclusively, white. At a glance, Stanislaus judged the mean age to be somewhere between thirty and forty, with a percentage of people who looked to be between sixty and seventy. Economically, there was no discernible common thread. The parking lot was a crazy quilt of Porsche SUVs, Toyota Camrys, and beat-up trucks with homemade camper shells. What was consistent with this population was their expression of grief, a sunken-eyed micro-separation from a common reality that put a twitch in their gestures and infused their movements with a hyper vigilance, as if an internal soundtrack kept them perpetually distracted, always a beat off, and jumpy.

At precisely eleven o'clock, a voice came over the sound system and announced, "We will now recite the Pledge of Allegiance." As if jerked, people who could stand did so and caps flew off heads in a wave, as the familiar rhythm of the words beat to their conclusion through the rooms. A recorded version of the "Star Spangled Banner" played immediately on the heels of the collective *and liberty and justice for all.* The twang of the famous country music star could scarcely be heard through the final *home of the brave,* sung at a strength of more than one thousand voices. No one moved as John Yearling walked to the center of the stage.

"Blessings to you all. My name is John Yearling, President of Value Our Family Traditions, and I am grateful to be here with you today. Now that we have all joined together in one of our most sacred traditions as citizens of this great country, let us talk about what brings us indoors on this beautiful summer day, when we could all be out enjoying the Lord's bounty, or working at our jobs for our families.

"And that is the question, is it not? Why on earth would we disrupt our homes and spend our paychecks on gas and motels, make whatever sacrifices have been necessary to lift us from our places of comfort, forsake the simple and fleeting pleasures of the season to crowd together in a stuffy convention center in an interstate hotel? Why are we here in this bland, sad space, instead of living our good lives?"

Yearling held the stillness, broken only by the crackle of air conditioning kicking in.

"We all know the answer. Naturally, we are here for the children. We are here for the children who are not here, who are lost to the world or to heaven, who for some unknowable, terrible reason have been taken from us. Now, I am a man of God. I know no greater mercy than the beneficence of our Lord, but I do not intend to stand up on this stage and convince a sea of grieving parents and relatives that the fact that their children have been snatched from their bosom is somehow a part of God's divine plan. I cannot know God's plan—it is neither my right nor my desire. I can say, however, that no God that I call mine would enact such a heartless punishment upon a loving parent.

"And loving is the word for you parents, grandparents, and family that have made this holy, if misguided, pilgrimage to this town, home to the ancient springs cherished by Native Americans for their healing powers. That you love is plain, that you are drawn to this place is plain, and that you suffer for your love and from this journey, is equally plain.

"I look out into this room and I see pilgrims, parents and grandparents and aunts and uncles and cousins whose love cannot be reconciled to their loss, the unimaginable loss of a child; pilgrims who feel they must search for something that will answer for that terrible, impossible absence, a bereavement Our Father in heaven knew all too well."

"Where's Eleanor?" a woman shouted. "I didn't come for all your God talk, I come for Eleanor!" A low, disorganized rumble rose from the crowd.

"Blessings on you, ma'am, you ask an excellent question," said Yearling, addressing the woman directly. His own voice boomed from the speakers. "Where is Mrs. Clay?"

A man stood up. "You run her off with those Chitter attacks. You and your church!"

"I thank you, sir. That is exactly the reason I come to you today, to talk with you all about my recent comments. It was never my intent to attack Mrs. Clay."

Yearling smiled sheepishly and chuckled. "You see, like many folks trying to navigate these new social media outlets, I haven't entirely figured out how to temper my passion to 280 characters. If I am guilty of the sin of overzealousness, I promise it was only because I am so eager to relieve good folks of their pain, lessen the pain made deeper by the irresponsible behavior of non-believers like Mrs. Clay. I have a passion in me I cannot deny, I will admit, a compulsion to protect innocent people from the devastation of godless charlatans, as I vehemently believe Mrs. Clay to be, though she, and you here today, may protest. I can see that many, if not all of you, have come to see her intentions and actions as honorable, and I mean no dishonor toward you all in questioning your faith, though I fear it is unwisely invested."

"But she's found those kids! She's the only one that's found them!"

The audience rallied. "That's right," some of them said, while others made "hm, hm," and "uh huh," noises in agreement. Here and there Eleanor's name floated above the collective, like the call of a chickadee, or a mourning dove.

Yearling filled his lungs, expanded his diaphragm, and projected, "it is the Lord's own truth: Mrs. Clay has found five children, has been the first on the scene in each and every incidence." He paused to gather and hold their silence before leaning in conspiratorially from the stage. "But how has she found them, I ask you? Let us lift the veils from our eyes and look plainly and with purpose at the conditions of Eleanor Clay's so-called miraculous recoveries. These precious children, all of them, have been found so close to death as to hear the Lord our God's gentle whisper in their ears. Each and every time, our children have been dug out of the earth broken and bruised, little bodies rotting. Brain damaged. I don't know, but is it not time to wonder, if we were not relying so heavily on the dubious talents of Mrs. Clay, if the police were not cobbled so by her heathen celebrity, how much sooner would we be recovering our children, whole and healthy, and not just barely alive? Is it not time that we, as loving guardians, questioned the ways in which our police force is weakened by this alien presence? Is it not time that we, as law-abiding citizens, challenged why our officers are having their power and authority drained by an infidel who, by her own admission, suffers mentally and emotionally from her own loss, a daughter she stood by and watched drown?"

Yearling held the moment for several seconds before he coughed lightly into his fist. "A tragedy, certainly, that I would not wish upon the devil himself: the legitimate loss of a child."

Gordon Stanislaus moved from the dining room and bar, throughout the hotel spaces filled wall-to-wall with people who were not tourists, who only superficially resembled, in their shorts and tank tops, the summer visitors whom he watched flow into the Springs to soak, play, and poke through bins and racks of Colorado magnets and coffee mugs, who came to drink, to eat pricey hamburgers and pizza or ice-packed cold cuts from a cooler, soothe travel-cranky kids, take pictures of wildflowers and deer and each other, and make the memories they'd revisit at the Thanksgiving table and share in holiday newsletters. He studied the faces of the somber crowd amassed in the hotel, a people denied their careless joy, their happy memories, and felt the collective desperation of those who would settle for, who would clutch at, any sort of story about their child—a medical chart, a police report—so long as it wasn't an obituary. He thought about how many unhappy endings he'd delivered over the years, how many times he witnessed a parent receive their own life sentence, could almost hear the clang and echo of their prison gate locking in place. He scanned the audience. Every face in the room come to listen today had the look of someone who hadn't yet heard the verdict, and despite an avalanche of evidence, thinks it might yet go their way.

Stanislaus turned to the lobby screen to watch John Yearling work the stage.

"Bastard," he said under his breath. He jumped to hear Marvin's voice right behind him.

"Yeah! What does he mean, bland?"

In the convention room, an older woman pulled herself up by the handles of her walker and spoke.

"Pastor Yearling, I watch your program on television and have many times heard you deliver an inspiring sermon. I don't follow the Chitter, but seems to me what you've been saying about Eleanor Clay isn't very Christian. We lost our Toby three years ago, and his mama and papa are never going to be right, Lord help them, but I know if they could have Toby back in any kind of shape they'd be eternally grateful for God's mercy and kindness."

"What is your name, ma'am?"

"It's Charlotte. Charlotte Wilcox. I come from Gentry, Arkansas to be here and meet with Eleanor, if I could, and I come today to see if you could make sense for me of the way you been talking about her. Don't feel to me like she's gaining anything for herself. She got more claim to humble than you do—a president, a TV pastor of a big church. You run a fancy beer company, too, as I understand it."

"God bless you, Charlotte. Let me tell you sincerely that I am first, and always, a humble servant of the Lord and His church. And yes, while God's love is available to every soul who lets Him in, while the blessings of his love are freely dispensed, I give praise that I and my family enjoy the beautiful earthly life that we do. While poor drifters like Mrs. Clay may seem to operate without evil motive or selfish cause—may even, in the costume of the martyr—appear selfless, I say let us be wary of false humility and dark methods.

"I openly acknowledge my good fortune. With a grateful heart, I offer all the hard work and service I can to my family, my community, my country, and my God each and every day. Each and every day, I praise the Lord for my bountiful life. I do not enjoy the wonders of this, my precious time on earth, nor could I share the word of Jesus Christ our Savior, without the support of hard working and open-hearted congregations of solid citizens such as yourselves. As part of my mission to serve God and his followers, I respect the structures that hold us together, support the intelligent and trained officers of our institutions to do their jobs free from the diluting, polluting influences of unstable, pseudo-spiritual carpetbaggers, and of elitist bands of self-appointed and so-called scientific consultants who may inflict more damage than they prevent or repair.

"My opposition to Mrs. Clay is not, as some of my misinformed critics have proposed, a vindictive witch hunt, but an honest attempt to flush our fine and valiant systems of a virulent, debilitating infection that is weakening our ability to truly care for and protect our children, all our sweet children, those precious babes we are blessed to hold close to us, as well as our defenseless unborn.

"We must say no to the corrosive godlessness of the Eleanor Clays of the world, say no to chaos, and give authority back to the leaders who can wield it with righteousness and results. If that means a change in leadership is in order, and I believe that may sadly be the case in Bristlecone Springs. I have faith that together in this country, in your hometown, and right here in Bristlecone Springs, we can commit to the courage that is required to make a change. We can restore strength and judgement to our police and legal systems and make our communities safe again. But we can only achieve this correction together. We can only rebuild our systems as a united and God-fearing, God-loving citizenry. I humbly call upon you, you who came here for salvation, to find the help that is already here, but that has been trodden upon by fakery. It is time to restore our faith in the leaders and heroes that show up every day to keep the peace and protect us, and it is time, if you are to be delivered of your pain, to invest your hope in something greater than chance and magic tricks. I am grateful for your time, and honor the sacrifices you make to be here today. Thank you, thank you, and God bless you all."

"Fucking prick," Stanislaus muttered.

"What's that, Detective?" Drubbs had exited the convention room, in preparation to manage the crowd once Yearling left the stage.

"Uh, nothing, Drubbs, nothing. Do we have uniforms in position for this exodus?"

"Yes, sir. We're ready for anything."

As it turned out, there wasn't anything to be ready for, nothing to control or otherwise contain. The crowd sat quietly for a full minute after Yearling disappeared behind the red curtain, then gradually got to their feet and shuffled out into the bright sunshine without incident. Those who'd been in the restaurant and lounge paid their checks if they had one, and joined the orderly queue leaving the hotel. There was not so much as a honk or beep from the cavalcade as they inched out of the parking lot and moved on to whatever cell they were inhabiting in the meantime of their lives.

Drubbs sidled up to Stanislaus as the last vehicle turned out of sight. "Well, Detective, I'm guessing that couldn't have gone better!"

Stanislaus pulled at his damp collar, the faint pressure of the backs of his fingers a hot poker on the welts rising and ringing his thick neck. "Too soon to tell, Drubbs. Too soon to tell."

CHAPTER
22

Nina opened her front door and smiled. "Althea, I was wondering when the happy day would come that I would see you in my home."

"You know you've never invited me, Nina."

"I've always wanted to. But ja, ja, you are right. What with brothers and boyfriends and bodies to look after, I suppose we've never been quite proactive about hospitality. I am glad you've taken the reins in your own lovely hands. *Willkommen*, at last."

"Thank you, Nina." Althea stepped through the heavy oak door into the vestibule of the old house. "Oh! Your home is beautiful!"

"Ha! You sound so surprised! What did you think, Althea? That I lived in a sterile box or a hovel?"

"I imagined someplace very clean and classy, like you. But I wasn't factoring in the warmth or the elegance. Anyway, ahem, you have a lovely home. There, I've recovered my manners."

"Althea!" Elan scooped her up in a hug, imprinting her with the flour from his apron. "It's about time."

"Well, hello, Elan. I see you're making yourself useful."

"I'm making Pfeffernusse from Nina's mother's cookbook. They're like my Nana's Mexican wedding cookies spiked with Christmas."

The trio moved into the kitchen, which was pleasantly cluttered with spice jars, bags of flour, powdered sugar, utensils, and bowls.

"How's Eleanor?"

"I'm fine," said Eleanor as she rounded the corner from the sunroom. The two women embraced.

Eleanor stepped back. "Weren't you heading home the last time I talked to you? I got the impression you and Cal were looking forward to a little uninterrupted domestic bliss."

"Yeah, I don't exactly know what happened there. Cal was at the cabin while I stayed in Boulder overnight, then he wasn't there when I got home. Point of fact, he abandoned me for your son, said Levi'd invited him to meet his students in Denver. I was sitting there eating turkey tetrazzini straight from the refrigerator when abruptly, I felt I had to come here." They settled into chairs in the sunroom.

"Also, I want to talk about what I found out about the other cases, areas of difference and similarity. I sent my findings—still speculation—to Bristlecone Springs PD, before I headed here. I didn't know if you were talking to Gordon, or vice versa, and I thought he should know what I'm seeing in the data from Canada, and how they may connect to the cases in Los Angeles."

"What are you seeing?"

"Patterns. Not like the kind you see, maybe, but a certain repetition in method and in the victim profiles. The kids are in the same age range, three to seven. Parents run the gamut from single moms to a pair of adoptive moms to couples with a houseful of other children. Weirdly, though, there was one mom who went public with her grief, just like Sarah Schmidt. Blamed her child's murder on her own prior abortion, saw it as God's retribution."

"That is a weird coincidence."

Althea picked through a bowl of cocktail nuts on the table next to her chair. "Hm, I wonder, though, how much of a coincidence it is. Cal was working for a clinic up there before we met, volunteering right up until he retired from his practice. He used to tell me how distraught, how depressed some women remained, long after an abortion, especially if they hadn't sought any support or had gone through it alone."

"Cal worked at an abortion clinic?"

"He would say no. He worked at a women's health clinic. I've often thought it was the intensity of that work, even more than his love of stringed things, that led him to take such an early retirement."

"Huh."

Elan hurried into the sunroom with his phone. "I just got a message from Bristlecone PD, with a link to a video of a forum John Yearling held at the inn this morning. Holy shit, Eleanor, there were over a thousand people there, all looking for you, all listening to him."

Elan sat on the floor as the two women watched the video over his shoulders. When it was over he said, "Why is it so quiet?"

Nina stood in the doorway. "It is like the cliché, the calm before the storm, no? I am not a trained meteorologist, but I know that Mr. Yearling there has sucked up all those people's air to fuel some kind of agenda. We're only witnessing the windless moment before the tornado lands. I wouldn't mistake that quiet for peace."

Eleanor asked, "Nina, what are you saying?"

"I am saying, dear Eleanor, that unfortunately I have seen

speeches like this one change the world for the worse, with the aid and support of reasonably good people who were experiencing more pain than they could manage. I am saying that I have seen violence erupt from such speeches. I have experienced it myself."

"Do you think there is something I can do? I mean, these people showed up in Bristlecone Springs for me—okay, maybe not for *me*—but for what they thought I could do for them. They think I can make them whole again, patch their families back together, find their children...but I can't. Of course I can't. No one can. But now, instead of facing them with that truth, I've run. And what do they get instead? What's come in to fill the vacuum? Certainly nothing they asked for. Nobody asked for Yearling, but it's Yearling who stepped into the gap to greet them with that ...speech."

"Seeding hope with fear," said Nina.

Elan raised himself to a standing position. "Whoa, whoa, whoa, there...I agree that our Mr. Yearling is an opportunist, but let's not give him too much power just yet. There's plenty you can do, Eleanor, even if you are just some flaky, godless— what was the word the good pastor used—*carpetbagger?* C'mon, who in this century says stuff like that? Whatever, Eleanor, if you want to be useful to these folks, it won't be by throwing yourself on the fire like Colorado's own Joan of Arc."

"Joan of Arc didn't throw herself on the pyre, Elan. Someone strapped her to the stake," said Althea.

"Either way, you know what I mean. No one in Bristlecone Springs needs a martyr. It was the right call getting out of town."

Eleanor stared out the picture window. "Maybe. But I can't stay here forever, and I can't go to Denver and make my family any more vulnerable. I've got to go back."

Althea said, "I agree. They're going to need you back. Those other cases in London and L.A.? They each report six victims. Five pictures are up on the board back in your home-town PD. There's going to be another one. I'm sorry to say it, but I'm afraid you're going to need to find another child, Eleanor."

Gordon Stanislaus stood in the middle of the basement office floor tiled with the police reports from Ontario and Los Angeles that Althea Giordano sent late that afternoon. He anticipated a long night, trying to assimilate the information and absorb Giordano's assessment, but all he could think about was the supposition that it wasn't over, that another abduction was yet to come. Was *inevitable*. If the criminal stuck to the program. If there was, in fact, a program. And if the goddamn internet didn't produce a copycat to raise the tally even higher.

At the moment, he thought, whoever was taking these kids will be hard pressed to find one to snatch. Stanislaus walked through downtown the day before without seeing a single child. Parents were keeping them under watch, out of the public eye. The public swimming pool sat empty, despite record temperatures. Summer swim lessons were canceled. A few young people with babies and toddlers huddled together around the wading pool, vigilant. The town had an artificial quality; it didn't sound right. Then he thought, it's probably better this way, for now. But September was coming up fast, and the first day of school wasn't far off. He didn't know how he'd be able to convince parents it was safe to let their kids walk to school, ride a bike, play in a backyard. Who'd believe him?

It was tough enough to keep your kid healthy and safe under the best of circumstances, which certainly didn't include having a child-stealing maniac in your midst. Hell, his kids never suffered more than a cold growing up, or so he'd believed. Safety was a myth. You never knew what danger was lurking around the corner, buried in the backyard, sitting across from you at the kitchen table. All you could do was take your head out of your ass occasionally and look around. Small changes were significant, worthy of your attention. He'd learned that the hard way, after the fact, and now took it as gospel.

He placed the toxicology reports adjacent to one another. Different drugs: heroin in Canada; curare, of all things, he thought, in L.A.; cannabis and valerian here. All administered intravenously. Heroin where there was an illegal opium market. Cannabis where there is a legal cannabis market. Curare, a poison and an anesthetic, originating in South America, not a street drug. Canadian case and southern California case tied to drug wars between local gangs and distributors. No evidence of gang involvement here. What was the pattern? Was there one?

All the victims were children. Why target children? None of the victims, here or elsewhere, showed signs of sexual abuse, though all suffered considerable physical abuse, mostly from the conditions of their abduction— exposure, dehydration, lack of oxygen. No one had asked for ransom, no demands of any kind had been made. Why kidnap children and subject them to this terrible treatment, unless it gave you pleasure to do so? Or it caused someone else immense pain. What did that prick say about a tragedy too horrible for the devil, the legitimate loss of a child? What the hell did he mean by that? Legitimate? Stanislaus could surmise what the pastor would mean by illegitimate. What was Yearling after with that grieving mob, besides his badge?

Revenge was a time-honored motive. Or could it be a warning? There was either too little information left on the scenes, in which case the criminal did it for their own reasons, and they'd have to wait for the bastard to make a mistake, or he was missing something critical.

Maybe the information he needed wasn't at the scenes. He'd talk to the parents again, and he'd see if he could get anything else out of L.A. and Ontario. He'd talk to Giordano. First, though, he had to go home and take a shower, pour some lotion on the carnivorous itch hijacking his body, change into a clean, dry shirt.

CHAPTER
23

Levi got on the ramp for I-70 from US-6 on his way to Cal and Althea's place in Genesee. The drive took less than a half hour, but by the time he passed the fossil beds, just north of Red Rocks, he was feeling worlds away from the Mile High City. Mesmerized by the hilly scrub and grazing buffalo and the hum of the engine at a steady seventy-five miles per hour, Levi failed to notice the billboards erected since he was last on this road going west a few days ago.

Levi exited the freeway, passing the entrances to two new posh-looking subdivisions and continuing on via the directions Cal had supplied via text, with the warning that Siri would land him in the woods. He took a right and followed a smooth dirt road about eight hundred yards until he came upon the structure Cal referred to as the cabin, a neat little jewel of a house set amid a field of pale butter and eggs, columbine, orange paintbrush, and alpine sorrel. As Levi approached the hand-carved maple door, he had an urge to snap off a corner of a shutter and taste it.

Instead, he ran a finger through the copper pipes of one of the wind chimes, floating a ripple of notes into the motionless summer air. He knocked and waited, then noticed Cal's truck parked backed up to a wooden outbuilding set a half-acre or so behind the house.

"Hey, Cal! It's Levi!"

"Hey, there!" Cal walked out of the building looking more than ever like the head of the elves, bedecked in a leather apron, wire-rimmed glasses, and his corona of white hair. "So glad you can make it! I've been tidying up the shop, getting a handle on inventory, and couldn't help thinking about you. I have a couple of fiddles I'd like to donate to the center, and one, I humbly suggest, you might be interested in for yourself."

Cal clapped a hand on Levi's shoulder. "Come on in, you can take a look. Want some iced tea? Althea blends the best herbal mix for ice, holds its own in a brew, doesn't even need sugar. She's a real kitchen witch, that scientist girlfriend of mine!"

"Sure, that sounds great. Is Althea here? I didn't see another car."

"She's not, no. Seems she had a few more loose ends in Boulder to tie up than she thought. Now you know the way, though, I bet she'd be happy to have you out—you and your mom, maybe?"

"When I've got a break, you bet I'd love to hang out. Can't speak for Mom." Levi entered the structure, bigger inside that it had appeared from the outside, and walked around the perimeter of the room, examining various violins and mandolins open in their cases and a bass leaning in the corner. The air smelled of sawdust, resin, wax, and varnish, with a layer of woody incense, and a faint undertone of herb. "Wow, Cal, these are super detailed. I saw one or two online, when I looked you up, so I had a preview, but up close they're really amazing! Think I could I play one?"

"Please. The look is supposed to complement the sound, and the sound's the point, right?"

Levi lifted a violin and played.

Cal sat at his workbench, listening with his eyes closed, tapping a boot. As the last note faded, he opened his eyes and smiled at Levi. The young man held his playing posture for another second, his own eyes shut tight, until he lowered the bow and relaxed his face, offering a small, shy smile in return.

"Ah, that's the stuff! Something you wrote? Sounds original."

"Yeah, just a piece I've been fooling around with."

"Spoken like a true virtuoso. I often wish I were a better player, but today I'm content to be a gifted listener."

Levi set the violin back in its velveteen bed. "Who are these for?"

"Oh, nobody, really, not yet. This is my surplus."

"But they look so ...specific. You know, custom."

"Yes, I suppose they do have some specificity to them. Most are scenes from my own dreams, or what I remember of them. Really, just a way to practice my craft between orders. Sometimes I sell them. These I'd like to give away."

Levi came and sat at the bench. "Cal, you've got almost a dozen beautiful instruments here. That one I just played sounds awesome. I'm sure you could get serious money for it, plus the rest of them."

"I could, you're right. But I'd rather the kids got them, had something of quality to play, know what that means. I'd like to contribute to their understanding that they are worth the good stuff. And I'd like you to have this one, if you'll agree to take it from me."

Cal unchecked the hinges on a battered-looking case set between them on the bench, and lifted the lid. Inside lay a classic violin, spruce and maple burnished a deep reddish brown, with no additional embellishment.

"This was my great aunt's. Now, don't panic, I own several more of her violins. This is one of them—the one I'd like you to have. If you'll do me the honor of letting me play Patron of the Arts in support of a budding talent."

"Oh, man, Cal, that's unbelievable, and super generous, but I don't know. Feels like too much, you know?"

"Levi, I'll respect any decision you make here, but I'd like to give you a little background on the instrument, shed some light on why I'd want you to have it in the first place.

"Not many people are aware of my great aunt's place in the timeline of twentieth century history, but as I hinted before, she played a pretty big role in hundreds of people's lives during the so-called Great War. Quite celebrated in her day, she was in Europe, not just for her shared bloodline with her famous composer uncle, but for her own musicianship, as well. Her all-female ensemble, The Waltzing Flowers, was one of the most popular performance groups on the continent. They played waltzes, of course—Viennese waltzes—almost exclusively. Dance music. But she was a composer, too, and was just beginning to be recognized for that talent when the war took a surge forward, and she was removed from her home in Paris and sent to Auschwitz, despite renouncing Judaism and marrying a Christianseveral years prior to her arrest. It was a tactic her uncle had employed with more success, although it must be saidhe took the added precaution of moving out of the Nazis' reach.

"The violins I have of hers are not the ones I'd hold sacred, if I could," said Cal as he brushed a palm over the belly of the instrument, "although I admit to being a little sentimental over this one. They're all special, of course, but I tell you I'd hand over the lot to have one of the instruments from the orchestra she conducted from the camp. You see, she helped keep dozens of women alive by teaching them how to play as a group—old women, teenagers, pregnant women—she made those prisoners more than meat to those cretins; as long as they could play sweetly, they could stay out of the ovens. Records have it my great aunt managed to get their rehearsal room insulated by convincing her music-loving captors a warmer room was better for the instruments."

"She didn't get out, though."

"No. She died of a lung infection, despite the insulation, not long before the liberation. At least, that's the story."

Cal lifted the violin and took a minute to tune it before he began to play the song Levi recognized as the one he'd put on the CD player at the Center. Cal's version was simple and sweet, the dewy tip of a honeysuckle blossom compared to the heavy nectar of the recording.

Levi said, "I don't know why you're always saying how you suck. That was amazing."

Cal chuckled. "It's the fiddle, or else I'm uniquely inspired. Probably both. My great aunt was a great violinist, Levi, a great teacher, and a great woman. This is a symbol of greatness. Accept it. While I didn't have the pleasure of meeting her, I feel okay telling you I think she'd be pleased."

"Thank you. I'll think about it, for sure."

The two men, separated by almost four decades, sat and talked music. Cal told some wild stories of shows he'd been to and musicians he'd met, Levi admitted his dream of packing the amphitheaters himself one day. Close to two hours had passed when Cal announced he was starving. Why didn't Levi join him for a sandwich in the cabin before he hit the road?

In the kitchen, Cal split a baguette and slathered the insides with homemade olive caponata, then layered on prosciutto, peels of asiago, a handful of arugula. He cut the sandwich diagonally in two, set the halves on plates next to a pile of truffle-dusted potato chips. "Pickle?"

Levi eyed the feast appreciatively. "No, I think I'm good. You sure know your way around a sandwich, Cal."

"Yeah, if I hadn't gone into medicine, I might've made a

decent chef. Althea and I have that in common, our love of good food."

Levi chewed and swallowed a sizable hunk of bread and meat before he asked, "How'd you guys meet again?"

"We were both living in Canada. I was about to retire from my practice. After we'd hung out for a bit and found we liked one another, I asked Althea if she'd like to move west with me. Surprise, surprise, she said yes."

"And you just quit medicine?"

"I needed a change. The move to Canada, my setting up in private practice, that was supposed to be the change that made a difference, but it wasn't. I'd spent too much time in the trenches. Good work, important work, but women's health around the world can be a grisly area of medicine. I'd worked in clinics around the globe, trying to help. Infant mortality, venereal disease, sexual abuse, unwanted pregnancies, unviable pregnancies, all manner of pain. I thought it was time I found another path, another way to do the right thing."

Levi lay his sandwich on the plate. "Did you perform abortions? I know that's a personal question. I'm sorry. You don't have to tell me."

"I worked for women's health, and that choice took a lot of forms depending on where I was working. How's that for a politely evasive answer? I won't lie to you, Levi. I've seen things go very wrong, particularly regarding abortions. I'm guessing you've probably never seen an ultrasound of a fetus at twenty-four weeks, though maybe you have, I won't presume in this age of digital access. And you're a well-traveled young man, been to corners of the world most people in this country will never experience. I stand behind my efforts in the field, and believe I have made a positive contribution to the lives of women and children, supported families around the globe, but I'll tell you plain, Levi, I still have nightmares over those pictures, so realized and recognizable. It's understandable, you're worried about your girlfriend."

Levi was staring into his plate. "It's not just Trista, though. Lately it seems like I'm hearing more and more stories of women, friends, people close to me, who've been up against hard and scary decisions. God, even my mom."

Cal sat still, watching Levi as he spoke. In the silence that followed, he placed a hand on the young man's back.

"You know, the Stoics believed that the animal soul was only realized after the body emerged from the womb, when it hit the air, and that the rational, human soul only developed after the age of fourteen. By that measure, you'd still be pretty new to your soul. You'll pardon my impertinence, Levi, but if you're any kind of evidence, the Stoics must surely have got it wrong—I can't accept that a deep spirit like yours is barely off its training wheels.

"My own struggling soul is grateful for the parameters set out by Hippocrates, the oath I took as a man of medicine: *Primum non nocere*: 'First do no harm.' A simple phrase, a difficult concept, and a near-impossible task, it seems like, for us mere humans. Thank goodness for the simple things, eh?" He tapped what was left of his baguette against Levi's in a toast. "Here's to a shared tune, a well-made sandwich, and a memorable afternoon."

CHAPTER
24

Annabelle lay her gym bag inside the door and called out, "Emmett? You home?"

"Hi, honey, yeah. I'm in here."

Emmett sat behind an old teacher's desk piled with loose papers in the small spare bedroom off the kitchen, tapping at his keyboard. It was a space they'd intended to keep free for Eleanor when she visited, but on those infrequent occasions when she stayed overnight, she always slept, or failed to sleep, on the couch in the living room. The desk was a scuttled refinishing project of Emmett's. He'd had big plans when he'd picked it up at a flea market several years back, but thanks to a busy schedule and, ultimately, waning enthusiasm, the yellow faux oak finish retained all its schoolroom nicks and scratches. Annabelle thought Emmett looked every inch the cute, frazzled high school teacher she knew he'd been years ago. She was surprised, though, to see him there, as the room, even with its desk, was functionally more storage shed than office.

"Hi. How come you're working from home? Are you okay?"

"I'm fine. Thought I'd limit my distractions, make headway on the new water project proposal. Didn't really feel like making conversation today."

"Sure. What's Levi up to?"

"He went to visit his new buddy, Cal, at his and his partner's house in Genesee."

Annabelle's knee buckled. She reached a hand to the desk, pivoted to sit on the edge.

"I don't like this new friendship, Emmett. It's weird."

"Is it? Looks like the two of them have a good deal in common, musically anyway. Levi appreciated his visit with the kids. I know he's interested in those custom fiddles the old guy makes."

"Grant you, I might be a little paranoid right now, what with all the internet energy around Eleanor ...Emmett, I made a few inquiries into Cal Abrams and Althea Giordano."

"You felt that was necessary?"

"I did. I do. The two of them have appeared so suddenly on the scene, and already seem to hold influence over Levi and Eleanor both. I mostly found basic stuff, easy to know. Like, for instance, that they've been in the state a little over ten years. Althea, at least, seems to be exactly who she says she is, a forensic botanist transplanted from a Canadian police force into herbal tinctures and food. Her work with CorpsPursuit is well-documented and highly regarded in scientific and criminal circles."

"Impressive, and non-threatening. And Abrams?"

"He's a little slipperier and has left much less of a paper trail."

"Annabelle, you sound more like a cop than a program coordinator."

"It's all about organizing resources. I'll bet they're not so different. Anyway, he had a private gynecological practice in London, Ontario, but only briefly. Before he got board certified in Canada and opened his practice, he'd volunteered at a women's health clinic. Prior to living in Canada, he held administrative and clinical positions in women's health centers in Singapore, New Zealand. South Africa."

"Okay, he had a career in women's health, and worked in global communities. That's interesting, and offers another area he and Levi might feel they have in common, the travel. But is it a concern?"

"Maybe not, but what if it is? The Canadian health center offered services ranging from annual exams and testing for STDs and HIV, to birth control and abortions. The overseas clinics, however, concentrated on what one of them called 'family health'. They offered, still offer, annual exams, testing, prenatal care, and adoption referral. Not only do they not perform abortions, they perform ultrasound exams for women who express, as one representative put it, 'ambivalence about their pregnancies'. You know who sponsors those ultrasound programs, don't you?"

Emmett said, "Well, probably more than one organization internationally, I'd guess, but for sure VOLT. You think Abrams—who's Jewish, right?—has connections to Value Our Family Traditions, an evangelical ministry?"

"Well, he might have been a clinician in their centers without ascribing to a rigid anti-abortion credo. It's possible, if he thought he was able to be effective in other areas he deemed more essential. Or he could be anti-abortion. He wouldn't be the lone doctor in the gynecological field to feel that way. Or the only Jewish man, I'd bet."

"It would appear, though, he's been out of the discussion entirely for ten years plus."

"It would appear so, sure, but somehow he really raises a flag for me. Too friendly. And the whole Santa thing creeps me out."

Emmett came around the desk and put his arms around Annabelle. "Bad experience at the mall?"

"Ha, ha."

"The timing *is* odd, though."

"What do you mean, timing?"

Emmet sat back on the edge of the desk. "Has Levi talked to you about Trista?"

"You mean about them being pregnant?" She folded her arms over her chest and looked at the floor. "No, in fact, he hasn't."

"Then how do you know?"

"I know, is all. Have you taken a look at how they are together lately? Everything's changed. I figured their energy was intense due to the impending separation, you know, but then, a couple of days ago, I was in the hall outside the kitchen while Levi was on the phone and heard enough."

"He blurted it out to me at dinner. I don't even think he meant to tell me."

"He did tell you, though. That's what counts. But—given Dr. Abrams's professional history, his presence feels weirdly superimposed on this moment. I can't imagine Levi confiding in him—Grandpa whiskers or no, he's a total stranger. Emmett, I don't like these new people so close to our little family, not now. Makes me feel vulnerable. It feels like we've lost our center. I don't like it."

Emmett wondered what Annabelle meant by center. It struck him suddenly that their center, their focus, such as she was, was Eleanor. He, Annabelle, and Levi were three loyal and competent protons to Eleanor's dark, dense nucleus, even though they all behaved as though the Denver family unit formed the critical mass, and Eleanor spun out in her own fragile orbit. Their center, he saw as clearly and suddenly as lightning, wasn't the cozy domestic core Annabelle seemed to be referencing, their status quo. He realized he didn't act from a fear of Eleanor's fragility; they weren't bound, as was his impulse all these years, to protect her. Eleanor's despair at once overpowered him and roped them together. Better to attach to the unstable force than be abandoned to the vacuum of his own grief.

"Emmett, honey, there's something I haven't told you."

He brought his focus back to the woman with whom he'd managed something of a real life, a reality he'd thought impossible after Freya's death and Eleanor's dissolution. "What, are you okay? What is it?"

She turned away from him, spoke to an old file cabinet. "I may have met Cal Abrams...well, not met, really, but we may have attended the same function, on one of my solo trips to South Africa. One of the beer dinners. It's not just conjecture on my part that he worked, maybe works, for John Yearling."

"Wait a minute, Yearling? The guy who's been dragging Eleanor over the coals on Chitter? My god, Annabelle, oh my god ...you're telling me you've known about Abrams this whole time ...were just this minute lying to me about— what did you say—'inquiries'?"

"I didn't know how to tell you..."

"For Christ's sake, Annabelle, you've had suspicions about this man that you've kept to yourself...while Levi's making friends with him! Why would you keep this from me?"

Just then, Levi bustled into the kitchen with a grocery bag in both hands, and a beat-up violin case under his arm. "Hey! I bought some stuff for dinner. It's been a while since we sat down together, right? Thought I'd sauté some lemon chicken, grill radicchio for salad. I bought ice cream...Is something going on? Are you guys okay?"

Levi didn't tell Emmett and Annabelle that he'd planned on cooking dinner for Trista tonight, that she'd said she wasn't hungry and wanted to be by herself. He didn't tell them Trista had an appointment at the clinic the next day. That he and

Trista had an appointment.

Emmett watched Annabelle as she took a bag from Levi, set it on the counter, and gave him a hug. "Sure, we're great. This is lovely, Levi. Dinner together is just what we need. Tell us how we can help."

CHAPTER
25

"911. What is the address of the emergency?"

"Please help, our baby's gone ..."

"Sir, what is the address?"

"Uh, shit, yeah, it's 7350 Bennett Dr. Listen, I was only asleep for a few minutes, right here on the couch, no more than a half hour ..."

"We'll have someone there as soon as possible. Sir, what is your name?"

"Me? I'm Noah Spicer ...look, someone took Jake, stole our baby, couldn't be more than a few minutes ..."

"Mr. Spicer, are you injured or hurt in any way?"

"No, no ...oh, God, Lorene, Lorene ...

"Is there someone else there with you, Mr. Spicer?"

"No ...Lorene, my wife, she'll be home any minute ...the baby's gone, oh, God, someone took our baby ...help us, for God's sake ...he can't got far ...I was only asleep for a minute ..."

Lorene Spicer pulled in behind the two Bristlecone Springs police vehicles parked in front of the rental house. She ran across the dry grass into the house, leaving her books and purse in the car.

"What's happened?"

"Lorene, oh Christ, Lorene!" Noah Spicer, tear-streaked and hyperventilating, stared wild-eyed at his wife. "I'm so sorry!"

"No ...it's Jake? Is Jake hurt?"

"Lorene Spicer? I'm Detective Stanislaus. Your husband called 911 to report your son missing. It appears he was taken from the portable crib on the screen porch while your husband was asleep. We're here to do everything we can."

Lorene sank to her knees and opened her mouth as if to scream, but instead pulled in a long breath and held it suspended and made no sound at all.

Noah knelt down beside her and covered her hands with his. "It was only a few minutes, the door was locked ...I'm sorry, Lorene, baby, oh, our baby ..."

Five minutes later the Spicers sat across from Stanislaus at the kitchen table.

"The department has issued a bulletin. Every available officer is out there combing the roads. Our job right now is to get down the facts, as you know them."

Lorene spoke with no trace of tears, no catch in her voice. "Our job, Detective? What about your job? If you were doing your job, the facts would be that my husband and I were watching Netflix while I did my homework and our baby slept safely in our own home. Those are the facts I'm interested in right now, Detective. Pastor Yearling had it right. Your department is incompetent."

Stanislaus paused before speaking. "Ms. Spicer, I'm sorry for your situation. I promise the department will do everything in its power, I will do everything in my power, to recover your child unharmed." He turned his attention to the man, bent into his wife.

"Mr. Spicer, can you please tell me again what happened tonight, from before you put Jake down to sleep until you called 911?"

"Yeah, yeah ...Lorene and I both got home from work a little after five, and then Lorene left for school around 5:30. I gave Jake a bath and fed him some dinosaur nuggets and apple sauce, we watched a video, and I laid him in the porta-crib on the porch, in just his diaper, on account of the heat. His bedroom was so hot, I thought he'd be more comfortable. We've done it plenty of times this summer. We just move him into his crib later, when the house cools off some. Right, Lorene?"

The young woman held onto her husband's hand, but said nothing.

"What time would you say you laid Jake down on the porch?"

"Uh, maybe seven? Yeah, seven, 'cause when I got back to the couch, the Rockies/Dodgers game was on, and I'd seen it was coming on at seven."

"And what time was it when you noticed Jake was missing?"

"I don't know, but I woke up quick, like from a nightmare, panicky...I went to the porch and he was gone..." He choked, and said, "He was gone right out of his crib..."

"You called 911 immediately?"

"Yes...no—I called Lorene, but she was driving I guess and not answering her phone, so yeah, then I called 911."

"Dispatch has your call at 7:38. You often fall asleep on the couch at seven o'clock, Mr. Spicer?"

"What the hell kind of question is that?" asked Lorene.

"I'm trying to assess if there was a pattern someone may have picked up on and taken advantage of, Ms. Spicer."

"Of course there's a pattern." She rose from the table to pace behind her husband's chair. "We work our asses off, I've got a day job, we have a two-year-old baby, Noah lugs rocks and lays sod all day, so yes, he's tired at seven o'clock at night, after working since dawn and taking care of a baby alone when I'm at school. Yes, we have a goddamned pattern ..."

Lorene stopped pacing and pointed a finger at Stanislaus. "Hey, are you going to have that Eleanor Clay woman help you find Jake?"

"We have not contacted Mrs. Clay at this time."

"Well, don't. Get the State Police, get the FBI, get the damn dog catcher, but keep that woman away from us. I want to see my baby again healthy and in one piece."

Stanislaus went to the small closed-in porch, covered patio, really, where his team was taking prints, completing their canvas. He peered into the portable crib, noted the tiny spot of blood on the sheet, no bigger than the tip of a needle.

Nina insisted they not leave until they'd had some of the supper she and Elan cooked, so they sat and ate brown bread, edam cheese, cabbage soup, and spiced cookies like it was winter in the Alps instead of a summer afternoon in Boulder.

She poured them each a demitasse of strong coffee she'd boiled on top of the stove, *to keep alert on your journey*, before Eleanor went to the guest bedroom to gather her few things, and Elan took his phone to the sunroom to call the station. He'd let Stanislaus know Eleanor was cutting her exile short, and that he'd be accompanying her back to town tonight.

Althea remained at the table with Nina, tracing the embroidery pattern in the linen cloth with a tiny spoon.

"Ally, tell me what it is."

"What what is, Nina?"

"What is the trouble that is weighing so heavily on you? It is more, I think, than Eleanor and the tragedies of her little town."

Althea was not about to unspool her ravel of free association onto Nina's generous table. She'd decided to keep her personal unrest to herself as stepped from her car onto the neat driveway edged in pansies. Her ride had been an erratic psychic power point of images of her and Cal, jumping from what had started as an impulsive May-September romance in Canada, somehow stretching across continent and time like the notorious roots of the aspen, movement as determined, yet as unnoticed, as a change in the meander of a river.

Had they ever had a conversation about children? They had, she recalled, a year, maybe two, after moving to Genesee. He'd said he assumed she didn't want to have any, given the trauma of her miscarriage. She hadn't remembered telling him, directly, of the miscarriage.

No, we talked about it, sure we did. I remember—one of those late-night-into-morning pillow talks; we had so many of back then. And, you know dear girl, you say all kinds of things in your sleep.

Well, why wouldn't she have told him? Althea had packed up her life and moved to Colorado, rock-sure of both the move and of her attentive, mature partner. Cal wrapped her in affection, made her feel safe, played fiddle music outside the kitchen window as she made supper, filled the little house with the first fragrant dianthus, left casseroles and love notes. She knew him, naked and close, could trace the hollows and the scars, knew the breath of him.

He was gone a lot. Or, at least, frequently gone—on the road, delivering and selling his wares, the stringed instruments he crafted with the precision of a surgeon, the vision of an artist. Always returning home to her with a pocketful of stories, outrageous and funny. They laughed so much. No mementos, though. He'd point out a concert shot of a musician playing a custom fiddle, but never a photograph of a bluegrass star with an arm around the craftsman himself.

What, you think I want to be one of those barnacles, always asking for a selfie with the talent? I'd rather paint you a picture. Play you a song.

Elan picked up his phone to call the Bristlecone station and saw a new text message from Terrance: *Call me.*

Elan called.

"Hey, baby, you been following Chitter?"

"Hey! Not so much in the last couple of hours. Why?"

"Don't overreact, I deal with this stuff all the time, and it's mostly hot air, but you should take a look at John Yearling's VOLT thread, a series of comments calling you out. You specifically. I just wanted to be sure you knew about them, and that I'm following them, too."

Elan put Terrance on speaker and brought up Chitter. Yearling, via VOLT, had recently posted,

> *@valueourloving traditions: BSPD, reduced to this: a sad, childless woman and a bike cop in short pants. When will see some grown-up leadership in BS?*

And among the comments:

> *@BringtheHurt: Sending a woman to do a man's job, and a man with only a bike between his legs. No, wait, and a lawyer husband, too! Department packed tight like a clogged sewer pipe. #snakethedrain*

And then:

> *@BringtheHurt: People ought to be careful about who they keep from their natural family, cop or no. #cantkeepmeout #mykidtoo*
> *@MadDad: Real men want justice. #takebackourtown*

Elan switched the screen back. "That last one's Jimmy Thorenson. Who's the other? The one that's made you my husband before I even got a ring?"

"@BringtheHurt is Catalina Escalante's ex, Kurt Davis. I don't think either one's on VOLT's thread because they found religion, Elan. By all accounts from your department, Davis is too stupid to do anything more than attract attention, drum up energy around some misguided Dads Too movement, which, I'm sure, VOLT will all too happily get behind. As well as angry bastards like Thorenson. Just be careful. Stupid plus angry wreaks its own havoc."

"Thanks for keeping an eye out, and for the heads up. I was just going to call you, by the way, after I checked in with Stanislaus. We're headed back."

"Back here? You just left. Why the quick turnaround? Not that I won't be ecstatic to see you, but it seemed like a good move, getting out of town."

"Eleanor feels like she's got more to do."

"I can't say I like the sound of that. You going to tell me she really is some kind of clairvoyant?"

"I don't know what Eleanor is, Terrance, except that she's the only person who's been able to get to these kids while they're still breathing."

"But how many more, Elan? Somebody's got to intercede before that critical point, don't you think? Snatching children from death is quite a spectacle, but this town needs to find its peace again."

"Terrance, am I hearing you align right now with the malcontents dissing the force? What the fuck?"

"Of course not. I'm just saying we need more than Eleanor's gifts. We need to solve this case, and shore up this community before it implodes and the buzzards come to pick at the rubble. I'm glad you're coming back, Elan. I, this town— we need you home, Officer DePeña."

Eleanor rode next to Althea, intermittently shoving a fistful of french fries into her mouth and wiping her fingers on a paper napkin in a doomed attempt to keep the grease off of Althea's tablet, which Eleanor was using to search for news articles on the abduction and murder cases in Los Angeles and Ontario.

"Don't even worry about it. I bought the most bulletproof one I could get just for this purpose—road research requires road food."

"I wouldn't have considered you the fast-food type, Althea. Figured you picnicked on homemade tarts and fancy cheese, you know, cloth napkins and whatnot."

"I resist the pigeonhole, thank you. Nothing wrong with a drive-thru burger and special sauce. You finding anything?"

"I can't tell yet. There's a whole weekend insert from an L.A. paper on drug-related crimes after the fact, mostly about gangs, from what I can gather with a quick scan. A load of articles on border patrol protocols and immigration issues in Canada. You're quoted in a couple of articles."

"Funny, I don't remember that."

"That's a thing with the internet, I'm discovering—it's a bottomless steamer trunk of memory, layers and layers far denser and deeper that any human capacity to remember stuff, that's for sure. Just got to dig. It's frightening, really. I don't know why anybody would ever Google themselves, subject themselves to that bag of horrors. Also, I don't know how the whole associative algorithm business works, but strange stuff comes up. I'm getting articles about cases in Asia, one from Africa ..."

Althea stiffened. "What kind of articles?"

"I don't know. Let me click on one. Okay, not travel pieces, I'll tell you that. Not surprising, I guess, considering I'm searching abduction and murder cases. Drugs, drugs, smuggling ring, pirate activity. Hm."

"What? What does 'hm' mean?"

"It means there's an article about missing and murdered children in Singapore. This article reports four."

"When in Singapore? Does it say?"

"This one piece is dated sixteen years ago, photocopied for posting. What's the matter?"

"I don't know, probably nothing. I'm under slept and over caffeinated. Hey, would you mind taking over the driving for a while? I'm feeling a little punch drunk, all of a sudden."

"Sure." Before Eleanor shut down the internet on the tablet, she bookmarked the Singapore article. They'd revisit it, she thought, when Althea had had a little rest. Eleanor had a strong feeling that *probably nothing* was very likely something, after all.

CHAPTER 26

Victor Tran noticed the birds first. He thought maybe the pair of ravens had the good fortune of finding a dead rabbit or prairie dog and was glad it was over in the refuse pile where he wouldn't have to deal with it immediately. He'd leave them to it. Tran had shown upextra early, a good half hour before sunrise, to finish his plantings in peace. Soon the construction would be done, and humans would fill up the five-bedroom homes in the new Rocky Vista development, park their SUVs in front of his hosta borders, and live their American dream-scape, but this morning he could be alone in his garden diorama.

As he unloaded perennials from the Honda Element, he noticed the ravens becoming more agitated, flapping and growling with increasing volume. He grabbed a long-handled steel garden fork and headed for the bluff of dirt, broken pavers, dug-up roots, damaged terra cotta planters, the odd cracked sink, and other construction detritus that awaited a final clean up. They'd need to clear it out quick if it was already attracting rodents.

Tran waved the heavy fork in the air to disperse the ravens, who had been intent on getting at something in a galvanized tub, against which leaned a pick-up sticks bundle of wooden planks. The ravens retreated to a nearby Ponderosa. In the weak light, Tran at first thought that the tub had been lined with peat or some kind of planting moss. Then he saw. End to end, the vessel contained a bundle, a three-foot cocoon of hemp rope with an opening like a balaclava at one end, exposing a small face partially covered in cloth. The ravens had pecked at the rope where they could reach it with their beaks, midway, and had succeeded in pulling up enough threads to reveal a tiny hand. The fingernails, like the corners of the mouth, were as blue as the larkspur he'd brought from the nursery to plant along the deer fence.

It was still morning when Althea returned to the apartment with a local paper and three coffees. She stopped outside the door to empty the mailbox, which was stuffed to bursting with messages from people who, like Althea herself, had managed to find out where Eleanor lived. She threw them into the trash can on the side of the building.

There was no news of another abduction. It wasn't until Elan checked his phone that they learned of the kidnapping and death of two-year-old Jake Spicer. His body was found on the site of a new housing development off Lost Valley Road early that morning by a nursery employee. The police announcement listed the cause of death as respiratory failure.

Eleanor sat and stared at her own phone in her hand. "Gordon didn't call."

Althea asked Elan, "Do we know from your feed that this child is related to the other abductions? Does it say?"

"I'm reading. Hemp wrap, not an exact match to anything

else, but close ...and similar circumstances, vis- a-vis bundling and hiding the body ..."

"Similar enough to be the sixth and not a copycat?"

"I don't know, not from this. Listen, I'm going to go to the station. I want to get the facts from a real person."

Althea threw him her keys. "Take my car."

Elan set them back on the counter. "Althea, I've got the station SUV, I drove it here, remember? You okay?"

"Oh, yeah, right. I don't know, maybe I'm not so okay. Sorry. Go, go, I'm fine."

Eleanor sat on the couch and stared at the phone in her hand. "Althea, I messaged Gordon we were coming back. Why wouldn't he call if another child went missing? I could have been looking last night. What's his—his?—name?"

Althea kept her back to Eleanor, her tone cold. "Jake, his name is Jake. Two-year-old Jake Spicer."

"Althea, what's wrong?"

"What do you mean, what's wrong?" She swung around, everything hot now, her face contorted in a mask of rage and despair, her skin mottled with shock. She wailed, "The boy's name is Jake. Isn't that what you asked me? Jake is the two-year-old baby who was found dead this morning, Eleanor. What else do you want from me?"

Eleanor placed her phone on the coffee table, folded her hands on her lap, and looked up at Althea. "I'll tell you what I want. I want to know why you lost your shit when I mentioned a sixteen-year-old article from Singapore. I want to know why you're acting the way you are now. Give me whatever you're carrying around Althea, whatever's tearing you up. What are you waiting for? What is it you're not telling me?"

Althea took in a deep breath. It caught in her windpipe, and she coughed. She rose and poured herself some water from the tap, knocked it back like a shot of tequila, cleared her throat. "Shit. Okay. You remember when you told me you thought you might be bringing the trouble when you find these kids? I'm wondering if it might actually be me, that I'm the one who's brought the trouble."

"What are you talking about? It's you? Wait, are you saying you have something to do with these kidnappings? Althea, what is it?"

"Listen, this may be crazy, and it's possible—probable—that I am making connections that aren't there, but..."

"But what?"

Althea sat next to Eleanor on the couch. "I don't know about L.A., but Cal has been everywhere else where these cases have occurred. At what appears to be the same time these abductions occurred."

"Cal. Cal?" Eleanor could feel her heart rate increase, her lungs tighten. She pulled herself into the room as the edges of her vision began to blur.

"So what exactly are you thinking about that?"

"I'm thinking it's weird. I'm thinking that there are a lot of gaps in my knowledge about my partner of ten years and that feels weird, too. And I'm having a hard time thinking at all, really, because my stomach is trying to escape through my esophagus. What if, Eleanor? What if I'm the one who's brought the trouble? What if it's Cal who is behind these abductions?"

"Let's not get ahead of ourselves—it may still be some sort of bizarre coincidence—but in any case, we can't hold on to this by ourselves. We've got to talk to Gordon."

Althea leaned back, let her head fall on the hard back of the couch, closed her eyes. "Yes, I know." She sat up, rubbing her skull.

"But what about Cal? What the hell am I going to say to the man I've been sleeping with for over a decade, 'I can't come home just yet, I suspect you might be implicated in the kidnapping and murder of dozens of children across several international borders?' I mean, what do I do here? And, whew!, *golly*, if it *is* a coincidence, where does that leave our relationship? 'Gee, honey, I thought for a minute you might be a psychopath, but I was mistaken, so what do you feel like for dinner ...?'"

Eleanor put her arm around her friend. Althea lay her head on Eleanor's shoulder, her shoulders convulsing as she sobbed into the armpit of Eleanor's t-shirt. In another minute she wiped her nose on Eleanor's short sleeve, reached for the phone, and placed it in Eleanor's lap.

"Okay, yeah, let's do this. But you first."

Eleanor called Emmett to tell him that Cal Abrams was under suspicion. She didn't want to deliver bad news over the phone, not to Emmett. She wished, as she hadn't in a long time, that she was close enough to him to talk face-to-face, but when her call went twice in a row to voicemail, she left a message. She then called Levi, got his voicemail, and asked him to call, before leaving a text that said, *I love you. Stay away from Cal Abrams.*

CHAPTER
27

Gordon Stanislaus sat sweating at his desk in front of a table-top fan, despite the fact that the digital thermostat read sixty-two degrees. On the other side of the desk sat a shivering Althea Giordano.

"So, Dr. Giordano, what do you want to share with me about this case that you haven't already? According to your last speculation, it's very possible Jack Spicer is our last victim of this serial criminal. Are you here to tell me different?"

"Detective, the reports from Canada and Los Angeles are similar to this case in that all the victims are young children, and all were drugged intravenously prior to being wrapped up and stowed somewhere. That five of the six victims in this case were found alive is a discrepancy."

"Yes. We know this."

"Right. But here's what you don't know. When Eleanor was Googling for comparable cases on our trip back from Boulder, she came across a series of similar crimes in Singapore, sixteen years old. I'm suggesting you check into those and do some research on possible incidents in South Africa in the last twenty years as well."

"Why would I do that? Search old cases that occurred on the other side of the world? It's not like North America has a lock on atrocity."

Althea intentionally slowed her breathing. "No, but they have something else in common. My partner, Cal Abrams, may have been present in those other locations at the time of the crimes."

"Dr. Giordano, tell me that once again—you're saying you suspect your boyfriend has something to do with our case? And possibly other cases?"

"My life partner, yes, the man with whom I moved here from Canada, and have been shacking up with for more than ten years, may not be the loving man I thought, and may instead, be responsible for several series of heinous crimes." She held her stomach, began to pant.

"And there's something else," she said in between breaths. "It's not in the report, but I think the valerian that was mixed with the cannabis and injected into these kids came from my house in Genesee." She leaned over and vomited into the wastebasket. Still bent, she said, "Like I said, that specificity is not in the report, but it could be tested."

Stanislaus pushed a box of tissues toward the edge of the desk. Althea straightened up in her chair, pulled at a tissue and blotted her mouth.

"Dr. Giordano, that might, only might, justify picking up your partner for questioning. We don't have any evidence other than your suspicions. And you know that what you're telling me makes you a person of interest, too, if not a suspect?"

"Truthfully, I hadn't got that far."

"Where is Cal Abrams now?"

Althea looked past the open door into the squad room

where Eleanor waited with Elan. "The last time we communicated, I'd sent him a text to say I was headed to see Nina, and Cal messaged back to say had an appointment with Levi Clay, Eleanor's son, at our house. He wanted to donate some instruments to Levi's youth orchestra and asked him out to the cabin to see them."

"You've had no contact for a couple of days, then? Is that usual?"

"It's not *un*usual. It's very usual for us to spend time apart. The frequency of our long-distance communications fluctuates."

"Christ, okay, so can we assume he doesn't know you suspect him? That's what I'm asking. Tell me this isn't a sudden silence, and he's not tracking you through your cell right now."

Althea remembered her and Cal's conversation about installing the app that would do just that, keep a bead of her physical whereabouts. He'd argued for it for lone hikes and travel, a safeguard. She'd nixed it, said it would turn her phone into a house arrest anklet, make her feel like a dog who'd been chipped.

"No, he's not tracking my phone."

Stanislaus nodded. "I hope you're right. If he's our guy, and he knew you were back here in this police station after going home, we'd lose our chance to pick him up easy. Call him."

"Call him? What do I say?"

"Just check in. Be casual."

Althea's stomach pitched. "I don't know if I can talk to him like nothing's happened."

"Nothing has happened, as far as we can prove. Call him."

Cal picked up on the second ring. "Baby! I thought you were finishing up in Boulder? When you getting your gorgeous self back here?"

Althea told Cal Nina had been approached for a new case

for the CorpsPursuit team, and they'd spent some time putting together a file for the group to study and consider.

"I think I'll hang out here another night. Get an early start tomorrow."

"Sure, I've heard that one before. All right, Dr. Giordano, do your thing. I'll keep the home fires burning."

"See you tomorrow, then?"

"Tomorrow. I'll take that as a promise. Hey—I love you."

"Yeah, me, too." Althea disconnected and pivoted over the wastebasket.

Stanislaus poured her a glass of water. "You got a picture?" He pushed a legal pad and pen toward her. "Write a description, the Genesee address, and what he's likely to be driving." Stanislaus picked up the phone. "Drubbs, call over to Golden Police and tell them we need a Cal Abrams for questioning on our abduction cases. Questioning only at this point. They can tell him we traced the drugs to his neck of the woods. Be general, but make it clear we need him back here." He hung up and faced Althea. "You stick around."

"Gordon? Why didn't you call Eleanor last night, when you knew the boy was missing, and you knew she was back?"

"I don't know, Dr. Giordano. Maybe I was hoping someone besides Eleanor Clay could keep him alive."

Levi sat in the parking lot of the downtown Healthy Families clinic and watched Trista and her mother pull away in their Suburban. He received a text from Emmett: *Hey! Where are you? How about we meet for breakfast?*

He texted back, *Hanging out with Bash. Maybe lunch?*

Emmett responded, *Sounds good. I'd really like to talk.*

Levi held his thumb over the tiny telephone icon at the top of his father's message, but then entered the thumbs up emoji in the field instead, hit send, and clicked to his contacts. He scrolled to Cal Abrams.

"Levi! To what do I owe the pleasure?"

"Hey, Cal, are you home? I was thinking about taking a drive out to your place on my way to a hike. Maybe we could talk, if you have some free time?"

"Sure! You all right, Levi?"

"No, I don't know. I don't know where to be right now. And I was thinking I wouldn't keep that violin you gave me after all. It's generous, Cal, but it doesn't feel right, at least not right now."

"Has something happened?"

"Trista's and my appointment was at the clinic was today. Her mom was there, too. She took her home, after. I thought me being with Trista at the clinic, us being there together, that that would make it, I don't know, not okay, I guess, but better, bearable. Her mom being there, though. I think that was the only thing that held Trista together, really. I know it was. I could have gone home with them, they both said so ...I can't explain it ...she felt so far away."

"I'm glad you called, Levi."

"I thought maybe you'd understand. Probably better than I do right now."

"I don't know if anyone can understand the path you and your girlfriend took today, Levi, but I'll be there for you any way I can. Hey, I'm running a few errands, but I'll be back on the ranch in just a bit. Head on over there, and if I'm not back before you, just let yourself into the shed. There's a key tucked in a pot of lavender to the left of the door."

They hung up and Levi checked again to see if Trista had texted. No messages. He saw a voicemail and a new message from Eleanor, which he ignored. He texted his dad that he and Bash decided to hike Red Rocks at the last minute, that they might backpack or car camp overnight somewhere and he'd let him know either way. He shut off his phone and tossed it in the bottom of his pack.

CHAPTER
28

Althea left Stanislaus' office to find a place to think and search. She planted herself in a folding chair in the Bristlecone Springs Police Department coffee room, at a card table covered in a vinyl picnic cloth inexplicably printed with cartoon cowgirls and baskets of fruit. She bent over her tablet, alternating between swiping the screen and taking notes on a legal pad. With each new link, her stomach tightened. An open box held the crescent remains of a powdered donut. She felt she might vomit again, but swallowed and turned back to the screen, the contents of which propelled the acid up her gullet with renewed force.

Unidentified, but easily recognizable, Cal Abrams' younger face shone out from grainy photos of volunteers and clinicians doing the good work overseas. There he was in Singapore, and again in South Africa. There were no pictures in the New Zealand stories in which she could make him out, but there was mention of a Dr. Calvin Albertson at a family health center in Christchurch. The Singapore dates fell within the time frame of the gruesome case involving the kidnapping and murder of half a dozen young children.

None of it was evidence. None of it revealed motive. All this exploration did was confirm he was in all the wrong places at all the right times. Althea rose and made for the hallway, plunging into the women's room en route to Stanislaus' office.

She hated throwing up. She lifted her head and observed her arms hugging the plastic toilet seat, in second position, she thought, suddenly reminded of tortured afternoons in ballet class when she was in primary school, and of their instructor, a French man who carried a baton he used to keep time. He used it, too, to tap a limb into position, trace a curve in a spine, or chuck under a chin to extend the neck. Althea had complained to her mother, who believed in a classical approach to discipline, and insisted she stick with it. She'd once mentioned her early dance career to Cal. He told her she was much too voluptuous for ballet—a bloodless art, in his opinion.

The last time she'd thrown up she'd been pregnant, not long before she'd met Cal. A layer of consciousness stubbornly clung to the fact that not once in all the time she'd been with Cal had she vomited, as if a fact like that had to count for something.

Stanislaus told Althea she was free to go, but made it clear she was to remain where he could find her.

"Of course. I'll get a room in town."

Eleanor stood in the doorway of Stanislaus' office. "Don't you still have my key?"

Althea turned around. She assumed her new and fragile-seeming friend would freeze her out, after revealing her suspicions about Cal, once the terrible reach of that information took hold...and she wouldn't have argued, not with a child in the balance, Eleanor's only living child. Certainly, the last thing she expected from Eleanor was hospitality. "I didn't think you'd want me at your place. But I'd much prefer to stay with you, of course. Thank you, Eleanor."

"Well, *yes*. Of course."

Althea cleared her throat. "How's Levi?"

"I didn't talk to him, but Emmett says he's meeting a friend at Red Rocks, and that Levi said he'd check in if they decide to camp overnight, which Emmett says he'll discourage. Why wouldn't I want you at my apartment? It's your boyfriend I don't want anywhere near any of us."

Althea needed to leave so Stanislaus could brief Eleanor on the most recent kidnapping but had trouble getting out the door without touching Eleanor, without giving her some indication of the gratitude—no, relief, maybe even a strange, grief-laced joy—she felt for being believed by this woman.

"That will be all for now, Dr. Giordano," growled Stanislaus, so in the end, as she passed she briefly squeezed Eleanor's elbow, which did not flinch.

She was surprised at how grateful she felt to be returning to Eleanor's sad couch. She'd have a rest, collect her thoughts, and go back to the station after the Stanislaus had contacted VOLT's offices about the overseas clinics. Entering the apartment, Althea considered the burrow appeal of the dim and quiet rooms. How their potential to isolate a body and insulate a mind could compel a human animal to hibernate. She tried to put herself in Eleanor's place. A woman with a grief so permeating it needed a tight, dark box, but she couldn't manage it. The hair on her arms stood up, not in fear but from an almost photosynthetic compulsion toward light, like seedlings groping their way through the topsoil to the air. After five minutes alone, she grabbed her phone to call Nina.

"I'll bet he's not even Jewish, Nina. Why is that the part of this that's sticking with me right now? The idea that he might have downplayed his fake religion so much—now it seems like the most important thing."

"Maybe it is, Althea, if it feels so. It's a complicated choice, as far as an alias goes. His downplaying, as you say, makes it all the more believable. Allows him to imply a history of suffering, wear the tragic mantle of a legacy that is not his, without having to talk about it. Of course, I imagine there is some sort of tragedy there."

"Nothing to justify murdering children."

"Nein, nein. But we are not searching for justification. We want now to understand process. What do you know?"

"I know I've been living with evil for ten years. I know that the hands I've known to make beautiful instruments, cook beautiful food, hands I've let touch me for ten years, hands I've wanted to touch me, hands I could describe in minute detail with my eyes shut, are the same hands that inject poison into young veins and wrap children up like spider food. I know I can barely sit here in my own skin, Nina. I know, now, that I brought this horror into Eleanor's life, into all these poor people's lives."

"Ach, Ally, no: he is the parasite, Althea. He is the flea."

"And I am the rat."

"Nein, he is the flea and the vermin both. Now, what can we do to help build the trap?"

"Yes, I know you're right, as usual. My impending break-down can wait. Gordon Stanislaus is requesting VOLT's records for people who worked in overseas clinics in the specific time frames, which would establish opportunity. I don't know what it says about motive."

"How has the ground he's walked on been disturbed, Althea?"

"I don't know if that metaphor's going to hold up, Nina. I'm a forensic botanist, not a detective on this case."

"You have ten years of observation of this man. You offer the most valuable insight available."

"I don't know who he is, Nina."

"But you know what he does, how he moves. You know

more than you think you do. We operate now from a different perspective. I am remembering, for example, a conversation I had with Cal about his mother. A music teacher, as I recall."

"What about her?"

"I don't know, except that it was clear he was fondof her and mourned her. Also, I remember, he said nothing about his father."

"That's already more than I know."

"Allow yourself to think, Althea. There's more. You must dig and allow yourself to discover what you know, what lies just below the surface."

Eleanor and Elan bought coffee at Bea's and sat on a bench in a park a couple of blocks from the station. The playground was empty except for a red squirrel skittering across the monkey bars.

The town had once again emptied out. Most of the people who'd come in search of Eleanor's help left soon after John Yearling's forum at the hotel. There were still a few families and individuals occupying campers at the KOA and paying by the week at the motor inn, but Eleanor was sure they'd follow the others out of town as news of the death of Jack Spicer bled into the atmosphere.

Elan spoke first. "You know, Eleanor Clay, you're a hard one to figure out. I mean, I really like Althea, she's fabulous, beyond great, but if she told me she knew Terrence's new best buddy was a psycho child killer, but she was withholding judgement until she could be sure, I wouldn't be changing the sheets in the guest room. How do you know you can trust her, Eleanor? Up until now, I didn't think you trusted anybody, except maybe Levi."

"I trust you, Elan. I trust Emmett and Annabelle.And I trust

Althea, too. She didn't suspect Cal when he and Levi drove back to Denver together. I think she's been as blindsided as anyone. And she just lost her partner. That's devastating. Just ask Emmett. Or yourself, for that matter. Do you lose all faith in someone because they've used some poor judgement, made some bad decisions? I notice you're still making those calls to your mother."

"Faith? Are you kidding me, Eleanor? You're talking to me about faith? Faith has nothing to do with why my mother can't bring herself to talk to me, why her relationship with her only son is as cold and rotten as yesterday's garbage. I'm talking about loyalty, Eleanor, and trust, the kind that comes from knowing someone is always going to be honest with you, even when it's hard, someone who has your back, and doesn't wait to jump in until it's convenient for them, or too late. By the way, Eleanor? Neither of us has killed or helped kill anybody. Neither of us has betrayed the other's trust."

Eleanor thought of the strain in Emmett's voice when they'd finally been able to talk about Abrams, could almost smell the adrenaline through the phone, the sulfuric stench of having just missed a bullet. She'd felt his fear, despite himself, of her.

And suddenly Elan's voice and face fades, and Eleanor is the red squirrel clawing her way across the grid, and then she is Eleanor, again, and sixteen, racing in her dream after a figure hell-bound for a craggy edge, racing and terrified she is too far behind to catch the back of a blouse, a belt, she is pushing into the wind that carries her suffering mother's howls, swimming into the dust storm of her mother's swirling, unmappable grief, a grief older than Eleanor, born before Eleanor, feeling the spent ground, the skid of gravel under her pumping soles, following the first lurching arc of the fall before the picture fades and she is looking again at Elan, the steam from his coffee condensing in the crease of his brow.

"No, maybe not, but the dead and dying lay everywhere just the same. Look, I'm not equating my own situation to these crimes. I'm just sympathizing with the sudden disappearance of the soul she thought loved her best."

"Maybe sympathy isn't what we need now. Since when did you get so touchy-feely that sympathy means so much to you now?"

They watched the squirrel run down the metal bars, across a bed of pine needles, and chase another squirrel up into the scaffolding of a colossal fir.

"Don't get me wrong, Elan. I'm as eager as anyone for Cal Abrams to get the punishment he deserves, assuming it's he who deserves it. And, yes, I'm angry with Althea for holding back until she did, but not so angry I want her to go away. She's my friend. Where is she supposed to go, home?"

"Well, I'm still a little shocked at your generosity. Come on, Eleanor, can a person live with a man whose done these terrible things, over and over, and not have so much as an inkling? Is that possible?"

"All things are possible. I'm sure you can quote a theorem or two from at least one of your classes. The catch is the *all things* part of it—the good things and all the bad stuff, too. It's all possible.

"From another perspective, we keep Althea close. We stay closer to our target. Gordon's having Golden PD pick Cal up for questioning, but we know there's not enough evidence to hold him. As long as Cal doesn't know Althea's onto him, I suspect he'll stay cool as a cucumber, assure the authorities that whatever dragged his name into the situation is an unfortunate coincidence. We'll have time to figure out the details."

"I don't know, Eleanor. What happens when they're done with their questions, and he wants to go back to the homestead? Althea's not going to want to play house anymore. He'll have to know something's up then."

"True. All the more reason to work fast." She stood to drop her coffee cup into the trash, saw that it was full to overflowing, and held onto the empty container. "Let's get back."

Emmett pressed the Find My Folks app Annabelle had insisted they all install on their phones in case of an emergency. All except Eleanor, who couldn't install the locator app on her flip phone, and who hadn't been known to move about much, anyway. The little icon indicating Levi's location blinked at a location downtown. *Not on the trail yet,* he thought. He searched Annabelle, whose icon blinked on the grid at the address of their offices, also downtown. He was soothed by their proximity, even though he knew they weren't together.

Eleanor's call informing him that Cal Abrams was a suspect in the abduction cases hit him like a sneaker wave. He wanted them home, in his sights and within reach. Annabelle had been right to suspect Cal Abrams, after all, even if she was wrong about the depth and speed of his agenda, or the why of it, as if there could be a *why* worth understanding, a reason to explain how a man can wreak so much unspeakable havoc. He was still angry she'd kept her suspicions to herself, and that she'd kept them to herself to protect her own secret plans. He couldn't think past his anxiety around his family's safety sufficiently to decide how angry he was that she had secret plans, had been making plans without him for some time. Why hadn't she trusted him? How was he supposed to trust her? She knew about Trista and Levi's pregnancy before he did, and hadn't shared that with him. Had she told him everything, even now? Their whole relationship was built on open communication. That's the premise he'd been operating under, anyway. *Non-violent communication.* Emmett paced, felt dizzy—not dizzy, but twitchy, buzzy—he wanted to hit something. Instead, he sat.

Annabelle's sins of omission aside, Abrams was too cozy with Levi too quick, he saw that now. Why hadn't he said something himself? How could he not pick up on Annabelle's distress? He thought of his boy in a truck for hours of lonesome highway between Bristlecone Springs and Denver with this monster and rippled with an aftershock of terror, as if he, himself, had rushed the tracks and narrowly escaped a fatal collision.

At least the authorities were on it, he thought, and Levi was safe. At least that.

"Blessings, Detective. I was sure we'd speak again, sir, but I didn't think quite so soon as this."

"Yearling, I need some information about a possible former employee of your organization."

"Value Our Loving Traditions, I assume you mean, of which I am only a pastor in service to a ministry. We have thousands of associates and volunteers, Detective, hundreds of affiliations, but surprisingly few actual employees. Who exactly are you looking for? Or maybe you don't have any actual sort of method, and would you like me to initiate a random search through our payroll history?"

"Listen, Yearling, we don't have time for your attempts to defame my competence right now. We suspect a doctor who served in several worldwide VOLT-friendly women's clinics may be implicated in the child abductions in Bristlecone Springs."

"'We don't have time?' Are you saying VOLT is somehow in any way responsible for these heinous crimes?"

"I'm telling you I need you to cooperate. Cal Abrams is his name. His partner says he worked in health clinics in Singapore and Africa, maybe elsewhere, too, as a gynecologist. In both Singapore and Africa, the clinics received funding and sonogram training from VOLT. As did a clinic in Canada, where Abrams volunteered before leaving a private practice and moving to Colorado."

"Cal Abrams ...isn't Abrams a Hebrew surname? Not that we discriminate, of course, but we don't attract many volunteers among our Old Testament brethren."

"He might have been traveling and working under an alias. I want the names of the clinicians working for your organization in the field over the last twenty years, and I want them quick."

"I want to be cooperative, Detective, but that sort of list could take some time."

"Like I said, Yearling, we don't have time for games. You don't get me the information I need, I take it."

"A court order would be required for that."

"In my hand in a matter of minutes. I heard you loud and clear the other day, Pastor Yearling. I may be on my way out after all this, but that badge you claim you have so much respect for? I'm the one wearing it right now. At the moment, the press, not to mention the social media outlets you're so fond of, know nothing of a possible connection between VOLT and the state's worse serial crime spree in history. But that can sure change. Easy for things like that to seep out of a leaky bucket like mine."

The two men held each other's eye. John Yearling considered the doughy, sweaty man for a moment before he pressed an intercom button.

"Estelle, hold my calls, please."

Levi found the key just where Cal said it would be, tucked under a large potted lavender plant outside the shed. It was wrapped in a note: *Levi, I was inspired to move our chat up the road to Genesee Park. Stone shelter, killer acoustics. Grab another fiddle if you want. I'll meet you in the parking lot.*

Levi sighed. He didn't want to get back in the car and wasn't all that eager to play music, either, no matter how cool the sound was. He'd been thinking of this little shed, and Cal's old records, and how easy it had been to talk to the old guy before. He'd wanted comfort, he realized. He considered just turning around and going home. He could talk to his dad, after all, instead of with this guy he barely knew. He was so tired. Too tired to dig out his phone and turn it back on to text, he decided. Plus, he was the one who called Cal—the decent thing to do would be drive up to the park, return the violin, and tell him they'd hang out another day if he had time before school or whatever. He got back in the car.

Cal watched the Outback pull into the space next to his truck in front of the stone picnic shelter. Weekends brought a happy cacophony of reunions, weddings, and other al fresco celebrations to the old Civilian Conservation Corps project, but today, in the quiet of a weekday afternoon, steeped in the scent of Douglas fir and Ponderosa pine, the crunch of gravel under the Subaru's wheels imposed too humanly on the summer song of the resident warblers.

"Hey, Cal. This place is cool. I'm surprised Dad and Annabelle and I haven't been here."

"Yes, I like this spot. Good acoustics, like I said, plus you can play in the rain and stay dry. And, strangely, there's never anybody here during the week. Lucky for us! I'm glad you came, Levi."

"Listen, Cal, I just rode up to say I need to take a pass on playing with you today. I know I'm the one who called you, but I feel like I've been hit with a tidal wave, and I think I've just got to go home." Levi extended the case with the antique violin. "I want to thank you for all those things you said, but I can't accept this."

"No problem, son, it wasn't my intention to burden you with a gift, and it's clear you've had a rough day." Cal reached out to take the case, grabbed Levi's hand and twisted his arm behind his back. He pushed the boy face first against the rock wall and injected a hypodermic through into his tricep. Then he turned Levi around and sat him, almost gently, onto the ground. The boy's body was already limp from the injection. He was conscious, but silenced. His open eyes broadcast a rapid-fire transmission of shock, fear, and panic.

Cal walked to his truck, reached into the front seat, and returned with a retractable measuring tape.

"I've got a few preparations to take care of for the next leg of our trip, so I thought, young Levi, that I'd tell you a little story." Cal measured Levi's body from heel to hip, hip to crown, and across his shoulders.

"I've been a little loose with my own personal mythologies, but as a wise someone once said—Camus, I think—'Fiction is the lie through which we tell the truth.' In my case, drama- tizing the truth has required, as in a complex piece of music, multiple variations on the theme, an arrangement of voices to flesh out the narrative.

"I have to say right off the bat, my boy, I was hoping for a different outcome in our relationship. Felt like you were truly feeling your heart as a father-to-be back when we were chatting in the shed. I could see that you atleast were seeing the destruction of life for what it is: a terrible crime against humanity. I sensed an ally in you, Levi. But today's events show how wrong I was. Your fate was sealed as soon as you allowed your girlfriend to kill that baby of yours."

Cal lifted Levi from the concrete slab and lay him in the rear seat of the cab. "We'll make one stop before we're on our way, and I'll tell you a little more about my journey."

He opened the passenger door to the Subaru and grabbed the backpack. "Ah, here it is!" he said as he fished out the phone. "You're a different kind of kid, I'll give you that, Levi, turning your phone off like that. Most teenagers would rather cut off a limb, or so I understand." Cal climbed into the truck and set the phone in the cup holder. "Yes sir, you are an exceptional young man. Your parents don't deserve you."

They drove east to the trailhead south of Red Rocks. Cal parked the truck, turned on Levi's phone, read his most recent messages and texted Trista that Levi would call her later. He was taking a hike to clear his head.

"Accommodating of you to skip the password protection. I read somewhere recently the new generation is skeptical of paranoid measures to protect their privacy." Cal wiped down the phone, threw it into a trash bin from the driver's side window, and turned west.

CHAPTER
29

"Here's what we know." Gordon Stanislaus had the storyboard moved from the basement up to the first-floor conference room. Eleanor, Elan, and the department's two detectives, Drubbs and Connors, were seated at the table.

"Cal Abrams, aka, Calvin Albertson, can be positively placed in Singapore, Ontario, Canada, and Los Angeles at the same time those locations were experiencing the serial kidnapping and murders of children. In each of those places he was working as a doctor in a women's health center, either as a paid clinician, in the cases of Singapore and L.A., or as a volunteer, as in Canada. He's worked in clinics in New Zealand and Africa, as well. According to John Yearling, the Singapore, New Zealand, and African clinics are affiliated with overseas branches or local versions of Value Our Loving Traditions and are current and past recipients of grants to promote sonogram testing for patients seeking what Yearling calls pregnancy counseling. In New Zealand, Dr. Calvin Albertson administered the training, which included technical procedure alongside a strong script of anti-abortion rhetoric to steer the patient toward adoption, the idea being that a pregnant woman was less likely to terminate when there was a picture. If she still wanted an abortion, she'd be on her own, as the clinic didn't perform them, nor would Dr. Albertson approve the procedure as one of two required 'certified consultants' allowing the woman to undergo an abortion in a hospital."

Eleanor said, "Why would a man, a doctor, committed to sparing the lives of the unborn abduct and murder young children? It doesn't make any sense."

"Sir," Drubbs asked, "do the victims in the Singapore and L.A. and Canada crimes have any connection to the clinics?"

"We don't know, and we're going to have to find out the old-fashioned way. Ontario police and LAPD have sent contact numbers for the families of the victims. We've got a call into the authorities in Singapore asking for names and numbers. Remember, Detectives, these are old wounds. Be compassionate. And get what you need."

Two of the mothers of abducted children in Los Angeles admitted to visiting Mission Pregnancy Resource Center, but neither knew nor had heard of either Dr. Cal Abrams or Dr. Calvin Albertson. Three of the numbers were disconnected land lines, and the person who answered the remaining number told Det. Drubbs he had nothing to say to the police.

A similar scenario played out with the Canadian contacts, with three of the women saying they'd been patients, without having ever met a Dr. Abrams. The mother of a fourth woman, who died of a heart attack five years prior, confirmed that her daughter had been a patient, but again, did not have knowledge of a Dr. Cal Abrams.

Eleanor studied the notes the detectives shared with her. She was no more comfortable among this team of men than she'd ever been and had expected some increased resistance to her presence from them, considering recent events. The department was feeling the pressure. But if the men were not precisely friendly, they were not shutting her out. The death of this last child had rocked the department hard. Whatever opinions they'd held of her were immaterial now.

She checked the dates the women or their relatives said they were patients at the clinics against Cal Abrams' employment history. In every case, the woman received treatment at least two years, and up to seven, before Abrams was hired. He hadn't known them. Why, then, Eleanor wondered, would he target their children?

One of the I-70 billboards flashed before Eleanor's eyes: *Choose life, that both thou and thy seed may live.*

Sarah Schmidt and Catalina Escalante both had abortions before having their children. What had Catalina said, *what it was, was private* ...but maybe not so private, Eleanor thought. As a doctor in the clinic, Cal Abrams had access to records. Hell, Eleanor thought, in those days they weren't even digital records, no password required, just a key to the room where they kept the files. Maybe. He's taking vengeance on women who've had abortions by murdering their children, she thought, and nearly passed out into another of her private movies, but caught herself and took two deep breaths before entering Gordon Stanislaus' office.

Stanislaus hung up the phone and came around his desk to Eleanor.

"Gordon, I know why he's doing it. He's taking the lives of children whose mothers have had abortions. I don't understand the bigger pattern yet, but I know this is what he's doing ..."

"Eleanor ..."

"Gordon, I'll bet if we scratch a little deeper, we can connect these crimes, and we'll have him ..."

"Eleanor, we're on the same page, but we don't have him."

"What?"

"He wasn't at the cabin in Genesee. Dr. Giordano tells me

he's not answering her texts. I've contacted Denver PD to put a BOLO out in the metropolitan area and alerted State Police. He's fled."

"Well, it's just a matter of time, then, right? With all that heat on the road? By the time he's hauled in, we'll have our case."

"Eleanor, there's more. Sit down."

The quiet intensity of his tone hit her like a pipe in the crook of her knee. She reached behind and grabbed the back of the chair and remained on her feet. "What?"

"Emmett Clay contacted Denver PD to report a missing person. Your husband noticed that the locating app on his phone indicated Levi had not progressed past the trailhead at Red Rocks. Police investigated and found Levi's phone discarded in a trash bin at the site."

"What? Levi's phone? Gordon, what does that mean? What are you saying?"

"I'm saying your boy's in danger. Eleanor, you need to go find your son."

CHAPTER

30

Eleanor dragged Elan into the women's bathroom at the station, saw the missed call, and pressed the call back button.

They stood in opposite tiled corners, each on their phones. She pushed against the freezing fog that weighted her limbs, filled her ears, clogged her throat, and shrouded her vision. She struggled to distinguish Emmett's voice, her own voice, over the roar in her head. However difficult it was to make this connection, this man still felt like a lifeline, and she held fast, though she could feel Emmett wanting to let go.

Elan called Annabelle, who then called Bash, and then Trista and Diane Bradstreet, Trista's mom. No one had heard from or seen Levi since that morning. Bash told them he'd had no plans for a hike or overnighter with Levi, that he hadn't spoken with him since the day before.

Emmett told Eleanor that he'd called the police when he noticed the Find My Folks app had Levi pinned to the same spot at the trailhead at Red Rocks an hour after he'd first looked. He then called Eleanor, who didn't pickup.

Emmett said, "This can't be happening. How can we be here again, Eleanor? I can't lose him. I can't lose my boy."

Eleanor heard everything then, bore the full weight of her husband's despair, understood clearly, in one whole piece, that under all that kindness, a kindness she knew to be very real, crouched the blame and resentment he'd been so careful to keep from her. Was he wrong to feel so betrayed now? All his efforts to protect Levi from being dragged under by the indiscrete eddy of Eleanor's grief, her contaminating shame, dissolved in one accident of fate. The first relationship Eleanor had let bloom—her friendship with Althea—plus her involvement with Elan and the abduction cases, had put their only child's life in danger.

She saw now that Emmett had kept her tethered to his and Levi's lives more to neutralize her ill effect than deny it. He'd sought to minimize her influence. The contrast between Eleanor's dark and pathetic mien, her shabbiness, and Emmett and Annabelle's domestic utopia was meant to put her in a sort of relief, amplify the light with the shadow. She'd done her part, she realized. Inarticulate and unresponsive, she'd been as useful, and as frustrating, as an old tube of glue, sealed shut with itself.

"I'll be there as soon as I can. We won't lose him."

Elan searched his contacts.

"Two, three hours by car is a long time, Eleanor. I think I can get us to Denver by helicopter. If I can arrange it, we'd be there in an hour, maybe less."

"You learned to fly a helicopter in community college?"

"I did, in theory, but no, I'm not going to be the one to fly. I bought Terrance a gift certificate for a helicopter trip for his birthday before I knew he was terrified of small open aircraft. I'll see if I can use the badge to bump the schedule."

The helicopter flew so low to the ground, Eleanor could make out individual petals on the milkweed blanketing Eagles

Nest Wilderness. She, Elan, and the pilot all wore earphones, but she doubted the pilot was listening to a recorded tour of Wildflowers of the West, as she was forced to, as she couldn't find a way to shut it off.

CHAPTER
31

Detective Stanislaus sat tall and cool in his chair.

"Word has it you have your man, Detective. I don't know what else I can offer you. Unless, for some reason all your own, I am still a suspect in this case. I can't imagine why else you'd drag me here, other than to harass a private citizen while there is real work to be done."

Gordon Stanislaus considered the man that sat across from his desk, polished as ever, though perhaps a little paler beneath the tan.

"The information your organization provided has been helpful, Mr. Yearling. Forgive me if I want to clarify any ongoing connection our suspect may have with you or with Value Our Loving Traditions. Or with Genesis 1:28, for that matter. I'm just trying to be thorough, Pastor, taking every precaution to ensure a private citizen such as yourself is cleared of any inappropriate or nefarious association."

"My conscious is clear, Stanislaus."

"It's Detective Stanislaus. And maybe you believe you've

done your housekeeping, Yearling, but I'm not so sure you haven't left a little dirt on your hands, after all. I shot down Eleanor Clay's theory that there might be a land issue involved in these cases. Now that we're looking at a possible vigilante motive, it would seem even more logical to dismiss a commercially driven agenda. But then there's this item we dug up in our search for Abrams."

He slid a paper in front of Yearling.

"Yes, I see. A hops crop venture in South Africa. If you knew anything about craft beer, Stanislaus, you'd know that South African hops are prized by brewers all over the globe. Sure, Genesis 1:28 has interests there. Along with hundreds of other producers."

"But you weren't solely interested in buying a share of the crop, isn't that right? Production was difficult due to unreliable water resources, and no one outside of the big boys was guaranteed a supply. You were after the rhizomes."

"And? You already know Genesis 1:28 has plans to grow a hops crop in Colorado. You're making something out of nothing here."

"Yeah, I'd agree, if it weren't for the fact that your bag man was our own Cal Abrams."

"I don't know what you're talking about."

"Okay. Then I'll stop talking." Stanislaus laid out a fan of documents to face Yearling, including an application for a Dr. Calvin Albertson to work at a clinic in Singapore, an employee roster from New Zealand listing a Dr. Calvin Abrams, and a photograph of a dinner party in Pretoria hosted by Genesis 1:28 at which both Abrams and Yearling are present.

"Look, Yearling, I could buy that VOLT would employ or manage a larger pool of individuals than you might be personally acquainted with across your many satellites. But this little Venn diagram of your two major concerns shows a troubling overlap. Meaning, of course, that it is a concern of this case that you have a more nuanced relationship with Cal Abrams than you've felt fit to disclose. Despite my asking."

Yearling sat silent.

"I'd love to take a moment to enjoy the beads of sweat I see developing at your temple, Yearling, but there's a young man in trouble here, likely abducted by your buddy, almost certain to die if we can't find them in time. What do you know?"

Yearling shifted in his seat and leaned forward on the desk, hands clasped together.

"*Detective*, it's true I know Dr. Abrams better than I previously indicated. He did work for VOLT at a number of our international affiliates. But he was just one of several people Genesis 1:28 engaged to bring back rhizomes. Small batch permits only, you see, and anyway, the hops growers denied our offer—a very fair, very legal offer—to buy their rhizome stock in bulk."

"Yearling, stop jacking me off, here. You've got to know that now, even a circumstantial connection to Abrams can hurt you. You might as well give me everything, before someone is able to tie your good name to another dead kid, a conclusion I would not go out of my way to suppress. If we find you're not involved with these crimes, then later we can play games to keep the stink off you and yours."

Yearling sat back. "Perhaps I shouldn't continue without my lawyer."

"You know, truth be told, I've been surprised to deal with you thus far without a legal team. Finally chalked my luck up to your mind-boggling arrogance. But I have to tell you, it's a little late to play that card, seeing how it's not just our little podunk PD on the case, but Denver, too. Maybe the FBI, soon. Plus, it would be downright fucking immoral for a good Christian man like yourself to withhold information that could save another man's life, just so he could save his own ass, now wouldn't it?"

Yearling kept his eyes on his lap. "You must believe, I never suspected Abrams of being mixed up in these horrible crimes."

"For argument's sake. Get on with it."

"I was a junior member on the board at VOLT when Abrams took the jobs at both the Singapore and New Zealand clinics. I know because one of my duties was to vet applications. This was long before I founded Genesis 1:28. I was in medical equipment sales at the time."

"If you were checking applications, you'd know Abrams worked under at least one alias. Wouldn't that have been a red flag for your organization?"

"Well, yes, it would have been. But Abrams had a good story for the name change, and I got to hear it at one of our conventions."

"Good enough to justify fraud?"

"I'm not sure it was. Well, legally, I don't really know. It didn't seem like he'd renamed himself for financial gain. He had reasons that had nothing to do with money."

"He operated as a doctor of medicine under at least two names. Under your organization's supervision."

"As I said, I'm not sure of the fine legal points of it all. When I first approved his application, I knew him as Calvin Albertson. That was for Singapore. By the time I met him in the States—at a VOLT training and conference for our ultrasound program—he was calling himself Cal Abrams. He said the renaming was in honor of his mother, an Albanian Jew who'd escaped imprisonment in the Nazi camps and eventually married an American—Gideon Albertson, Abrams' father—a pharmacist from Connecticut. She died when he was still quite young—the way he told it, from a broken heart. She'd wanted more children and couldn't have any. Insult to injury, the father provided illegal abortions out of his pharmacy. From the perspective of our mission, we couldn't have asked for a clinician more dedicated to our cause. And, truth be told, having our message delivered by the doctor with the Jewish-sounding surname lent a certain, ah, *credibility* to our endeavors."

"Unbelievable. What about the crimes in Singapore and New Zealand? He never came under suspicion? VOLT didn't clean up his mess?"

"Heavens, no. Unfortunately, we at home weren't apprised of any local crimes overseas, and we'd certainly never been aware of any violent activity connected to Dr. Abrams."

Stanislaus frowned. "And I don't imagine you would've looked too deep, even if you'd heard something."

"VOLT operates in foreign countries to preserve the lives of children and promote healthy Christian families. I resent your implication that we don't care."

"Resent away. How and when does Africa play in?"

"Did the South African community suffer a similar series of crimes?"

"We have not uncovered evidence of any abductions and murders that relate to our case. Yet."

"Abrams ran our ultrasound training there, traveling back and forth to multiple foreign clinics. He was still doing it, right up until about a year ago, when he told us he was definitively hanging up his clinician's coat. I'd invited him to a few beer industry dinners when our schedules overlapped, as you already know. Somewhere along the line I expressed my frustration at not being able to get ahold of the hops rhizomes I wanted to grow for Genesis 1:28.

"It was Abrams who suggested a smaller scale approach. As a gesture of goodwill, he said, he'd be happy to bring back the dried rhizomes I sought before he left Africa for good."

"How?"

"I left the details to him."

"You said there were others, too, who did your importing for you."

"Yes, well, that's what Cal—Abrams—told me, that he'd set it up so that several people coming to the States would transport small packages."

"So you lied."

"Not that I'm aware. It's true I never saw any of those hops. Not any of them. Abrams and I parted company for good after he failed to produce even the amount that he was supposed to have brought on his person. He said he'd been relieved of his package at customs. I assumed he'd kept it and was either going to sell it to a competitor or have that botanist girlfriend of his create some designer variety from it. Either way, he screwed me out of a crop."

"Do you know Dr. Althea Giordano?"

"The girlfriend, right? No, I don't know her. It comes as no surprise that Abrams kept his mistress separate from his other associates. I knew *of* her, of course."

"They've lived together for more than ten years. She's hardly a mistress, Yearling."

"You might tell that to his wife."

"Wife, huh? This guy certainly gets around. Where would this alleged wife live? Not Colorado?"

"Oh, no. As I understood it, she was back east. I don't know where exactly. She was listed as his contact on the first application, a Catholic. I don't recall her name, or a wife, on later documents. They might have separated. Wouldn't wipe the sin off his current arrangement."

"That's a lot of attitude coming from a compassionate man of God."

"He'll be judged for worse, by the looks of it, and not by me."

Stanislaus stood, circled the desk, and sat back on the corner. Arms crossed, he leaned into Yearling's profile.

"I don't know, Yearling. I'm not *feeling it*—your latest story. Why shouldn't I entertain the theory that you and

Abrams schemed up this nightmare to facilitate a land grab?"

"What?"

"I'm not saying he doesn't look good for these other crimes, but what if, let's say, you became aware of his grisly history, and decided a version of it could jibe with your plans to expand your beer empire?"

"That's crazy."

"Not so crazy, if you saw your competition, the cannabis folks, poised to move in and willing to pay the asking price for the land you thought should be yours."

"Ridiculous. I told you, I never even got the hops starters I wanted."

"Yes, you never got the hops, illegally or otherwise, so you said. Or just maybe not yet, if Giordano—the *mistress*—was designing you your own special clone."

"I told you I don't know Dr. Giordano."

"But you do know Abrams, we've established that. Maybe you're lying and she's in on it, maybe you're lying and she doesn't know you're using her. Either way, Pastor Yearling, you're a lying sack—hold the ashes—and you're not out of the shit yet."

As Stanislaus collected his materials, he stopped at the photograph of the Pretoria dinner. The memory of the framed family portrait in Eleanor's apartment flashed in his brain. He pushed the picture back across the desk.

"Yearling, who is this woman?"

"The photo isn't the sharpest, you know, but I believe that is Annabelle Gibson."

"What is she doing at one of your beer dinners?"

"Ms. Gibson works as a private consultant. She's supposed to be an expert on water use."

"'Supposed to be'?"

"Well, that's my understanding. I can't say I know the woman very well."

"Well enough to invite her to dinner."

"What are you getting at, Stanislaus? Look, I've indulged you, but please stick to some semblance of a theory. Those dinners are for the local players to get to know one another. Annabelle Gibson was an influencer, if you will, a *person of interest*, to use your parlance. And guessing by the look on your face, Detective, Ms. Gibson's much more interesting than I imagined."

CHAPTER

32

Elan typed on his phone to the drone of the recording: *The basal leaves of aquilegia elegantula grow on long stalks, up to twelve inches, and are divided into three leaflets, each partially divided into three smaller, lobed segments, which have rounded tips ...*

Dear Professor DePeña,

I'm sending this to your university email in the hope that you think it's from a student and open it by mistake. I know you're getting my texts, because what kind of mother blocks her son's texts, even if she chooses to ignore them?

I'm sorry it wasn't me who delivered the news of my graduation. I didn't think you'd want to attend the ceremony. I thought I could figure out a way to tell you that would help you understand, but then, I realized I didn't really understand it either, how I came to wear a uniform, after everything. Terrance said you didn't hear it from him, but Terrance is a terrible liar for a lawyer. Anyway, it was my job to tell you I'd completed my training and was taking a position at Bristlecone PD, and I didn't trust my decision enough to respect you that way.

I apologize.

I don't know, maybe going to the academy was some kind of rebellion on my part. Or maybe you're right, and I was still in denial over Pop's death, or too steeped in a corrupt monoculture to know my own mind...I wish I could at least say I took it seriously from the beginning and have that count for something. Not that I believe that would make a difference to you.

I'm serving as an official escort to a woman who is trying to find the person responsible for kidnapping and drugging kids here in Colorado—maybe you've followed the news from Arizona. Maybe not. She's a different kind of person—very sad, with a particular brilliance (so unlike your high-polish smarts). She had a daughter die by drowning, and has a son who grew up without her in Denver. She's kind of lost herself. But she's found these kids.

I don't know if police work is my destiny, Mom, but I've felt like I'm part of something important, helping with this case. I know where you stand on police, but I can't see where I'm on the wrong side of this, if I'm trying to end the violence. I love you.

I am writing you from a frighteningly low-flying helicopter and feel compelled to attach a short aerial video of what our virtual guide is now pointing out as *subalpine larkspur*. But he's wrong. They are, if I remember my Western Botany, *silky lupine*—wolf plant, so-called symbol of happiness, creativity, and imagination, occasionally poisonous. They're in such beautiful bloom. We're hovering so close I can almost touch them. Funny, even as I look at them, I'm missing them a little.

Always, your Elan

CHAPTER
33

"What exactly are you so sorry *for* Annabelle? I'll tell you right now, keeping your side hustle in corporate real estate from me is nothing compared to letting our boy become bait for a serial killer! *Levi*, Annabelle! Our Levi is in the hands of a maniac we—you and I—could have protected him from!"

"I'm so, so sorry ...I know I should have taken stronger action ..."

"Oh, my god!"

"But it was you I was trying to protect, before we knew how dangerous Abrams really ...before ..."

"Oh, Christ, just don't."

"I'd met him, yes. But I didn't know him, Emmett. Or Yearling, either, really. He invited me to a dinner or two ..."

"Two!"

"Yes, two. I only remember seeing Abrams at the first. Yearling approached me at the second dinner to discuss water rights in Colorado, said he was interested ingrowing a local hops crop for Genesis 1:28. Somehow, he knew about my background in real estate. He lost interest when he discovered my water expertise was limited to African land."

"Why all the secrecy? There was nothing wrong with you giving some advice to those hops farmers, no conflict of interest, as far as I can see. No reason for this."

"Emmett, I wasn't ready to tell you ..."

"Tell me what? Oh, my god...are you leaving us? Is there someone else?"

"No, no, Emmett, never. Of course not."

"What, then?"

Annabelle took a step back, crossed her arms over her chest, stared at the floor. "I was going to leave DRINK. Start my own consulting firm. The South African beer industry wants my help and is willing to pay for it."

"Leave DRINK? For corporate work?"

"Yes. Lucrative corporate work. But also to help grow a sustainable industry that has the potential to employ thousands."

"Or exploit them."

"And you wonder why I waited to tell you ..."

Annabelle stopped herself, moved toward Emmett and took both his hands in hers.

"Emmett, please ...I'm not sorry for wanting to grow, to make a change, but forgive me for not trusting you, for not trusting that we could talk about it. Believe me, I wish I'd handled all of this differently. I just wanted to be able to secure this new start, make a break that wouldn't reflect negatively on you or undermine DRINK. Maybe I didn't like this guy, maybe I thought he...it doesn't matter, but I never, *never* suspected he'd be capable of this kind of horror."

Emmett released himself from Annabelle's grip and turned his back to her.

"I thought, at worst, he was an opportunist. We talked a little. He asked if I would transport some hops rhizomes back to the States. I said no. Later in the evening, when he was drunk, he whispered to me that I didn't need to be so high and mighty, considering I was selling out. I assumed he knew that I was talking to people about working on my own, leaving the NGO. I was afraid, now that he was here, he was going to make some kind of trouble before I could tell you my plans. I never considered it could be worse than that."

"That's what happens when you swim in infested waters. One predator looks just like the next."

"Emmett."

Annabelle's phone rang. She answered.

"Detective, yes, that's everything I have in those scans. Yes, including the financials. I won't, no. Yes, I understand. Thank you."

"You've shared your secrets with the police, Annabelle? So it's just me you left in the dark? What isit about me that compels the women in my life to imperil my children and conspire with the authorities?"

"Okay, Emmett, okay. I get it. I'll leave you alone. For now. But I'm not going anywhere. We'll get Levi back. The rest can wait."

CHAPTER
34

Althea approached the little house as she might a Smithsonian exhibit, a replica of an iconic moment in history. She needed the distance to see where she could begin to separate the tendrils of her life with Cal. They could, always would, share history, but she was determined to sever the perennial roots of them, and today— the sooner to sow a future without him.

What could she claim as hers? Just a few weeks earlier she would have said it was all hers, this home she'd cultivated for their pleasure; she would have said, and believed, that the carpets of flowers, the fragrant herbs, even the bees—these were the threads of her glorious web, were the intoxicants she used to keep her companion rapt. How did it take that turn, she wondered now, when it was he who had courted her so arduously? He who had begged her to start this life together in this place? It was she who was under the influence all along, drunk on the sweet music, the daily morsels of affection. It turned out that Cal had had devotion enough for the both of them, his attentions a kind of anesthesia.

He'd worn her like a costume, disguised himself in her mantle. Althea got out of the car and sagged with fatigue, sank into a bed of Scorpion grass, dotted with the last of the pale blue forget-me-not petals.

Enough with all this goddamn romanticism, she thought. She got up and walked around the back of the shed, wheeled out the gas-powered Husqvarna rototiller and pulled the cord. In a matter of a couple of hours she'd plowed under the wolfsbane, the dianthus, and the yarrow. She hesitated at the ranunculus, still shy of its autumn bloom, and then put her weight into it, watched the earth turn upside down and brown again. She'd pick the vegetables before she tore up those beds, transfer the garlic and asparagus, compost the rest. She wouldn't waste the food. As she pushed the blades through the soil, she imagined burning the shed, setting fire to the house. But as the day progressed and she sweated through her shirt, she reconsidered. The police would confiscate the cannabis plants, empty out thegreenhouse, and she would always want a greenhouse. She loved the cottage, could keep loving it. Dismantling the shed with a sledgehammer, though—that was an idea with legs. Maybe, when this was all over, Eleanor would join her.

CHAPTER
35

As promised, Eleanor and Elan touched down on a pad at Denver International an hour after they left Bristlecone Springs. Annabelle was there to meet them.

"Officer DePeña, it's good to meet you in person."

"Thank you, ma'am. I hope I can be of service."

"Getting Eleanor here so fast—we're already grateful."

"Yes, ma'am." He turned and spoke to Eleanor as she disembarked. "Stanislaus called for a cruiser to pick me up. I'll check in from Denver PD."

Eleanor looked past Annabelle as she stepped on the helipad. "Where's Emmett?"

"Eleanor..." Annabelle stepped in to hug Elanor, who shrank out of reach.

"He's home, talking with the police."

"What don't I know?"

"Well, we talked to Trista. She and her mom left Levi in the parking lot at the downtown Healthy Families this morning around ten. No calling or texting since."

The moment Anabelle's words hit the air, Eleanor understood everything. A complex diagram of the events leading to Levi's abduction projected onto the blue sky in a burst of perfect clarity before the whole world swirled to a choking gray that poured into her nose, her mouth, made cold steel of her lungs, and eddied in her stomach. Eleanor stared at her feet, tried to feel the solid ground beneath them.

"And he was alone, after?"

Annabelle stiffened. "Levi didn't tell us, either, Eleanor. Emmett only found out about the pregnancy by accident. We've done our damnedest. It was you he turned to."

Her boy had come to her. What did he hope to get? She knew all too well what he'd hoped for, what she didn't give him.

She looked at the elegant figure in front of her, saw the customary poise undone like a loose thread, felt her own terror reflected back at her as radiant heat. She knew nothing about this woman, she realized, except this heat. Eleanor grabbed Annabelle's hand.

"I'm sorry. I know I've let Levi down, left it all to you and Emmett." Annabelle gasped, sagged, and then, like a hinge released, let her full weight fall onto Eleanor, nearly bringing the two women down. Eleanor felt Annabelle's tears drip into her ears, run down her neck.

"I can feel him," she muttered into Annabelle's hair, "I haven't frozen him out, not all the way. I feel him. He's not lost, not yet."

Annabelle sniffed aggressively and straightened, bringing them back to plumb.

"Let's go home."

Eleanor jerked back from the warmth of the embrace, shocked by the voice outside of her own head.

Emmett was a body in recession. Leaning on the kitchen counter, he was a river in drought, bones exposed, edges drying to dust. Looking at her husband, Eleanor was struck by the way she'd always seen him, in motion, catching and reflecting the light, myriad life force teeming beneath the surface. In this moment, she thought, a good wind would pick him up and scatter him.

"What does he want with our boy, Eleanor?"

Our boy. At that, she understood how complicit she'd been in her own failure to show up for Levi. She'd told herself she hadn't deserved him. It was clear to her now that deserving him was beside the point. He was not a reward she'd earned; he was not a gift. Levi had chosen her. She was the parent he needed. She and Emmett. Never more so than now.

"He wants to punish us, Emmett. He wants to break us."

"How can we be any more broken?" Emmett jackknifed over the soapstone counter. Annabelle folded herself over his back and held him as he shook.

"My god, it's me ...I'm the one that put Levi in danger. I told him about the time before Freya, before Freya and he were born, about the abortion. Levi must have told Abrams and made himself a target."

Annabelle straightened. "There's Trista, too, don't forget. I doubt it was just yours and Eleanor's story he told. Whatever information was or was not shared, our sweet Levi trusted this fuck. And you know what? It doesn't matter what Cal Abrams thinks he knows about our boy or us. He's not making some martyr or example out of our kid. We know who—what—we're looking for, now. What did the police say, Emmett? Emmett!"

He'd sunk to the tile floor. "I thought we'd figured it out. I thought we'd won. Here he was, healthy and whole. Safe. Across the world and back, he'd been safe. Now I can barely say it out loud, it feels so ridiculous. I'm ashamed to think I believed in something so impossible."

Eleanor struggled to hold herself up, to keep her eyes on Emmett, to resist the blur that erased his edges, softened his pain.

"Emmett, please don't get lost in that now. So, safety's not a thing we can guarantee. It never was. You haven't been making Levi safe all these years, you've been making him strong. We need you now—Levi, Annabelle, and me, too. If we've got each other, we've got resources. Someone said to me recently, *family will figure this out.* We can do this. Stay with us."

Annabelle knelt on the floor to face Emmett. "Eleanor's right. Our tender, complicated, variously skilled family will find Levi."

He looked up at Eleanor. "Alive?" he choked.

The doorbell rang. Annabelle rose to answer. She returned with Elan, who kept his expression blank as he took in the scene—a man curled up on the floor, a pale woman standing as if hung from an invisible hook, sagging and limp-limbed, an empty coat.

"Denver PD confirms it was Emmett's Outback parked at Genesee Park. Tire tracks indicate another vehicle, likely a truck, was parked alongside the Subaru, then pulled out of the dirt lot."

"Mrs. Clay ..."

Eleanor stopped staring at Emmett and looked up, irritated. "For god's sake, Elan."

"*Eleanor,* from the other cases we can assume Abrams will need supplies, and he'll need to get them from somewhere other than his home."

Emmett had pulled himself to his feet. "So?"

"So, sir, while Denver's looking for the truck, we can find out if any music stores between here and Genesee have sold significant quantities of catgut today, check the hardware stores for sales of hemp rope and tubing."

Eleanor paced. "Abrams took six children in Bristlecone Springs, the same number involved in the other cases. Taking Levi was a spontaneous decision, and you're right, Elan, one he would have had to restock for. I'll call Althea, see if she's got anything new, and focus on the map. We know he likes water."

Annabelle was relieved to do what she did best, which was prepare for the worst. Though there'd never been a worst, not since she'd been with Emmett, she kept the gas tank filled, their passports updated, and a stash of cash at the ready at all times, just in case.

Emmett sat on the sofa, one hand on his laptop, the other thumbing his phone. He was having no luck with the music stores, until Levi's buddy, Bash, messaged him a screenshot from his Snapshoot account, with the caption: *St. Nick out of uniform! Check out those guns! #SummerSantaSighting.*

Bash wrote, *This our dude?*

Emmett's lungs tightened. Sure enough, there was Cal Abrams at a checkout counter with baling wire, tarps, and what looked like an inflatable pool float. The blood ran from his head.

He texted Bash, *Where is this?*

Bash responded. *I asked in comments, waiting to hear back.*

Emmett found Eleanor in the little office, sitting on a cardboard box, talking on her phone.

"Hold on, Althea, it's Emmett."

"Bash found a photo of Abrams."

"Where?"

"He bought a flotation device and wire."

She dropped the phone. "Emmett, where was he?"

"*Wire*, Eleanor..." he gasped, pressed his palms to his eyes, sputtered, "I don't know, I'm waiting for Bash ..."

Eleanor picked up the phone. "Althea, email what you got directly to Gordon. He's talking to Denver PD Emmett thinks he's got a lead." She hesitated a second. "Althea...?" The connection was cut, *call ended*. She flipped the phone shut.

"It's better he's following a pattern. Makes it easier for us to narrow the search."

"Shouldn't we be out searching now?" His phone buzzed. A message from Bash read, *Big D Supply, Silverthorne, CO.* "Silverthorne. He bought the stuff in Silverthorne. Dillon Lake?"

Eleanor rounded the desk and sat at the computer. "He's going back west ...no, it won't be a lake ...he'll take Levi to the river, he'll go back to a river..."

Emmett looked over her shoulder at the interactive map. "There's a lot of Colorado between us and them, and a lot of river."

"Elan!" Eleanor yelled, and the young man appeared the doorway, tapping into his phone. "Get a hold of Gordon and tell him Cal's been sighted in Silverthorne. If Abrams is on the interstate, Bristlecone Springs and Denver PD can sandwich him in."

"Yes, ma'am."

"And us?" Emmett asked. "What do we do?"

"We do what Gordon told me I had to do back at the station, find Levi. Let's go."

"Go where? Where should we be while the police cover the interstate, throwing darts in the wilderness? I want to be someplace I can be reached when the police have something."

"When they recover our boy's body, you mean? Didn't you just ask me if we should be out searching? I can't sit here, Emmett, cozy in your lovely home, waiting for bad news."

"Jesus, Eleanor. Who the hell do you think you're talking to?"

"Emmett ...look, I'm sorry. You're the last person I want to hurt, but I can't just keep talking right now. We can't stay here another minute when I know I can find him. I can find Levi. Before it's too late. I need you, and Elan, and Annabelle, too, to get him back. Please, Emmett, let's go get him back."

Annabelle came into the room and slipped an arm around Emmett. "I'll stay here. Let you know the moment I hear anything." She pressed the key to her SUV into his hand and hugged him tight.

A flash of lightning jerked everyone's attention to the window.

"You'd best grab the rain gear, too."

Eleanor and Elan waited in the driveway while Emmett stowed the slickers and rain pants from the storage closet in the garage in the back of Annabelle's Honda, which she had stocked like an emergency larder—water, packets of dried fruit and nuts, two flashlights, a blanket, a first aid kit. He guessed if he opened the glove compartment he'd see his phone charger. His heart hurt with the ways she protected him, him and Levi both, how she reached out to Eleanor, even. He opened up a dusty safe, removed his grandfather's Colt, tucked it under the blanket, and closed the hatch. Then he slid into the front seat, pushed the remote to open the garage door, and backed out.

CHAPTER
36

Cal sat in the back of the truck, brushing pine pitch onto the interior of a plastic canoe. A steady rain beat onto the camper shell. Levi lay along the long edge of the truck bed, bound at the wrists and ankles, awake and woozy with fumes, turpentine, and the lingering effects of an injection of cannabis and valerian.

Cal pressed and smoothed strips of burlap over the sticky pitch. "Not my best work, I admit, but this is a larger scale project than I'm used to, and perfectionism will just have to take a back seat to expediency. Too bad. You deserve better, Levi."

Levi struggled to clear his throat, which felt coated with its own layer of tar. "You...why...?" he rasped.

"You really shouldn't try to talk, or breathe deep, at this stage of our journey. Me, though, I'm used to it, so I'll tell you. I'm not doing anything you yourself haven't put in motion. Merely the consequence of your choice. Consequence always accompanies choice, Levi. Always."

He rubbed resin onto a length of rope.

Levi coughed and choked on his phlegm before he managed to turn his head and spit.

Cal continued. "I really thought it was going to go another way for you, son. You seemed genuinely attached to the life that you and your girlfriend murdered, but I see now that you had no real influence over your woman."

Levi growled, "Who the fuck are you...?"

"Ah, I'm just a humble witness, is all. I heard the regret in your voice, son. And if I'm not mistaken, more than a touch of resentment for your impotence in the matter."

Levi gasped. "*No...*" He coughed and tried to spit again, without the benefit of saliva. Cal tilted a sip of water into his mouth. Levi choked. The next mouthful he swallowed.

Cal sat back on his haunches, tipped the bottle into his own mouth. "No, you say. I suppose, then, it was a *relief,* and let me guess—because you two weren't *ready?*"

"No, asshole...not my...*choice.*"

"So you seem to think, more's the pity. You people always point to the suffering in the world as an excuse, 'Take care of the babies that are already here,' blah, blah, blah. But clearly, suffering is part of our human experience, and no amount of human intervention, I humbly suggest, prevents it. 'Participate joyfully in the sorrows of the world,' said the great Joseph Campbell. Buddha agreed, I would argue. Tell me, what if Moses' mother had killed him instead of leaving him to be found in the rushes?"

"My mother...."

"Hm, yes, your mother. It's a fact she's added an unusual layer to my protest. Who knows, but the wan Eleanor Clay is a modern mystic? We shall test her, as the good Lord has already tested her. A trial she failed disastrously, I understand. I'm willing to bow to the mystery that would save your precious body tonight, Levi. There's nothing anyone can do for your soul."

Cal reached into a bag and withdrew a hypodermic needle.

CHAPTER
37

Emmett had a hard time seeing the road through the angry sluice of rain, but the Honda kept its grip. Eleanor contacted Stanislaus to tell him she and Emmett and Elan were headed to the hardware store to find out what they could about where Abrams was headed. Stanislaus told Eleanor he had uniforms and detectives from Bristlecone Springs PD on the lookout along the I-70 corridor up to the confluence of the Colorado and Eagle Rivers. Eagle County Sheriff's Department was keeping an eye out between there and Silverthorne.

Neither Emmett nor Eleanor spoke after she hung up with Stanislaus. Elan sat in the back seat plugged into his phone, the electric green wire of his ear buds pooling on a notepad on his lap. The only sound in the cabin unrelated to the rain was the scratch of Elan's pen. Finally, Emmett broke the sloshy rhythm of the windshield wipers.

"How do you find them?"

Eleanor didn't answer.

"You don't know, is that it? Or you won't say? How is it

that you've been able to find these kids, when all the others, everywhere else, have died?"

Eleanor looked up from her lap to see Emmett focused on the road, hands bleach-knuckled at ten and two.

"I don't know."

"I don't believe you, Eleanor."

"What *do* you believe?"

"That's a good question. I used to believe in bare feet and camping in the backyard, in kitchen table homework and haircuts, in holding a little one under the armpits while they learned to ski, in whispering with my wife while kids dreamt in their beds. I used to believe I could protect my own. I used to believe in us."

"You and Annabelle have a good life."

Emmett shook his head. "Don't. Just don't. I'm talking about us—for the life of me, Eleanor, I still can't understand it, how we...*disintegrated*. Even after we lost Freya, at the worst of it, I'd thought we'd survive, you and me. I mean, *you* and *me*, Ellie."

She turned to look out the passenger window, scanning the roadside brush through the rivulet of rainwater that coursed along the glass.

"I can't believe you let us go."

They approached a billboard, one of VOLT's. Across Sarah's looming despair someone had graffiti'd, in red paint, *"Proverbs 19:8, 'He who gains wisdom loves his own soul.'"*

"I see a pattern ...and a disruption in the pattern, or that's how I think of it, if thinking is what I'm doing. I get a sense of the energy of a thing, of a body, and start to... sort of... *see* where the energy is incongruent in the field of loss."

She thought about the five children she'd found barely alive. She remembered a vision, a picture, of the disturbed bank of the river where they'd recovered Lizzie, pale little snail, curled and translucent.

She saw the top of Freya's sun dappled head, an ear, an unsubmerged finger, slipping under the surface, swallowed.

"You want to know why I'm finding the living instead of the dead, like I used to? Practice. Maybe it's as simple as that. Maybe I've just practiced enough to get it almost right."

An hour and a half after leaving Denver, they turned off the interstate toward Silverthorne and Big D Supply. Emmet sprayed a wall of water and mud onto an adjacent pickup as he swerved into the parking lot. In the few steps from the SUV to the automatic door, the rain pounded off the ground and rebounded straight up Eleanor's PVC jacket, soaking her to the waist.

Emmett rushed the clerk at the front counter with the Snapshoot picture of Cal Abrams. "Hey! Did you sell this guy some supplies earlier today? Did he say anything about where he was headed?"

"Yeah, I saw that, but I wasn't here when it was taken. My dad helped him late this morning, I think. He was pretty tickled—my dad, that is—when my kid pointed out how many people commented on that picture, liked it, or whatever. Who wants to know, anyway?"

Elan lifted the flap of his raincoat to show his badge. "Bristlecone PD. You heard about those children getting taken in Bristlecone Springs? This man is a person of interest in these kidnapping cases."

Emmett gestured to Eleanor, who was scanning the room. "He's got our kid. We've got to find him."

"Jesus." The man lifted his cap and rubbed a hand through a clipped bristle of dirty blond hair. He looked at Eleanor. "I know who you are, don't I? You're the woman that's found all those kids."

Eleanor didn't divert her attention from the walls. "I am."

"And now you gotta find your own? Son of a bitch. There's nothing right about that."

Emmett looked at the embroidery over the man's left shirt pocket. "Gilbert?"

"Gil'll do."

"Gil, look, anything you can tell us would help. Anything. We're running out of time."

Elan added, "Along with light, visibility, and traction—this rain's not gonna let up anytime soon, according to the forecast."

"Hang on a minute." Gil disappeared into a doorway behind the counter and returned with an older man, plainly blood related, evidenced in a matched set of gray eyes and a shared bear shape, slightly convex at the belly in the senior figure. The old man nodded to Elan and extended a hand to Emmett.

"Howard Brickel. Santa Claus was in here a little before noon. Bought an odd mix of supplies, though I'm sorry to say I see the sense of it now, knowing how those kids were found. Paid cash, or I'd have more for you." As he spoke, he kept his eye on Eleanor.

She stood in front of the wall next to the counter. Fishing reports and boat regulations were papered over with lost pet flyers, inkjet-printed jet skis for sale, and summer rentals. Scanning the announcements, Eleanor stopped at a poster for a band playing a local bar. Under the headliner she read, *with special guests, Pop the Chute*. She pressed her hand over the name, and leaned into the wall, felt the wood floor buckle beneath her.

"What is it, Eleanor? Do you see something?"

Elan was at her back. She could feel his hands on her upper arms, holding her up. She stood up, pushed herself off the wall. He let go but did not step back. She turned and saw the look on his face, not mere concern, not worry, but another energy altogether, willing her to keep on her feet. Across the store she saw Emmett, who looked back at her as if she'd driven them to the edge of a cliff, and the old man, who looked like he'd like to push her off.

A faded topographic map of Colorado hung left of the notices. Delineated by an angry red border, Summit County resembled, unambiguously, an erect phallus. With a nod to the obvious, a handmade banner tacked beneath the map read, *Welcome to Summit County! We're Happy to See You!*

Elan pointed to the map. "You'd think I would've noticed that before."

"Noticed what?" Eleanor edged in front of the map.

"Look where we are, at the base of this, uh, projectile." She could see they were at the northwest end of Dillon Reservoir. She had thought to keep west on the interstate toward Bristlecone Springs, toward the confluence of the Colorado and Roaring Fork, assumed Abrams would revisit the geography of Freya's drowning and death, use Levi to compound the devastation. But as she stared at the map, her eye traveled the vein that marked the flow of the Blue River, stopping at Green Mountain Reservoir and its Roosevelt-era dam and hydroelectric plant.

"A different confluence."

"Maybe a different river. He must know the police would be canvassing the interstate. He wouldn't try to take Levi all the way to the springs."

Eleanor asked over her shoulder, "Did he say where he was going?

Howard Brickel stood silent, staring at Eleanor.

"Where was he going?" Emmett yelled. He was shaking.

Brickell just shook his head. "If he said so, I didn't hear, though he was as interested in that map as your woman seems to be. Asked if the area'd had many tourists this season, I said sure, though this storm was likely to clear out the boaters for a day or two."

Emmett rushed to Eleanor and the map, pushing Elan out of the way. Her finger was tapping the blue Rorschach splotch of reservoir.

"You said a river, Eleanor. You were sure it wouldn't be a lake."

"I know. It might be both, or maybe we can't separate them out this time. I don't know. But I've got a feeling."

"Are you seeing something?"

"No, nothing like that. It's my gut, is all."

"But it hasn't been your gut that's found the others, has it?"

"I don't think we can separate that out, either, Emmett." She turned to the old man, ignoring, or oblivious to, his clear animosity toward her. "Mr. Brickel, what's the road report for Highway 9?"

Elan had his phone in his hand. "I've got it right here. 'Heavy rains, flooding'. No closures yet."

"Call Gordon. I want to tell him we're headed north to Green Mountain."

Howard Brickel watched the rain out the storefront window. "Yep, floods are likely, this keeps up. You know," he said, looking at Emmett, who was watching Eleanor and Elan with their heads together over the phone, "I got a neighbor, nice old gal, went to see your wife when that preacher was at Bristlecone Springs."

"Yeah?"

"Near to broke her heart, not getting to see her—your wife, that is. I told her—my neighbor lady— if a person can't show up for all those unhappy folk took the time and trouble, she's probably nothing but a fake, maybe worse."

Emmett clenched his fists and leaned in, but Elan stepped in.

"Mr. Brickel, thank you for your help."

Emmett's mouth was still twisted in a snarl as he put the key in the ignition. He put the SUV in reverse and spun the Honda around to face the road, sending a wave of water several feet into the air. "What if you're wrong? What if every mile we drive away from here takes us farther from Levi, then what? Eleanor, please god, tell me you know what you're doing!"

She stared through the wipers, pushing at the rain.

"Shit," said Emmett, and pulled out of the parking lot.

CHAPTER
38

Stanislaus stood staring into the middle distance, out of his office, to an unfixed point in the reception area. The air was muggy, somehow, even with the air conditioning. He rubbed his shirt over his chest at the place where the gold crucifix lay, until he noticed the heat of the metal on his skin and stopped.

He read the notes on his desk. Giordano said if Abrams was using the same concentration of drugs for Levi that he's used on the little kids, Levi might not be affected as much. He could use more, of course, but he might not have it, or, too, she speculated, he might miss that detail, given the spontaneity of this kidnapping. Giordano had delivered, Stanislaus thought— filled in a lot of gaps, provided a number of connections that would come in handy when the lawyers got their turn. Couldn't be easy, helping to build a case against your boyfriend of ten years.

Nothing is easy, he thought, not a goddamned thing.

Eleanor had a feeling. Well, who doesn't? he thought, and picked up the phone.

CHAPTER
39

No billboards dotted CO-9 as they kept pace with the Blue River, flowing north up the shaft of Summit County to Green Mountain Reservoir. Unlike the concrete expanses of I-70, massive Brachiosaurus tails of industry seemingly cut by gods and suspended through the canyons, this was a road built by humbler aspirations. It was not a road of infinite possibility— not a road for caprice or for destiny, undefined—but a purposeful road, a road that led only to the specific and immediate aim of its traveler.

Eleanor sat in the passenger seat of the SUV like a prisoner at a slow-motion screening of her life—not her whole life— just the last corridor, the slip of time she'd been unable to escape. She wasn't dreaming now, in that way that she could, and sometimes did, wide awake. She was watching herself, in the wash of a Colorado landscape, alongside a river. From inside a vehicle, dry, open-eyed and calm, she watched herself sink and surface, sink and surface, and tried not to go under.

Through the rain-mottled glass, Eleanor watched watercolor splotches of the green and brown spread and blur, watched the earth succumb to wet. She closed her eyes and took a deep breath, could feel the mineral rush of river flow into and fill her mouth, displacing the air. Her eyes shot open. No, she thought, not now. She would maintain, she would *enforce*, some distance from her sunken self, propel free of that sucking gravity, keep her head above water.

How do you find them? was Emmett's question to her. She knew what he really wanted to know: *How could you trade us for them?*

She'd tried, after Freya was lost, after regaining consciousness, after someone pulled her out of the river, after she'd left her daughter to be carried away, never to be recovered. After she'd awoken, sputtering, lying on a muddy bank, after she'd awoken to a world without her daughter, she tried. And each morning after that, after she awoke next to the warmth of her husband, with her young son asleep and fragile as tissue in the next room, after she emerged drenched and quivering from her raging dreams, she tried.

She took the drugs. She tried to respond to Emmett, after the initial wave of his pain had ebbed and he sought solace in sex, searched for a way back into their intimacy like a man lost in space, collapsing from want of oxygen. She tried walking among people, taking Levi's hand as they walked to school, picking him up, navigating the misguided intentions of the parents who had not let a daughter drown in the Colorado, who smiled and chatted at her with set expressions and eyes clouded with fear. She'd felt for them, really. She wished she didn't have to be the one to penetrate their ignorance, reveal the world for the terrifying circus it was.

She had compassion for all the awkward parents, all except the one·who'd asked if maybe she'd missed Eleanor's thank you note in the mail for the veggie lasagna she'd sent over after the funeral, and by the way, could she have her dish back ...but even that stupidity was a kind of gift, her disproportionate rage the first real emotion she'd experienced after Freya's death. Of course, she'd made a mess of that, too, shattering the woman's baking dish on the tile floor of their bright suburban kitchen, in plain sight of Levi, scrunched deep into the banquette of the breakfast nook, curled with terror. Emmett had come home to find her kneeling in shards of Pyrex. The room had gone gray in the oncoming dusk. Levi lay asleep on his belly on the banquette, one tear-streaked cheek stuck to the vinyl. Emmett swept the floor around Eleanor, put her to bed, and took a sleepy Levi out for pizza. Although Emmett would say different, Eleanor knew that after that, it wasn't only she that had let go, allowed her to drift into her dark waters, out of reach.

Levi. She had tried to forget about time, marked it as dispassionately as she could, was herself marked dully by it, while her son had courted time, grown strong and beautiful in it, grew eager to leap into the dazzling ribbon of it. Eleanor realized, in this claustrophobic moment, what a miracle it was that her son survived their trauma as he did. But another? Eleanor and Emmett and Elan would find Levi, would bring him home; of that she was sure. After, he'd have to learn what he'd need to be himself. After this time, she'd be there, and not on her bloody knees. After this.

CHAPTER
40

Cal Abrams paused to catch his breath in front of the brass plaque: *Green Mountain Dam and Power Plant, 1943, United States Department of the Interior, Bureau of Reclamation.*

"The machine never stops, Levi, even—no, not *even, most particularly*—in war. What we won't sacrifice to keep our industrial fires burning!"

There was a sign posted next to the plaque:

Caution! Rapidly Rising Water Poses Extreme Danger.

Cal had kept up a running narrative and commentary since the truck pulled out of the parking lot at the last place they'd stopped, a campground, Levi guessed, where he had built the craft in which Levi lay bound and prone. The old man chattered on as Levi floated in and out of consciousness in the pickup, as he lay Levi's body in the makeshift vessel, as he hauled Levi by rope though the brush and rushes, the rain beating the atmosphere clean of anything but itself. Although Levi hadn't caught much of Cal's monologue en route, and now none of it in the downpour, he felt the persistent weight of the language seep into his skin, snaking his insides with corrosive rivulets of rant and rhetoric. Random speech sprayed and blistered his cracked consciousness in patches, like a noxious, rootless memory.

Emmett drove north through the pooling water, around the debris, making its way by wind and rain to the road— rocks, leafy limbs, gritty veins of mud. It was dark as a November dusk, summer's sun vanquished behind a thick bank of sky.

"Flash flood warnings for Summit and Eagle counties," reported Elan.

Emmett jumped. He kept forgetting about Elan in the backseat.

"And hey, looks like we won't be on our own for long. Det. Stanislaus issued an alert to Silverthorne PD, and the local emergency alert system has sent out an SOS on behalf of the dam. Summit EMS and local police should be bringing up the rear any minute."

Emmett checked the rearview mirror. It hadn't taken him long to decide Eleanor was right, to convince himself of the inevitability of finding Levi and Abrams at the dam. He'd follow Eleanor's intuition, or whatever it was, but he'd make sure he'd be the one to find Abrams. The desire to meet, head on, the cretin responsible for this hell they were in dug deeper with every mile, filled every pore, even overwhelming the desire to hold his son again. He hadn't admitted as much to himself when he loaded the old revolver into the back of the SUV. He hadn't really understood his own motivation, his movements had felt automatic, but the longer he drove into the blinding storm, the clearer he was on it. He told himself he'd kept that shameful weapon all these years as a reminder of how far he'd come from the days when the men of his family, like all the men who *tamed the west,* would shoot first and ask questions later. As he drove into the rain, the need to grasp the why of it all drained away, along with his aversion to the weapon waiting in the rear. No, he would have no questions for Cal Abrams. In his new resolve, he was sure he'd brought with him the only answer that served.

Cal bent to tie the plastic canoe to a stump next to the spillway, securing the rope under a whorled knot in the wood. He had perforated the edge of a tarp and laced it over the small craft like a corset. Levi awoke from his last slip out of consciousness to find himself thusly swaddled. Now, pelted painfully awake by the rain, he held his face as still as he could. The water in the craft had risen to the soft impressions behind his ears, lapped incrementally higher with every breath.

Breath, he thought. Control the breath. He was not high. There was no drug in between him and his terror, but neither was there anything messing with his brain. He could focus.

He found, with his hands still bound behind his back, that he had just enough room for his long, strong fingers to manipulate his bindings, to begin to loosen himself. He plied his fingers into the geometries of the knot, digging and wriggling until the hitch released and came undone.

Hands freed, he worked his arms around to his sides, and considered the trussed tarp, already frayed where Cal had punched holes in it. The material would rip with enough force, Levi thought. Still bound at the ankles, Levi watched Cal crouch over the stump, his back turned, torso balanced on his haunches. Levi breathed in deep, expanding his chest, pressing the top of his skull into the ground. Water filled his ears, rushed from either side of his head to cover his face. The tarp strained against the pressure as Levi arched his back. A thread popped, then another. Levi rolled on his side toward Cal, his mouth barely above water, sipping breath, inflating, blooming his body to fill the plastic shroud until the low, slow growl of the fabric gave way to an ecstatic zipper of release, louder than the rain.

Cal spun into the trajectory of Levi's arm and was thrown backward into the slippery weeds. The old man spiraled around on his knees and threw himself at Levi, who had himself fallen forward and was struggling to undo his shackles. Cal had his hands around Levi and was hauling him back into the canoe when he was blinded by a bright light aimed directly into his face.

"Police! Hands in the air!"

Cal stared wildly into Levi's eyes before releasing his grip and scrambling up onto the bridge.

"Police! Stop!"

Cal ran to the center of the bridge. He slipped and skidded on the reeds that clung to the sole of his boot and reached out to grab the cement wall of the winch, groping for purchase on the wet gears. An alarm punched the air as the mechanism engaged to heave the gates, release water from the rising reservoir into the river, and pull Cal's fingers into the grinding steel. Arch-backed and open-mouthed to the broken sky, he screamed. The wail of the siren swallowed his agony. Then it stopped, leaving only the static of heavy rain.

Eleanor rushed to Levi, followed by police and EMTs. As the ties were cut from his ankles, Levi's knees curled into his chest. Eleanor kneeled in the mud and held him to her, wedging his head between her chin and clavicle. She unfolded herself from him and stepped back as two of the crew checked him for injuries, leaned in to hear him answer their questions. They helped him to his feet and supported him under the arms as they walked him onto the bridge toward the hydroelectric plant and the emergency vehicles parked in the lot.

The Sheriff radioed to get someone to override the gate program and get Cal's hand out of the gears. Levi kept his head down as he and the EMTs passed Cal, captive in the works. They were three-quarter way to the other side when the alarm blared once again. The electric winch engaged and reversed its direction, releasing Cal's hand and with it a bellow that bludgeoned the air and breeched even the rain. Levi reeled to see Cal twist out of reach of one uniform and grab the canoe from under the arm of another. The old man scuttled fast as a crab toward the spillway. Levi pulled away from the EMTs and ran after him.

Forty feet away, Emmett crouched on the emergency platform on the dam wall, ten feet below the bridge, his two hands wrapped around the grip of the Colt. He snapped toward the moving figure on the bridge and saw two bodies. He lifted the weapon with two hands and fired at a mass of white, willing it to be Abrams' mane.

At the sound of gunshot, Levi slipped and fell to one knee. He regained his footing and lurched toward the edge as another shot ripped through the rain. He turned to see his father, coiled low on a platform, pointing a gun straight at him.

Cal leapt, threw himself belly down onto the spillway as though into the curl of a wave, one hand clutching the tip of the canoe, the other tucked under the barrel of his torso. Down a near-vertical concrete drop of three hundred feet, he shot into the rising river.

Levi teetered at the edge. He swung his head once over his shoulder to see Eleanor running, unseeing, in a mad arrangement of light. He lowered himself, swung a leg over the rim, then the other, and crossed his arms over his chest. Face up, chin tucked, he jumped into Cal's wake.

Eleanor, running after Levi, swerved at the gunshot to see a darkening sky slashed by a chaos of flashlight, then turned back to see her son fall from view. She raced to the spillway.

He moved from her, her boy, diminishing at impossible speed, as if propelled by a rocket, losing mass and headed for the black bottom of the river. She tried to track the disappearing body of her son in the current, but saw no bodies, only the buzz saw chop of rushing water.

Eleanor ran to Annabelle's SUV. The other emergency vehicles, seconds before, had filled with police and emergence crew in pursuit of the fugitive. Keys hung from the ignition. She steered the vehicle into the narrow access road adjacent to the river, now thick with mud. Foot on the gas pedal, eyes on the water, she scanned for she knew not what, a scrap of fabric, a human limb among the rafting wood. The SUV stalled in the muck. Eleanor jumped out and ran the pathless bank to a bridge some dozens of yards from the dam. Hands thrust out, plowing the rushes that cut her fingers like the flap edges of envelops, ankles hinging to navigate the disinterred roots of the thick willow carr, she ran blind, oriented only by the sound of the river on her ear, the grasping vegetation under her feet. She stepped into the water and struggled to stay conscious as the force swept her in and took her downstream.

The kickback from the second shot knocked Emmett back against the safety rail. The gun dropped to the metal platform. He reeled to retrieve it, throwing his weight forward. The wind and the rain at his back extended his momentum and Emmett, still reaching, followed the arc of the falling gun into the churl of water. No one was left on the bridge to witness how fast the river swallowed both the gun and the man.

Elan was a step behind Eleanor when he heard the gunshot, then the next, and ran to the bridge rail, scanning the banks for movement. His flashlight rolled over the empty emergency ladder. He directed the beam back to the ladder and tiny deck and spotted a shining colorless shred of something flapping in a metal joint, a scrap of rain slicker.

"Human in the water!" Elan shouted.

No one was there to hear his call for help. Emergency personnel had dispersed to chase down Abrams. Two police officers followed Eleanor's direction on foot. A crew of EMTs had jumped in the emergency response truck to position the vehicle for medical service downstream. He called out again, directing his flashlight beam across the expanse.

A single responder ran toward the SOS from across the bridge.

"What's the situation?"

Elan removed his rain jacket and pulled a life vest from a pile of equipment. He grabbed the end of a coiled rope and threw the end to the EMT. "Man in the water! Rig me up!"

"Are you qualified?"

"Yes! No! ... Look, there's no time! We'll lose him!"

The EMT shouted back, "It's my job, Officer. You spot me. You know your rigging as well as your Morse code?"

Elan nodded and went to work securing the rope to the bridge rail. "White man, gray rain suit, 165 pounds. Name's Emmett Clay."

The EMT climbed over to face the wall and lowered herself as the blistering skin of the water and the curtain of rain rose and fell to meet.

Fewer than two hundred yards from Eleanor, Levi Clay held Cal Abrams' neck in the crook of his right arm. With his left, he pulled them both over an island of river thicket to the bank, then hauled his catch onto a remnant of matted thatch. He leaned onto Cal's prone torso with an elbow as he undid, with his free hand, the belt from his own pants. Cal was conscious, and cold, immobile but for the bellows of his diaphragm. Levi crossed the old man's arms over his ribcage and straddled him, sat on his chest facing his legs as he wrapped the woven belt around Cal's ankles. He reached for a fistful of river grass, twisted it around his hand and pulled at the root. Levi climbed off and used the grass to bind him at the wrists.

The hand that had been mangled by the gears appeared to pulse, lurid and shapeless as a beached glob of man-of-war jellyfish.

Cal choked and coughed. A tremor rippled his whole body. He opened his eyes. He had to squint in the rain to measure the yard or so distance that separated him from Levi, who sat staring back at him.

"So, you've hogtied the old goat rather than leave me to the river. Now what, young Levi?"

Levi said nothing.

"Why wouldn't you want me dead? Go ahead, appease whatever secular gods you think you love, maybe your ego, with a sacrifice! Throw me back into the drink. The river won't tell anyone your secret—you'll be as blameless as your mother when she sent your sister to her watery grave."

"Shut up."

"Oh, Levi, how else will you quench your revenge? End me here. Make mine the second life you take today. Tell me, and I'll tell you, does it get any easier?"

Levi palmed a rock and rolled it in the silt.

"Maybe you think you're saving lives, taking mine. Go ahead, Levi, but the river won't wash the blood from your hands or from your mother's."

Eleanor grasped and released her way downstream, the rush of the water and pelt of rain unable to drown the sound of her own voice in her head.

Levi! Levi!

Mama?

Levi, run get your dad! Freya's in the river! Run, Levi!

In her mind, the rain gave way to the heat of a summer day. Eleanor felt herself back in that younger body, sunburnt and dusty. She was once again the woman who leapt into the river on that cloudless day at Veltus Park, into the current spiraling around the downed tree, the wet moss-patched log that her Freya had skidded over and rolled from seconds before. Eleanor could see Freya's hair, a shoulder, another felled branch, twenty, then thirty feet downriver. Eleanor's flip flop wedged into a root. She struggled to free herself, her eye pulled down and away from Freya long enough to see her naked foot break the surface. She lunged forward, searching the moving water. Freya was gone. She saw her flip-flop pop up and get carried by the current to where Freya had been a second before. Eleanor heard herself scream as she dove into the channel. Immediately, her limbs worked to move her horizontally toward the bank. She grabbed a branch near to where Freya had held on, then let go, trying to steer herself to the next thing she could grab. Past an overgrowth of chokecherry, she saw her daughter holding onto a feather of willow with both hands. Eleanor saw her baby's fingers slip.

Freya, hold on, Honey! Hold on!

Eleanor fought through the water until she was so close she could smell her daughter's shampoo, see the pale skin beneath the wet fabric of her shirt at the collar bone. She grabbed her daughter's forearm and pulled, had the length of the child's body along her own when a rotted trunk hit her broadside above her hip, pushed the air from her lungs and broke her hold. Freya was sucked back into the current. Eleanor grabbed the piece of wood that rammed her and ruddered toward her daughter, shrinking the distance between them, narrowing the gap until Eleanor could touch the stitching of Freya's t-shirt, feel a pinch of wet cotton between her forefinger and thumb. She tightened her pincer grasp and yanked. Freya's body cracked like a whip, her body folding into a vee as the boiling water pulled her, hips first, below the surface. Eleanor funneled all her strength and focus into holding onto both the limb and her daughter, blind to the metal beam of bridge that met her skull and released her grip.

And then Eleanor was back in the rain, in the dark, pulling herself into a little pool and up onto the bank, sobbing into the muck.

"Levi! Levi!" She called into the rain. Coming to her feet, she crashed forward into and through a dense tangle of growth to a small clearing and saw her son sitting in the mud.

"Levi!" She thought, *Am I dreaming?*

"Mom!"

Eleanor ran to embrace Levi and tripped over a mound. She fell across Cal, landing knee-first in his gut. He let out a howl, and she jumped up and back as though she'd dropped onto a trampoline in a snake pit. Levi ran around to catch her before she fell backwards into a sharp tumble of dead wood.

Cal coughed and sputtered, "the amazing and mysterious Eleanor Clay! In the nick of time, once again."

"Shut up!" Levi kicked Cal in the ribs.

"Levi ..."

"Mom. Oh, my god, Mom." He wrapped himself around his mother and pressed his face into her slick plastic shoulder.

"Levi, honey, you're safe!"

Levi lifted his head and stepped back, holding Eleanor at arm's length. Eye to eye he said, "I'm not safe, Mom. I'm not, you're not—nobody's safe with him still breathing."

"We'll let the police deal with him. He can't hurt us, or anyone, not now."

"You don't believe that, Mom. I know you don't."

Cal shouted, "I don't much believe you either, Eleanor!"

"I said SHUT THE FUCK UP!" Levi kicked him again, threw himself at him with so much force he lost his balance and fell back into the mud. Cal groaned. Levi sat up, removed a shoe, and peeled off a sock. He replaced his shoe, then filled the sock with several handfuls of wet silt and small rocks. Cal gagged as Levi kneeled over him and stuffed the heavy knotted sac in his mouth.

Levi stood to face his mother. In the nearly drained light, through a filter of rain, Eleanor appeared blurred to him, distant. He almost laughed, to see her this way, as if through a filter. This is how he knew her.

"Levi."

"What, Mom? What do you want? What can you possibly want from me now, when you've never wanted anything—not from me, not from anyone, not for as long as I can remember?"

"It's not that I don't want anything..."

"Fine, then...you don't want anything. Well, what do you *need?* What do you need from me, Mom? When's the last fucking time I really mattered to you?"

"You've always...I never..."

"Don't, Mom. Don't hand me some *it's not you, it's me* bullshit. I know, everybody knows, it's always about you. Whether you're around or not."

Levi squatted at Cal's feet and stared into the old man's eyes.

"I'll bet that you've *for sure* got your own seriously sad mommy story, don't you?"

He leaned in close to Cal's face.

"I guess you thought maybe that was our place to bond. You *recognized* something in me...thought you could *relate* to me... well, sorry—I'm not going to be some poster child for your fucked up past-due greatest generation moral apocalypse...

"You know what you were right about, though? You should die. I should kill you. I don't know what the hell you are, Cal. Maybe human, once, but now? Now you're—I'll use your word—*unviable.* You are definitely one unviable son of a bitch." Levi kicked him again, with purpose. To rupture a kidney, to splinter bone.

"Do not for one fucking second think that I can relate to you."

The thrum of the rain was interrupted by the snap and rustle of bodies breaking through the brush. Behind Eleanor, Levi could see the dot end of a beam of flashlight. He looked at his mother, standing a few feet from his reach, and felt himself tunnel away from her, as some force, the light, the shouting voices carried on the current, sucked her away from him. He stood in a vacuum of anger and fear, of his own breathless grief, past the brink of himself. He leveraged his foot under Cal's hip.

"Levi!" Eleanor was pleading with him. "Don't! He can live, he can die, it doesn't matter! But you do, Levi, you matter!"

"One push, Mom! One push and it's done! One push and the river can take him, too." Levi squatted to roll Abrams toward the water.

"You don't have to watch—just turn around, Mom, or zone out, like I know you know how."

The voices rose behind her. "Levi, please! I left you. I'm sorry, but please don't leave me now."

Levi stood. "I'm not leaving you, Mom. I'm protecting you."

"You're not, son. You can't—just as I can't protect you. But I can love you, Levi. I love you. Don't sacrifice yourself to him or to me. Don't do this, please, you can't do this."

Levi looked hard at his mother. He heard the noise of the responders, still out of sight but close enough to distinguish one voice from another.

"You're wrong, Mom. This is something I *can* do."

With both hands he shoved his mother into the brush. He bent down to Cal and threw his weight against the bound and shackled body, pushing up a sandbar of mud between them and the river. Furious, Levi crabbed around the body and pulled at the legs, tugging as Cal fought to shake him off. They struggled, skidding and digging, entrenching themselves deeper into the wet earth until Levi slipped and lost his grip, and fell backward into a bed of horsetails.

He did not rise to resume his attack, but felt his rage drain like water from a dropped vase, replaced with an unfamiliar heaviness that sank him deep into to the ancient ferns. Flattened, Levi kept his eyes open to the swift-moving sky, letting the rain needle his face, mix with his salt.

Cal, no longer besieged, lay like a shipwreck, heaved onto the sandbank created in the scuffle.

Eleanor crawled to her son's side and laid her cheek on his belly. Levi tilted his head to see Cal trying to slither backwards out of the depression. He lifted a knee and stilled the squirming man with the thrust of a heel to the groin. The rain stopped, the new, raw silence broken only by the squeak of grass beneath breath.

A crescendo of crackle and shout rose through the trees. The first EMT to come upon them nearly fell across the bodies by the riverbank.

An officer from Silverthorne PD was close behind. "You two are mighty lucky to be alive after that river run! Guess we'll be finding our kidnapper with a dragnet, if at all."

Levi looked at the slipped earth where Cal had lain just moments before. The river had already filled the hollow where his body had been, washed flat the man-made spit that had held him. Cal Abrams was gone.

CHAPTER
41

Minutes passed like hours from the moment the EMT dropped into the darkness until she recovered Emmett, snagged on the bank, until help and a Stokes basket arrived to lift him out, until the helicopter landed. There was some discussion over whether the air lift was the best option, given the persistent storm conditions, but the wind had abated, and it was clear Emmett would need more than what the nearest Urgent Care could provide.

On the ground, the noise of the propellers had drowned out everything except the static of falling water and the shouts of the responders. In flight, Elan could still hear nothing but the whoosh of blades and his own blood in his ears. Emmett's eyes were closed, but his lips were moving. The medic bent low over Emmett's body, secure in its wrappings, and listened, like a safecracker trying to pick a lock, Elan thought, and then turned his mouth to the prone man's ear and spoke back to him.

At St. Anthony's in Lakewood, the EMT—Francis—stopped

to talk with Elan in the waiting room.

"The doctors will tell you what they can once they get him set up in the ICU. You can't know with spinal cord injuries right away, but he's in good hands. Looks like he might've been lucky, his breathing was pretty good, he could talk. English teacher, your friend?"

"Not as far as I know, but I don't know him all that well. He's the husband, or ex, of a woman I work with. He builds wells in Africa, something like that."

"Well, he knows his Yeats: 'Things fall apart; the center cannot hold; / Mere anarchy is loosed upon the world, / The blood-dimmed tide is loosed, and everywhere.' Not the most comforting words, maybe, but it's not every SPI could quote from 'The Second Coming' under the circumstances."

While Elan waited, he looked it up on his phone. *The ceremony of innocence is drowned; / The best lack all conviction, while the worst / Are full of passionate intensity.*

"Jesus, I thought Eleanor was dark," he said aloud. Then he wondered about EMTs who could swap verse while they threaded tubes through cavities, measured a pulse.

How do you ever really know the whole of anybody, he thought, *when they keep breaking? The parts, they never add up the same again.*

To be changed, he realized now, was his greatest terror.

"Huh."

Stanislaus ended his call with Elan DePeña and reached across his desk to switch off the fan. DePeña would stay in Denver to sort things out with their PD, offer what support he could to Eleanor and her family, then take the Zephyr back, unless the lawyer boyfriend wanted to pick him up. *The kid did all right,* he thought. *He hung in there.*

Eleanor, though. He didn't know what to do about Eleanor, how to do right by her, and he wanted to do right by her, but how? To his eye, she was hardly better off on this side of the horror than she was before. Could be things were even worse. He couldn't guarantee her a job, not after this case. The department was too small for so much notoriety. And god knew what shape the boy was in, damaged, like the other kids, both visibly and in other, un-seeable ways. At least the ex-husband had that Annabelle. He was glad there'd been nothing more than a bit of marital subterfuge there, and he was glad Emmett Clay had someone, though he didn't know the man from Adam. He was getting sentimental, he thought.

Eleanor Clay. For all they'd been through, he didn't know her much better than the day they met. But maybe they knew each other well enough. Lonely knows when it's looking in the mirror. They each wore their solitude with some resolve.

It was summer, still, but a dissident chill made him grab his jacket and head to the break room for a hot cup of coffee.

CHAPTER
42

"There was a poet, an American, who wrote ...ah, nein, nein, I won't remember ...but wait, I have it here." Nina crossed the room to a tightly packed bookcase and dragged her finger along several spines before pulling a pale hardback, faded and frayed at the corners. In her lap, the book fell open to the page she was after.

"The women at Dachau knew they were about / to be gassed when they pushed back the Nazi guard / who wanted to die with them, saying he should live. / And sang for a little after the doors closed.

"What do you think? That death was a blessing he didn't deserve? Or that living was what you did when—and if—you could?

"This is what I think I think: we act with our bodies. What is moral is what we do, when we do, compelled by the blood of us."

Althea, who had been swirling her glass on the side table, gazing into the ruby liquid, pushed it away, spilling the contents. She tore a tissue from the box.

Nina came to Althea and draped an arm over her shoulder. "You have a right to feel what you feel, and it is good that you feel something. Tender tissue, yes," she said, picking up the pink soggy wad of paper, "but new growth."

"Thank you for turning to botany for your metaphor and not forensics. I do feel somewhat spliced and sappy." Althea stood, unfolded, and shook herself like a great blue heron drying her plumage, starting at the shoulders and ending with a wring of her fingertips.

"And you know what else I feel? Hungry. I'm going to inventory the fridge and open a real bottle of wine."

Eleanor sat running her fingertip around the rim of her full glass of brandy.

Nina said, "You know, we had the pleasure of hearing Rose Mahler play with her group once, my brother and parents and me, in Germany. She was very famous on her own, without the uncle. Uncommon, to say the least, for a woman in those times. She was a *role model*, as they say, very gifted."

"And now she's what, a footnote on a serial killer's Wikipedia page?"

"Footnote or no, she was someone."

They sat. Nina cleared her throat. "Tell me, Eleanor, what is next for you?"

"Oh, I don't know. I told Gordon I was taking some time. I got the feeling he was relieved...to be honest, despite ten years with the department, it never felt like a real job. More like a cover, or worse, some kind of punishment. I was never a true member of the force—more like their disturbing little secret. And after all this, well, I don't know what I am, what I could or should do. In the department or anywhere else."

"You don't know if you can disappear back into your burrow? No, I imagine not. And what a waste that would be!" Nina leaned toward Eleanor from the edge of her club chair. "Eleanor, I wonder if you would consider working for Corps-Pursuit, after all?"

"Nina, I'm hardly qualified, and besides, it's volunteer based. I'll need an actual job."

"Ja, ja, this is an actual job I'm discussing."

"Working with you?"

"As my assistant, if you will. Also, if it is agreeable, perhaps you would consider taking a room in this big house of mine."

"I don't know what to say, Nina."

"Say nothing. Let your brain do its thinking and your heart do its feeling. I will only emphasize that it is my most sincere desire that you accept."

"Thank you. But, Nina, I've got to ask—why? I mean, if we agree that it isn't my resume that qualifies me."

"I have many reasons, Eleanor, so many. First, we do not agree, after all, regarding what you insist is your lack of credentials. You are not a scientist, no, but you are perceptive in ways that cannot be taught.

"And then I feel what I will call a kinship. Something in my body recognizes something in your body, like those female elephants on that property in—where, Georgia, perhaps? The ones that, when they find themselves together again, nuzzle the scars of the other."

The casement windows in the kitchen were open wide to the late afternoon breeze. The scent of rosemary stopped Eleanor at the doorway.

Mama! Here you go!

Ladybug, what a lovely bouquet of what looks like all our blooms. Freya, honey, between you and the deer, I think I might just give up on a flower garden. Where's the rosemary I asked you to clip for the bread?

I got that, too. And there are plenty of flowers left for the deer. Plus, they grow back.

Yep, they do, Smart Stuff. Thank you for the flowers. Wanna grind up some of that rosemary with the garlic for me?

Eleanor watched her younger self next to her daughter, who stood on a stool using two small hands to grind a pestle into a wooden bowl set atop a bleached dish towel.

Mama?

Hmm?

What are you going to do when I go away?

Well, I don't know. Are you leaving?

Someday.

I guess I'll just love you wherever you are, then.

You will. And me too, you.

"Eleanor, you okay?"

The room came into focus, and it was Althea at the kitchen window, sorting through a pile of herbs.

"Yeah, I'm fine. I was just thinking I used to have one of those, back in another life," she said, gesturing at the mortar and pestle on the counter.

"Hey, speaking of another life, I'm thinking about taking a job with Cannabis Cumulus."

"For real? Give up forensic botany?"

"No, never. I won't leave CorpsPursuit. A representative from the consortium approached me about a research and development gig, heaps of money. I need a change, and I'm ready to be intoxicated with cash."

"Nina just offered me a job here. Well, not here. The lab. As her assistant."

"You know, I knew the minute she introduced you, you'd be her favorite."

Eleanor looked past Althea out the open window.

"I'm kidding, Eleanor."

Eleanor blinked and turned to look at her friend. "I'm going to accept."

"Excellent. Welcome to the team! That is, if you're sure you want to continue looking for dead people for a living." She poured Cote du Rhone into two glasses and clinked hers to Eleanor's. "Here's to recovery!"

Elan loaded a box into the back of the Volvo.

"I don't know why we don't throw this paltry haul straight into the dumpster, Elan, seeing as she's moving into Nina's house. I mean, dear lord, are these full-size sheets? Do they even make these anymore? Guaranteed they don't fit a grown-up bed. Not that you'd want them to. I wouldn't. Want them."

"You're right, Terrance, but what can I say? We volunteered to move Eleanor to Boulder, and I'm not authorized to make the call regarding her sad, small, ugly sheets. How would you feel if I callously tossed your fun-run t-shirts?"

"What? That's a specious argument. You know I'm delighted to help Eleanor move ..."

"Almost too delighted."

"Now, now. I give full props to Eleanor for encouraging you in your career."

Elan laughed. "Down there, Tiger. I told you, I'm not ready to try for detective. I need to put in more uniform time, and you know, I really do like the bike. Plus, there's a class or two I haven't taken from Colorado Mountain. Avalanche science. Rage yoga."

He lifted a rusted kazoo out of a shoebox of odds and ends and blew. "Levi's going to fill me in on the Julliard experience. Maybe I'm a gifted musician and I don't know it."

"Yeah, and I should dig out my skates—maybe I'm the next

Brian Boitano. Hey, are we going to see Levi before he leaves for New York?"

"He's already there. Once he got his acceptance letter it came together super quick, thanks to Annabelle, of course. She caught me up a couple of days ago. Emmett and she plan to spend the last two weeks of December in the city, assuming they're both up to it—Emmett's been killing it at physical therapy. She says the doctors think he'll be home in another month."

"Amazing. Lucky man, after all." Terrance took Elan's hand and kissed it, then wiped his eyes with the cuff of his sleeve. "Not as lucky as me."

Elan squeezed Terrance's fingers tight before grabbing a last box.

"Speaking of optimism, Annabelle's got Eleanor scheduled for a visit to Gotham next month, after Levi's settled a little."

"Eleanor's going to travel to New York? Wow."

"Yeah, just look at her go. Next thing you know, she'll be packing a driver's license. And a passport."

"Don't you and Annabelle go expanding her universe too quickly, Elan."

"The Brain is wider than the Sky— / For—put them side by side— / The one the other will contain / With ease — and You— beside— "

"You sneaking in a little online intro to poetry?"

"*Poem du Jour*, daily download, my latest obsession. From yesterday: 'We took new stock of one another. / We wept to be reminded of such color.'"

"That's right, that's right."

CHAPTER

43

He stood at the rail at the spot he stood every day at this hour since he arrived in New York, a figure in a frame familiar from dozens of TV shows and movies, in all the tried-and-true plots—blossom-bright love stories inspring, salt-kissed summer romance, chill November dramas, sodden March mysteries. In each viewing, in sunshine or fog, he saw the bridge as the poet did, as harps in the skyline. The moment he set foot on this island, he could hear the steely music, feel the taut keen notes of urban aspiration singing in the high-strung expanse.

But not today. He looked down into the Atlantic, at the blurred edges of flotsam sunk under the murk. From this perspective, it was hard to imagine the cold magnetic sea as a living place. It appeared only a repository of the spent. Today, for Levi, even the sky was held in its chop.

A gull bobbed in his downcast line of sight, its eye flat black, trained dead ahead. Several yards out its colony screeched over a garbage tug. Levi eyed the water, scanning for the thing he wished and dreaded would break the surface—

a bearded monster, bloated with death. Proof. Peace.

Levi jumped up and down a couple of times, shook his hands as if to release the gloom from his fingertips. He'd finish his run, take a hot shower, feel like himself again by the time his mother's plane landed. It was Eleanor's first trip to New York. She was coming to him, and that felt like something. He'd made no plans for her visit; there was no itinerary. He thought he might take her for pizza, or let her choose, let the glitter-gritty city reveal to her how it wanted to be seen.

CHAPTER
44

Eleanor watched out the little window as Jamaica Bay rose up to meet the airplane in its approach to Kennedy. The little basins that stretched into what she assumed was Brooklyn reminded her of the spikes on the crown on the Statue of Liberty, symmetrical and finite, but like baby fingers, too, stubby in their salty reach. She wasn't fooled, however, by these calm channels. Though the civilized shores of this bay looked nothing like her endless river, she knew that all waters took what they could in a storm.

"First time in the Big Apple?" her neighbor asked as he latched the little table to the seatback. He'd put on his headphones immediately after takeoff, drank a Coors Light, and commenced to snore softly ten minutes into their three-and-a-half-hour flight. Eleanor liked him.

"Uh huh. My son moved here for school this fall."

"And ready for a visit from Mom so soon? That's a son loves his mother."

She smiled. She'd been happy when Levi announced his

decision to go to Julliard. And then, abruptly, she felt herself caught in a familiar undertow, feeling it would be better if her son cut his ties to her completely, embarked on the life he deserved free from her drag. She could sense something similar in Levi, though he said nothing. It was almost a relief, his doubt.

She reached into her carry-on, a snack-filled bon voyage gift from Althea, for a stick of gum, and pulled out the card Elan had tucked into the bag before they said goodbye at the terminal. The front was a photograph from Elan and Terrance's recent rafting trip on the Colorado. He wrote:

> *Photo of me and Terrance getting soaked by the Shoshone Rapids, taken by the rafting company staff. I could've done better. Anyway, a big trip calls for a benediction, and Lucille Clifton says it better than I can:*
>
> *may the tide / that is entering even now / the lip of our understanding / carry you out / beyond the face of fear / may you kiss / the wind then turn from it / certain that it will / love your back may you / open your eyes to water / water waving forever / and may you in your/ innocence / sail through this to that ~ blessing the boats*

She'd been feeling she should somehow be mourning the loss of innocence in her boy and feeling the shame of her part in that loss. But Elan, via the poet, was right. Innocence isn't something that lives once, for a time, and dies. Innocence is not ignorance, in the end, but a strength so tenacious it can *sail through this to that.* It was resilience—something more grounded, more substantial, than hope. It wasn't lost to Levi. Even she could have it back.

Notes

Chapter 41: "The Second Coming" by William Butler Yeats

Chapter 42: "The Great Fires" from THE GREAT FIRES: POEMS, 1982-1992 by Jack Gilbert, copyright © 1994 by Jack Gilbert. Used by permission of Alfred A. Knopf, an imprint of the Knopf Doubleday Publishing Group, a division of Penguin Random House LLC. All rights reserved.

Chapter 42: "The Brain— is wider than the Sky—" by Emily Dickinson, c.1862

Chapter 42: Tracy K. Smith, excerpt from "An Old Story" from Such Color: New and Selected Poems. Copyright © 2018 by Tracy K. Smith. Reprinted with the permission of The Permissions Company, LLC on behalf of Graywolf Press, Minneapolis, Minnesota, www.graywolfpress.org.

Chapter 44: Lucille Clifton, "blessing the boats" from How to Carry Water: Selected Poems of Lucille Clifton. Copyright © 1991 by Lucille Clifton. Reprinted with the permission of The Permissions Company, LLC on behalf of BOA Editions Ltd., boaeditions.org.

Acknowledgements

Thank you to all the people and other entities that helped this book find its form, especially M., who booked the trip that brought Bristlecone Springs to life; and B., who saw herself in the pages; and other M., through whom I found myself.

About Atmosphere Press

Atmosphere Press is an independent, full-service publisher for excellent books in all genres and for all audiences. Learn more about what we do at atmospherepress.com.

We encourage you to check out some of Atmosphere's latest releases, which are available at Amazon.com and via order from your local bookstore:

Dancing with David, a novel by Siegfried Johnson

The Friendship Quilts, a novel by June Calender

My Significant Nobody, a novel by Stevie D. Parker

Nine Days, a novel by Judy Lannon

Shining New Testament: The Cloning of Jay Christ, a novel by Cliff Williamson

Shadows of Robyst, a novel by K. E. Maroudas

Home Within a Landscape, a novel by Alexey L. Kovalev

Motherhood, a novel by Siamak Vakili

Death, The Pharmacist, a novel by D. Ike Horst

Mystery of the Lost Years, a novel by Bobby J. Bixler

Bone Deep Bonds, a novel by B. G. Arnold

Terriers in the Jungle, a novel by Georja Umano

Into the Emerald Dream, a novel by Autumn Allen

His Name Was Ellis, a novel by Joseph Libonati

The Cup, a novel by D. P. Hardwick

The Empathy Academy, a novel by Dustin Grinnell

Tholocco's Wake, a novel by W. W. VanOverbeke

Dying to Live, a novel by Barbara Macpherson Reyelts

Looking for Lawson, a novel by Mark Kirby

About the Author

Irene Cooper's previous books include *Committal,* poet-friend-ly spy-fy about family (V.A. Press, 2020), & *spare change* (FLP, 2021), a finalist for the Stafford/Hall Prize for poetry. In 2020, she co-edited *Placed: An Encyclopedia of Central Oregon.* Poems, stories & reviews appear in *Denver Quarterly, The Feminist Wire, The Manifest-Station, phoebe, The Rumpus, Witness,* & elsewhere. Irene teaches in community and sup-ports AIC-directed creative writing opportunities at a regional prison. She lives with her people & Maggie, the corgi, in Ore-gon, where she thinks about gardening, but mostly just watch-es the birds. Find her at www.irenecooperwrites.com & on Twitter @icooper435.

CPSIA information can be obtained
at www.ICGtesting.com
Printed in the USA
BVHW040441121022
649201BV00001B/8